May home always have a
special place in your heart.
Frances Davis
2006

Homeward

By Frances Davis

ISBN 0-7414-2847-4

Artwork for front and back covers by Cathy Kitchens.

Published by:

PUBLISHING.COM

1094 New DeHaven Street, Suite 100
West Conshohocken, PA 19428-2713
Info@buybooksontheweb.com
www.buybooksontheweb.com
Toll-free (877) BUY BOOK
Local Phone (610) 941-9999
Fax (610) 941-9959

Printed in the United States of America
Printed on Recycled Paper
Published November 2005

DEDICATION

In memory of

Virginia D. Bergmann

Daddy's Mama

to

Martha Ann Johnson,

college classmate

cherished friend

PROLOGUE

Secrets were burdensome liabilities, especially when partnered with advanced age and failing health.

Marcus Trent sank wearily into his desk chair as the pain in his chest intensified, a piercing discomfort that had plagued him the last three months and had become a grim reminder of his mortality. It was also a reminder to Marcus that the time had come to tell someone about the secret he harbored, the current urgency wrapped in a twenty-five-year-old crime.

Energized by his decision, he pulled open his desk drawer and scrambled through the assortment of odds and ends that had accumulated in the quarter century Trent's Pharmacy had been in existence. He pulled an envelope from the conglomeration and removed the small newspaper clipping it contained, then tucked the paper into a plastic cassette tape box.

He fervently hoped that Leigh Parrish had continued to have a keen interest in crossword puzzles and that she would come to the pharmacy before his earthly days were over.

CHAPTER 1

CRESCENT ORCHARD
NORTH GEORGIA MOUNTAINS
MARCH 16

There was something ominous about the black BMW parked in the lot adjacent to Trent's Pharmacy. Its well-defined lines contrasted sharply with the hundred-year-old brick building, where the continual attack of the elements had loosened the mortar and faded the walls to a nondescript red. The car was very much out-of-place in the mountain village, where there were never showroom-new cars that boasted a matched pair of side mirrors and a series of aerials just above the rear window.

Even the town surrendered to the influence of the car. Twilight had hovered ever so gently at the edge of Crescent Orchard until the afterglow of the fading sun provided just enough energy to send it gliding quietly into town, almost unnoticed. It settled softly, cueing the halogen lights to pop on, and instantly, the little town nestled in the mountains of North Georgia was magically transformed into an Alpine village.

Leigh Parrish scrambled to rescue the contents of her purse that spilled on the street as she stepped from her fifteen-year-old Toyota. Piece by piece, she stuffed items into her faded blue denim shoulder bag. Her lipstick rolled down the street, narrowly missing the opening of the rain sewer. As she retrieved it and turned back to her car, the BMW drew her attention. Its sleek finish was unmistakably elegant, undeniably expensive. The *License Applied For*

3

cardboard tag was enclosed with a brassy chain border that succeeded only in being gaudy.

Leigh secured an errant strand of blonde hair behind her ear. She lingered briefly at the car, finally noticing a deep scratch on the rear quarter panel on the passenger side. *Not good on a new car,* she decided.

§§§

In the office of the corner drugstore on Main Street, Marcus Trent labored over the ledger spread open on his desk. His head, crowned in white as pure and brilliant as the patches of unseasonable snow outside, was bowed low. Eyes red-rimmed with exhaustion stared at the endless columns of numbers. With a trembling hand, Marcus picked up his wire-rimmed glasses and hooked them over his ears. He spoke slowly, his voice barely audible.

"I don't have the money now. You said March 18. To-day is just the sixteenth."

The man Marcus addressed was medium everything: height, build, weight. He wouldn't have earned a second look except for the jagged, purplish-blue scar on his left cheek that extended from the corner of his thin-lipped mouth to just below his temple. He yanked a chair across the bare wooden floor, straddled it, and folded his arms across the back before replying to the pharmacist.

"So what's two days? You knew the payment was due this week."

"I'm sorry."

"*Sorry* don't get it." He got up from the chair, giving it a sharp kick with his foot. "You know my boss expects me to bring money when I return. And I expect you to provide that money so that I don't have to give him a report of your bad behavior."

"Terrence—"

"*Mr. Elliott,* old man. Don't forget your manners when you address me."

Terrence Elliott strode across the small office and stood at the end of the desk. "Now, you were about to say something."

"It was nothing," Marcus Trent replied.

"Then I'll take the money and be on my way."

"I do not have the money. I will not have it on the eighteenth. I will not pay you ever again!"

Elliott perched on the corner of the desk. "That is not a good decision. You should know how important it is to make your payments on time. Besides, my boss will be very unhappy when he hears about your unwillingness to pay. Especially when he learns your company safe has thousands." He waited for the stunned expression to disappear from Marcus' face. "The safe was open. I took the liberty of looking in and making a swift estimate while you were going over your ledger. Mostly fifties and hundreds. How long have you been stuffing this Fort Knox?"

He stopped suddenly and slid away from the desk as the pharmacy door opened, then closed. When the tinkling bell grew silent, he whispered to Trent. "Who is it?"

"Probably just a late customer."

"Get rid of 'em. Fast."

Marcus rose from his desk chair, pausing a moment as dull pain ebbed across his chest.

Elliott produced a .380 semi-automatic from inside his sport jacket. "This one-way glass?" He jerked the gun toward the enclosure that shielded the front of the office from the store area.

Marcus nodded.

"Good. I'll have my eyes on you. Don't try anything smart."

Marcus shuffled from his office. As he approached the customer, a smile broke across his weathered face and he greeted the young woman at the magazine rack.

"Good evening, Leigh. Haven't seen you in weeks. Is there something I can get for you?"

"Hello, Mr. Trent. I wanted to pick up a magazine on my way to the hospital."

"How's your grandmother?"

"There's no change. It seems the painful hours outnumber the good ones, but she doesn't complain much."

"She's never been one to complain."

"You're right." Leigh glanced at the collection of magazines. "That's what I want," she said, selecting the current issue of *Detective Code*.

Marcus smiled. "Still like trying to solve things, don't you? That was inherited from your Grandfather Bracken. He loved creating puzzles out of anything, then challenging someone to solve them."

Leigh nodded. "I'll keep the tradition going with this magazine. Real mysteries don't happen in Crescent Orchard, and I don't anticipate ever leaving here."

"The Bracken roots go back many years," Marcus said, handing her the change. "By the way," he continued, pulling his hand from his pocket. "Take this and listen to it. It's a recording of big band music, like your grandparents and I grew up with. It's music with an odd twist—it actually *sounds* like music. I thought of you when I heard it and wanted you to have it."

"Thanks, Mr. Trent. I'll take my cassette player to the hospital tomorrow so Daddy's Mama can listen with me. You know music has always been an important part of her life. You're very kind to think of doing this." She smiled. "Daddy's Mama told me you and she have been friends for many years."

"The friendship of our families has a long history," he replied. He was silent for several minutes, then rubbed his eyes. "Forgive me, Leigh. I just got to remembering the past and couldn't quit. And you need to get to your grandmother. Give her my love, will you?"

"Sure, Mr. Trent. And thanks again for the tape."

Marcus Trent watched as Leigh closed the door behind her. He thought about the note he had hidden in the cassette box several weeks earlier. It wasn't much of a clue, but Leigh was intelligent. She'd figure it out, he was sure of that. The bell became quiet and he turned toward the office.

"Lock the door."

"What?"

"You heard me. It's closing time. No more customers tonight. We have some unfinished business to complete."

Slowly, Marcus Trent moved toward the door, then turned back without locking it and moved haltingly to the office.

He clutched his chest, stumbled on the threshold plate, and crumpled to the floor.

§§§

Across the street, Chester Leverett lingered quietly in the shadows. He had been there when the BMW drove up, and now, twenty minutes later, it was still parked.

Chester shuffled to a more comfortable position. He needed to see his Uncle Marcus before the pharmacy closed at six-thirty, but he couldn't take the chance of being seen, not even by some stranger in town. He would have to wait.

7

He watched as Leigh Parrish left the drugstore, walked briskly to her car, and drove away. He turned his back to shield an unsuccessful attempt to light a cigarette and a moment later, he heard the ignition of a motor.

The fancy black car was leaving.

§§§

Rookie Patrolman Brian Porter swished his hand across his badge, then surveyed his dim reflection in the plate glass window of the police station. He adjusted his cap to a ridiculous angle, moving it back, then forward. Finally satisfied with his efforts, he congratulated himself with a mock salute.

"Go get 'em, tiger."

Brian turned on his heel to face Sgt. Adrian Hendley.

"Sorry, sir," he apologized.

The sergeant grinned and his burly appearance softened. "That's part of what that word *pride* on your badge means. But don't get carried away with that part."

"No, sir. Or, yes, sir."

"Relax, son." The sergeant chewed his toothpick. "Like this shift?"

"Just fine. Kinda dull, though. Nothing's happened."

"Be thankful for that. Things will change one day and you'll wish for some dull nights." The sergeant drew in his breath and wiggled a button through the hole on the opposite side of his navy uniform shirt, only to see it slip out when he exhaled. He moved his tie, discreetly covering the gaping breach. "Oh, by the way, any word on the street about Marcus Trent's altercation with Chester Leverett?"

"Nothing except Chester was in a rage."

"Keep your ears open. I got bad vibes about that guy."

"Why is that, sir?" Brian asked.

"You haven't heard the story?"

"No, sir, can't say that I have. At least, not all of it."

Sgt. Hendley exchanged his toothpick for a handful of jellybeans from the jar on the desk. He offered the jar to Brian. "Want some?"

"Thanks, no. Just finished supper."

"You won't stay in that good habit long working here. These *are* my supper on many nights."

Brian waited.

"As I was saying, Chester and Marcus had a little fracas a couple weeks back. Chester can't talk, you know, but he can yell. Folks heard him across the street as far down as Ginny's Diner."

"What was it about?"

"Marcus won't say. He and Christine took Chester when the boy's parents died—they'd be Christine's sister and brother-in-law. The big fight happened three, maybe four years ago. Don't know what that was about, either. At any rate, Chester moved out of Marcus' house, found him a shack up on Providence Hill. Bikes the six or seven miles from Providence into town a couple of times a month. Nobody knows what sparked the latest riot between them two."

Brian waited while the sergeant poured another handful of jellybeans, then asked, "Any idea why Chester can't talk?"

Sgt Hendley frowned. "Chester's dad was a fireman when they lived in Canada. Chester saw him go in a burning building to attempt a rescue, and he never came back out. Marcus said it had such an effect on Chester he never spoke another word."

"What was his age?" Brian asked.

"Barely four. There was not money for special help for him and the regular schools eventually declared him not suited for the mainstream curriculum. I don't think he got any further than the first grade. His mother died about a year after his father, and that's when Marcus and Christine became his foster parents."

"What a story," Brian said softly.

"You got that right. But just listen. You may pick up some valuable information. And keep an eye out for Chester."

"Will do."

Brian synchronized his watch with the clock over the desk. "Six fifty-two. Time to move out and see if the town is locked up and bedded down for the night."

As the door closed behind him, Brian stood for a moment reflecting on the winter scene. The moon hung low with only a few early stars dotting the heavens. The snow, a rather unseasonable surprise to North Georgia in March, was clinging tenaciously to protected places. The sidewalks and streets were clear and the few vehicles out were moving freely.

Brian proceeded on his foot patrol along Main Street's business district. He stopped at the corner and glanced at the brightly illuminated upstairs windows in the courthouse. County commissioners must be having another of their highly publicized citizen discussion groups. He smiled at the thought of small-town politics.

Brian continued to walk. The post office would be open until seven, the fast food store until eleven. He made a mental note to check both on the midnight stroll.

A car came in his direction and stopped for the traffic light. Brian waved to Leigh Parrish as her battered Toyota turned right on Stanley Drive.

Headed for the hospital, he thought. Most people around town knew that Leigh had dropped out of night classes at the community college and had given up her part-time job at Spring Flowers Florist to spend time at the hospital with her terminally ill grandmother. The community gossip declared that with no income, Leigh had been forced to mortgage Jeaneen Bracken's home, Carmela, to pay escalating medical costs not covered by insurance.

Brian turned his attention to the street as a dark BMW headed out-of-town on Northern Boundary Road. *Just another humdrum patrol*, he thought, reaching out to check the door of Trent's Pharmacy. The knob turned easily and the door swung open.

Brian hesitated. Mr. Trent always closed promptly at six-thirty and double-locked the door. Cautiously, Brian entered and glanced around. Instinctively, his hand came to rest on the Colt .45 automatic at his side.

No one was behind the counter and no customers were in the store.

"Mr. Trent?"

No response broke the silence. Brian moved toward the back of the store. Nothing seemed disturbed.

A dozen steps brought him to the cubicle that was the pharmacy office. The door was partially open and Brian reached it just as a low moan drifted out. With gun drawn, he flattened himself against the wall just as another moan escaped.

He listened intently. Only the sound of labored breathing came from the office. In a swift movement, Brian twirled from the wall and through the door.

Marcus Trent was huddled face-down on the floor. Brian yanked the two-way radio from his belt and yelled an SOS.

"Trent's Pharmacy. Need an ambulance! Quick!"

He holstered his gun, then knelt by the pharmacist.

"Mr. Trent, hang on! Help's on the way!"

"Chest..."

Brian leaned closer to hear. "Sir?"

"Chest..."

"You're hurt in the chest, Mr. Trent?"

"Chest..."

Brian glanced hurriedly around the room. A chair was slightly out of place and a ledger was open on the desk.

"Chest..."

Brian turned back to Marcus Trent and at the same time heard the welcome wail of the ambulance siren.

§§§

Leigh Parrish hurried down the hall of Crescent Orchard Hospital to Room 106. She gently opened the door and entered, quietly approaching the bed.

"Daddy's Mama?" she whispered.

Brown eyes, weary with suffering, looked at her searchingly.

Leigh caught her grandmother's hand, then bent over the bed to kiss the forehead that was knotted in a frown. "Are you in pain?"

With great effort, Jeaneen Bracken nodded.

"I'll call the nurse to get you something."

Jeaneen labored with her reply. "No, Leigh. It does no good. And it confuses my mind." She sighed heavily. "The pain will be over soon. I am looking forward to that."

Leigh squeezed the frail hand gently. "We're going to find a medication that will help, Daddy's Mama."

"Permanent healing. In Heaven," Jeaneen said weakly, turning her head ever so slightly. Leigh fought to keep back the tears that were stinging in her eyes.

"Leigh?" It was barely a whisper.

"Right here, Daddy's Mama," Leigh answered softly.

"I'm—very—tired…"

"Just rest. I'll be here with you." Leigh pushed back the gray hair from her grandmother's forehead.

"Good night, Leigh."

"Good night, Daddy's Mama. I love you."

Just a hint of a smile floated across Jeaneen Bracken's face and a sigh escaped her lips. Leigh bent to place a kiss on her forehead and knew that her beloved grandmother had slipped quietly into the Lord's waiting arms for her eternal rest.

§§§

At 38, Creede Kelly was the undisputed current king of mystery writers. His Erin Wintergreen series had occupied a prominent place on the New York best seller list for six consecutive years. Erin was a global success. Her prowess at sleuthing was nothing short of phenomenal. In and out of danger, she waged war on corrupt politicians, infiltrated the Mob, jerked environmentalists-gone-astray back into line.

But after six years, Erin had hit a snag. Or more correctly, Creede Kelly had. His previously unlimited fountain of ideas was drying up, his wellspring of plots was stagnant. No new novel was hiding in his computer despite the frantic urging of his editor.

And so, on March 16, he had left Atlanta with his detective friend, Max Benedict, to wander around the North Georgia mountains for a couple of days. Writing was on the back burner.

Creede studied the road sign ahead.

"You sure you know the route?" he asked, glancing at his lifelong friend.

Max ran stubby fingers through his salt-and-pepper hair.

"Sure, I'm sure. I grew up in these mountains. Know 'em like the back of my hand. We want Northern Boundary Road. Go straight through Crescent Orchard on Main Street, which becomes Northern Boundary just beyond the city limits. You can't miss it."

Creede slowed his truck to a crawl.

"What's with all the lights ahead?" he asked.

"Somebody probably slipped in the snow. Nothing spectacular ever happens in Crescent Orchard," Max answered.

"For nothing to have happened, there's quite a commotion." Even as Creede voiced his observation, he angled the truck into a parking place in front of Trent's Pharmacy.

"Only in an Erin Wintergreen book would this happen," Max observed dryly. "A parking place at the front door."

Creede smiled as he opened his door. "Some days I'm just lucky."

"Max Benedict!"

Max turned as he stepped from the truck. "Adrian Hendley! Haven't seen you in a coon's age! How's it going?"

"Staying busy. What're you doing in this neck o' the woods?"

"Took some days off. Sgt. Adrian Hendley, meet Creede Kelly, my chauffeur for this hunting trip."

Sgt. Hendley raised an eyebrow. "Hunting? Nothing's in season now, Max."

"Exactly what we're hunting. Nothing." Max pointed to the pharmacy. "What's going on here?"

"Marcus Trent apparently had a visitor. Left him on the floor."

"How serious?"

"Dunno. Ambulance just left with him."

"Who found him?"

"Rookie cop. Porter. Been with the department all of five days. Just tonight he was complaining about the lack of excitement."

"Did you say Porter?" Max asked.

Sgt. Hendley nodded.

"Brian Porter?"

"The same. Know him?"

"Well. Bright fellow. He was in a crime scene course I taught a few months back. Tried to get him to go into private investigation and come to work for me, but he told me his application was in here. Said he wanted to get into small-town law enforcement. He's got the credentials to make an outstanding cop." Max looked around. "Is he here? I'd like to say hello."

"He followed the ambulance. Should be back in a half hour or so. Want to wait?"

"Think we'll drive by the hospital, maybe catch him there."

Creede followed Max to the truck and was about to step in when something sparkled at the edge of the front tire. He bent to pick it up. By the glow of the street lights Creede examined what appeared to be half of a bracelet charm. On one side was engraved *HJ*, on the other side the numbers *1271*. He studied it for a moment before handing it to Max.

"Think this is a clue?"

Max looked at the charm with the scrutiny of a well-trained detective.

"I doubt it," he said, returning the charm to Creede. "Probably something from the gum machine. Already broken. Those things aren't made to last, you know."

"Guess not." Creede absently dropped it in his pocket and climbed in the truck. "Which way to the hospital?"

"Turn right on Stanley at the corner."

Moments later, Creede pulled into the hospital drive. "Where to?"

"Emergency entrance. In the back."

Creede maneuvered along the drive. He had just rounded the corner when he hit the brake and screeched to a halt.

Max threw out his hand to steady himself. "Hey, man, that's dangerous!"

At that moment, Max saw her.

"Well-ll," he said slowly, "aside from her being blonde and drop-dead gorgeous, what other reason did you have for slamming me into the windshield?"

"She walked right into the road—never looked up," Creede answered, somewhat shaken. "I didn't want her to be a statistic."

Max Benedict noted with profound interest that Creede watched the blonde in the long plaid coat until she climbed into a dilapidated Toyota, coaxed it to life, and crept out of the parking lot. He was almost sure that no other woman had gotten that much attention from Creede Kelly in the last sixteen years.

Creede rubbed his chin with its two days' growth of beard. *Mountain village...cold winter night...mysterious invader...drugstore robbery...victim...* He thumped the steering wheel. "Any objection to heading back to Atlanta, Max?"

"And miss an opportunity to rough it a couple of days? You bet I've got objection!" Max shot a glance at his friend. "Uh-oh. Don't tell me you're letting an anonymous blonde muddle your mind."

"Actually, a brunette. Erin Wintergreen. She has a new mystery to work on. *Murder in the Mountains.*"

CHAPTER 2

Terrence Elliott walked steadily, determined to leave the events of the evening far behind. The journey led him along the edge of Northern Boundary Road, still slippery in spots and edged in patches of snow made dingy by the sporadic traffic. He clutched a Trent's Pharmacy plastic bag filled with Marcus Trent's money and mentally cursed the salesman who had insisted the BMW was faultless. The twenty-degree weather did little to cool his rising anger over being stranded in the middle of nowhere, all because of a car.

He walked hurriedly, his patent leather shoes occasionally slipping on the road's icy spots. Getting back to Crescent Orchard and finding a mechanic became an obsession. There was no oncoming traffic to provide light, and a shy moon finally faded in an ebony sky. His flashlight gave little assurance of enduring much longer.

Elliott's gloved hand reached to pull his overcoat collar closer to his neck, then slid along the scar on his face. Almost numb with cold, he wondered if hypothermia would claim him.

"Ye—ow—ow!" he muttered as he slipped on a rock on the shoulder of the road and rolled down a short incline. His fall ended abruptly against a pine tree, and he sat for a moment waiting for the ringing in his head to clear and allow him to focus on the situation at hand. Reporting to his superior would not be pleasant. The Trent Connection had not gone smoothly, but it wasn't his fault. Terrence groaned. The way the boss had chosen to conduct this mission was less than brilliant.

Right now, though, there were other things to consider. The money was his first priority. He had to find a place to temporarily conceal what would belong to him because no other person in the organization would ever know about it.

He groped on the ground through icy leaves and tangled undergrowth until he found the bag. The flashlight was gone.

Pulling himself up, he struggled toward the highway. The darkness was aggravating and confining, and more than once he threw profanities into the wind. Slowly feeling his way, he reached the top of the incline and finally stood on the road. Three steps later his foot struck a metallic object that rolled a few inches in front of him. His dignity already severely wounded, he dropped to his hands and knees and felt for the object.

There it was. His flashlight. He shook it vigorously, then clicked it on. It was still as dim as ever, but it was light. Fortified, he walked on.

The road made a sudden curve, and just as suddenly the moon reappeared. To Terrence, it was perfect timing. Not fifty feet beyond was the outline of a building.

He hurried forward, tightening his grip on the plastic bag. He focused the flashlight on the door and was surprised there was no lock. With a slight tug, the door quietly swung open.

Terrence stepped inside the barn, pulling the door closed. He stood in the darkness, barely breathing, listening for sounds in the winter night.

The cold was biting, sending a chill through his body. From somewhere in the building came a peculiar scratching sound that he could not identify. He shivered, his normal response to a combination of the cold and a severe case of nerves. He heard it again, a scurrying sound that wasn't too far from where he stood. *Must have been a mouse*, he thought. A moment later, he heard a thud from the same direction and hoped it meant a cat had found his dinner.

The door bumped and Terrence whirled around. Nothing there. He shook the flashlight and a tiny glow dimly illuminated the immediate vicinity.

He walked slowly, deliberately. The weakening arc of light came to rest on a small trunk. Perfect!

He set the bag of money at his feet, then turned his attention to the trunk. No lock. What incredible luck!

The lid opened easily and Terrence waved the flashlight over the contents. Stacks of newspapers! They would make a perfect cover for the money. He slid the papers to one side and buried the bag in the middle. After shoving the papers back to their original position and lowering the lid, he turned and left the building.

Terrence closed the door, and from habit took his handkerchief and wiped away any fingerprints he might have left, forgetting he was wearing gloves.

Something rattled in the rhododendron bushes next to the barn, and Terrence swung around as two bright spots glowed from within the bush. He stumbled briefly, dropping the handkerchief, as a cat raced from the bush toward the barn and some secret entrance.

Terrence almost ran the short distance back to the road and resumed his journey. The moon was now shining bravely, the beams glittering on icy patches of snow that dotted the shoulders of the road. The cold stillness of the night made him gasp for breath as he hurried along.

He stopped for a moment at the top of the hill and surveyed the immediate area. A glow of light shattered the darkness, providing hope that a vehicle was approaching.

Terrence stood on the edge of the road and waved his arms as the vehicle drew nearer. With the tires spraying slush, it stopped, and a youthful voice yelled through the open window, breaking the stillness of the night.

"Howdy, sir! You 'bout scared the life outta me! You okay?"

"Fine," Terrence answered, crossing the road to the driver's side. "What kind of vehicle *is* this?"

"A 4700 model International, 230 horses, six plus one, with full air brakes," the driver said proudly. "It's a wrecker."

The door opened and the lanky, bearded driver stepped out. "You got a car broke down?"

Unbelievable! "Well, yes, as a matter of fact, I do," Terrence answered.

"Close by?"

"A mile or so down the road. I was walking to the nearest town to find a mechanic."

"That'd be Crescent Orchard. And I'm the mechanic. Bo Patton."

"I'd appreciate some assistance."

"Climb aboard," Bo invited as he heaved himself up to the driver's side. "It ain't no easy ride in this Sherman tank, so just hang on." He drove to the lane that led to the barn.

"What're you doing?" Terrence asked anxiously.

"Turnin' around. That's the only way to get to Crescent Orchard from here."

Terrence shook his head. Somehow in the darkness he had gotten completely turned around. *No patience and no sense of direction*, he thought.

A couple of miles down the road, Bo pulled alongside the BMW.

"This it?" he asked.

"Yeah."

"I saw it just now." He shifted the wrecker into neutral, opened his door, and jumped out. Terrence followed.

"Pop the hood for me," Bo directed.

Several minutes of careful inspection revealed nothing.

"What'd it do?" Bo asked.

"Just died. No warning—nothing. It's brand new. I punched all the buttons I could find, but nothing worked."

Bo slid under the wheel and looked over the gauges. "Keys?" he asked, holding out his hand. He turned the ignition several times with no results.

Terrence stepped closer. "Got a lemon, didn't I?"

"Wouldn't say that, exactly," Bo drawled. "Nothin' that can't be fixed."

"How much?" Terrence ventured.

"Oh, I'd say about twenty bucks oughta do it. You're out of gas."

§§§

Leigh Parrish sat in the white wicker rocker in her grandmother's bedroom, her head resting on the back of the chair. For almost an hour she had barely moved, consoled by the ticking of the Seth Thomas clock and surrounded by the soft lavender accents in the room and the variety of memories that settled in her mind. More than that, however, she felt overwhelmed by the spirit of her grandmother's love that lingered tenderly in this house.

Jeaneen Holt came to Crescent Orchard as the young bride of Samuel Bracken. They settled in the family home where five generations of Brackens had lived and raised their children. Samuel's great-grandfather, Edward Bracken, had helped his friend, Philip Patton, propagate a new variety of apple. The popularity of the apple grew rapidly, as did the Bracken orchard. When trees covered 40 acres, Edward decided it was time to name his real estate. On the day the Crescent apple was patented, the sleepy mountain community that was its birthplace officially became Crescent Orchard, and Edward Bracken christened the homestead Carmela, the Latin for "bountiful orchard." He had watched intently as the glass of apple juice trickled along the banister before dripping into the flowerbeds at the edge of the porch, declaring that from these humble beginnings would rise orchards to supply the world with the best-tasting apple yet developed and assure Crescent Orchard a choice spot in the annals of historic events. The years were proving him correct on both.

Jeaneen and Samuel worked hard to preserve the legacy bestowed on them and often reminded each other that although apples were their livelihood, Carmela endured because of love. When extremes of rain and drought threatened the crop and their finances, they focused on getting through one day at a time. The same philosophy had guided Jeaneen when Samuel died, two months into the tenth year of their marriage. Jeaneen steadfastly refused to leave Carmela. Through years of struggle, she raised their son, Mark; saw him married to his childhood sweetheart, Melanie Thomas; rejoiced in the birth of her granddaughter, Leigh.

Mark died before his thirtieth birthday, and a couple of years later Melanie married Gordon Parrish. Jeaneen did not object to the marriage. Gordon had been educated at the best schools and enjoyed an excellent reputation in the field of corporate law. His wealth was moderate and he could easily afford the responsibilities of a family. The only obstacle— the heartbreaking event for Jeaneen Bracken—was when Gordon insisted on adopting Leigh and changing her name to Parrish.

Eventually, Melanie and Gordon Parrish accumulated more substantial wealth and decided it was time to see the world. Leigh was in the tenth grade when she came to live at Carmela, and Jeaneen Bracken's life assumed new meaning.

Together, she and Leigh redecorated the modest cottage to suit the needs of a fifteen-year-old. The wisdom of age and the determination of youth bonded in a rare love, and Jeaneen Bracken and Leigh Parrish were comfortable with each other.

The Parrishes returned for Leigh's high school graduation, then announced they had decided to live permanently in Switzerland. Communication had been limited to Christmas, and visits became obsolete.

Leigh was 20 when tragedy invaded Carmela. A routine health examination had revealed an abnormal growth on her grandmother's back. For years, Leigh lived in the shadow of the diagnosis. She worked at the florist shop and attended evening college classes until tuition money was needed for more urgent expenses. Just after her twenty-fourth birthday, she dropped out of college and reduced her working hours to part-time in order to care for her grandmother.

The Bracken nest egg had long ago disappeared and Leigh's tiny salary from the florist shop barely covered the necessities of life. The darkness seemed to fall more heavily when Leigh made the trip to the bank to mortgage Carmela, deeded to Leigh on her twenty-first birthday with Jeaneen's admonition to "hold on to it, whatever the cost." Leigh knew the mortgage was necessary to pay for medical treatments not covered by insurance, but Daddy's Mama must never know about the loan.

Leigh turned to switch on the bedside lamp and for the first time since leaving the hospital, she was overcome with grief. As tears filled her eyes and splashed down her face, she reached for her grandmother's Bible. It fell open at Luke 15 where a delicately crocheted white cross marked Jeaneen Bracken's favorite passage—the account of the prodigal son. In neat, precise letters she had written a brief note in the margin: *He came home.*

It was no surprise to Leigh that *home* was the focus of her grandmother's life. As she read the verses a second time, it became clear that the eulogy for Daddy's Mama would define *home* with overtures of earthly dwellings, but from the perspective of eternity.

§§§

Nine Rockingham East was in Atlanta's northeastern upper class section. Surrounded by dogwood trees, redbud, flowering fruit trees, and a few fashionable magnolias, Creede Kelly's house was a perennial favorite on the Tour of Homes list. It had spacious, well-manicured grounds, a kidney-shaped pool with water the color of the Mediterranean, and all the elegant appointments of a twenty-first century mansion that *Southern Living* photographed for holiday editions. It was the socially correct place to live.

Creede paid handsomely for the upkeep of his house, but found little to enjoy about it. His success as a novelist had provided this luxury, so it seemed incumbent that he bury himself in writing as a feeble payback for the exquisite house.

The kitchen door slammed behind him and he automatically turned to reset the alarm. The kitchen was spotless, as it always was when Pauline cleaned the house. There was a note on the refrigerator, the agreed-upon message center. He slipped it from the magnet and read the carefully written block letters:

Mr. Kelly. I will be back Thursday afternoon and cook dinner. Your blue jacket needs to go to the cleaners. Pauline Barnes. P.S. Patti called.

Creede smiled as he tossed the note in the trash can. As a housekeeper, Pauline was a gem. She cooked the meals and looked after him and his daughter. She hated entertaining almost as much as he did, and by mutual consent they agreed any necessary parties would be hosted at the country club.

He thought about the postscript on Pauline's note and wondered about Patti's call. She was almost eighteen, but he felt a fierce protectiveness toward his daughter. Some of that undoubtedly would end, come October, when Patti would marry her prince and move out of the country.

Something about that thought created an ache in his throat. How could he function without her around? Effervescent Patti. Tempermental Patti. Melancholy Patti. So many emotions made up his daughter. Like her mother, she was a study in contrasts.

Creede stopped at the breakfast nook and sorted through the mail that came after he left on his aborted mountain trip with Max Benedict. There was the usual assortment of circulars and bills, the *Atlanta Constitution*, and a letter from his editor.

Creede slit the flap of the envelope and read the one-line message from Zachary Bennett:

Where is it, pal? Still waiting.

Creede made his way through the family room to his study and flipped on the light. The digital clock on his desk changed to twelve-o-one as he watched. The next day, already. The day before had been a strange one. What had begun as a pleasure trip had ended in drama, one that he hoped to turn into the next Erin Wintergreen best seller.

The dust jackets of all the Erin books stared at him from the bulletin board above his desk. There was Erin in Spain, her brunette beauty highlighted by a crimson toreador outfit; Erin in the Alps, flying down a snow-covered mountain on one ski; Erin in Washington before a Senate committee investigating a high-tech money-laundering scheme; Erin in Hawaii, balancing on a surfboard above a huge wave; Erin in Mexico discovering hidden treasure; and the most recent, Erin cooperating with Scotland Yard and involved in international intrigue. The seventh book was to be a sequel if he could link a North Georgia mountain mystery with Scotland Yard.

He unfolded the newspaper and the headline announced another hit-and-run to add to the city's infamous list of such accidents. He read the article hurriedly, then threw the paper to the floor. A flood of thoughts suddenly rushed through his mind, a reminder that he had almost had that dreadful experience a few hours earlier when a young woman walked in front of his truck. How did people deal with those accidents? Suppose he had hit the blonde, injured her—or worse, killed her? He shuddered at the thought and turned back to his desk.

Creede angled his six-foot-two frame in the desk chair and clicked on the computer. He selected the program, then waited for a blank document to pop up. His fingers flew over the keys and in short order, he had produced a very rough draft of the prologue. The printer ground into action, spilling out the pages. He leaned back to proof the first sentences:

Erin Wintergreen slid to the edge of her chair, her plaid coat slipping to the floor. "No. That is not the way I want to handle this case, Inspector. I will not put innocent lives at risk just to draw a criminal out of a hiding place that we're not even sure he now inhabits."

Inspector Daly frowned. He was positive this blonde beauty sitting across from him had not the vaguest idea about apprehending criminals. Scotland Yard could do without the likes of her and those notions of hers.

Creede blinked hard, staring at the sheet of paper in his hand. Erin Wintergreen was not overweight, but a plaid coat on her just would not work.

And what on earth had possessed him to describe her as a blonde?

CHAPTER 3

MARCH 17

Jason Trent sank against the plush royal blue velvet cushion and told himself again that he had the very best of the political world. It was the only world he wanted. Screaming through the air in Senator Jorgenstein's Learjet at 30,000 feet over Kansas and employed by the senator as his personal aide at a terribly inflated salary, Jason knew he was an important man. It was his intention for everyone around him to recognize his importance. He had begun to move forcefully in Washington's political scene. In the close confines of the inner circle, it was whispered that Jason Trent would be the next senator from New England who would impact the political world. He had the encouragement of the staff to pursue the goal if Senator Jorgenstein's quietly rumored appointment as an ambassador materialized later in the year. At 34, Jason had the intellect, the charm, the charisma that drew people like a magnet. *Any* cause identified with Jason Trent automatically gained instant approval and a devoted following reminiscent of the legendary Pied Piper. In Joseph Jorgenstein's state, Jason Trent was as popular as the senator.

"Jason?"

He struggled to rouse himself from the reverie that had settled in, opening his eyes to see the senator standing in the aisle. Hastily, Jason scrambled to his feet.

"Sorry, sir," he apologized. "I must have dozed off."

28

The senator motioned him back to his seat. "It's been a tiring journey, Jason. Overnight trips to California are a bit burdensome on the best of us." He paused. "I've just received a message for you from the office about your uncle."

Jason slid to the edge of the seat. "Uncle Marcus?"

Senator Jorgenstein nodded. "Someone apparently surprised him in the pharmacy last night. He's in the hospital. An undetermined amount of cash is missing."

"Cash?" Jason asked. "Couldn't have been much. Uncle Marcus never kept more than a couple hundred dollars in the register." Jason shook his head, glancing cautiously at the senator. "He was injured?"

The senator nodded. "Don't know the extent, but he was carried by ambulance to the local hospital."

"How'd you hear?" Jason asked.

"Sgt. Hendley with the Crescent Orchard Police Department called the office and left word for you." The senator watched as a blank expression settled on Jason's face. "I've instructed Captain Holmes to drop me off in Washington and then get you to Atlanta."

"Thank you, sir."

The senator returned to his seat, and Jason settled back. His thoughts turned to the gentle, white-haired man who was his father's uncle and the only remaining Trent of the older generation. Many years had passed since Jason had seen his uncle. His job was demanding and his social obligations kept his calendar filled. It simply left no time for visits. Neither could Jason deny the unfortunate fact that the fire had made his visits less frequent, and Chester Leverett's presence always made them less cordial.

Jason remembered spending a couple of summer vacations in the Georgia mountains where his great-uncle took him fishing in the sparkling trout streams. Uncle Marcus believed in the inalienable right of every boy to a few weeks a year spent in the country soaking up the purest way of life. For Jason, it had provided a fantastic childhood memory.

There had been Yule celebrations at the Trent home where the Christmas tree touched the ceiling and a bright fire threw cozy reflections about the room. The tidy bungalow, situated at the edge of Crescent Orchard with 30 acres of lush mountain real estate as the backyard, was always decorated tastefully but simply. He was almost seventeen when the family was last together for the holiday. They had arrived the day before Christmas Eve in a sprinkling of powdery snow, chilled by temperatures that hovered in the mid-twenties. Aunt Christine was troubled with a hacking cough that continually grew more annoying. Three days later, she was taken to the hospital, diagnosed with pneumonia. A few months after that, she suffered a debilitating stroke, and before the next Christmas, Uncle Marcus had made the painful decision to move her to the nursing home for better care. Jason vaguely remembered being notified a month or so ago of her passing, but he was out of the country at the time and failed to make contact with Uncle Marcus when he returned.

The plane dipped a few feet, and Jason reached to retrieve a file that dropped to the floor. Other memories were lurking in his mind, but they seemed opaque and disconnected. There was something about a house a few miles down the road, a small cottage where two rocking chairs graced the front porch that was bordered with red verbena and lavender petunias. Watermelon-colored crepe myrtle outlined the lawn where it met the road in front; in the back, apple trees paraded as far as the eye could see. There was a mountain rising in the foreground, and Jason remembered sitting on the porch thinking if the mountain ever fell, it wouldn't stop until it rolled through the front door. He thought about the elderly lady who lived in that picturesque place that Uncle Marcus had said was a very good friend to him and Aunt Christine.

Jason was in his late twenties when he met his uncle's friend, and right now, no amount of coaxing his memory produced a name for her. He could see her ever so clearly—warm brown eyes, a dimply smile, and baby-soft gray hair. And she cooked apple pies that were absolutely divine.

Despite his mental searching, no name came to mind. He closed his eyes and slid down in the seat, ready to admit defeat—not easy for Jason Trent—when suddenly, he recalled that the nameless woman had a beautiful grand-daughter named Leigh.

§§§

CRESCENT ORCHARD
MARCH 22

Leigh Parrish firmly believed that she maintained abso-lute control over every area of her life. She was one semester short of a college degree; she owned a house—with a hefty mortgage—but thankfully, she had a job at the florist shop. She was convinced that time would bring consolation to heal the grief surrounding her grandmother's death.

One tiny tear pushed its way down her face. She brushed it away impatiently and firmly reminded herself that Leigh Parrish did not cry. The renegade tear had begun its journey as she sat at the small desk in the living room at Carmela writing acknowledgments for the flowers, food, and visits. She clutched a florist's card signed *Melanie and Gordon*.

Just like my mother and stepfather. Nothing more than a funeral wreath to acknowledge Daddy's Mama lived.

Leigh tossed the card aside, irritated with her mother's failure to attend the funeral. She pushed back from the desk and walked resolutely to the bay window. Just beyond the tree line, Providence Hill rose majestically, a prelude to the higher peaks of the Blue Ridge mountain chain. Soon, it would be dotted with color as the rhododendron announced the coming of spring to North Georgia.

Daddy's Mama loved this time of the year.

Leigh stood for several minutes caught in the emotions of this special house, realizing again her need for the security it provided to deal with the loneliness that overwhelmed her.

§§§

Leigh's drive from Carmela to Crescent Orchard was almost always predictable: Jeremy Canton's tricycle would be just at the edge of the family's driveway, Mr. McKinley's mailbox would still resemble the Leaning Tower of Pisa, and Mrs. Radison's clothesline would be propped up with a bright red two-by-four.

Crescent Orchard proper was the result of sprawling apple orchards gradually convening to a central point and the establishment of a town that some 2000 inhabitants called home. With a mayor and council, police and fire departments, and a hospital, Crescent Orchard had carved out a significant place in the foothills of the Blue Ridge Mountains. The financial district, consisting of one bank and an investment firm, took pride in the fact that each was locally owned and not influenced by national overseers.

"Miss Parrish?"

A well-dressed forty-something woman with black hair winged in gray at the temples came from behind the teller's window and stood almost at Leigh's elbow.

"Miss Parrish?" she repeated.

"Yes, I'm Leigh Parrish."

"I'd like to speak with you, please. Just follow me." Piercing brown eyes were cold and unfriendly.

She led Leigh along a narrow corridor, opened a door with a brass plate at eye level that proclaimed *Ms. Fain*, and indicated a chair in front of a cherry desk. The office was small but tastefully decorated. Williamsburg blue walls were accented with off-white trim. The lone window was outlined with a paisley print lambrequin hovering over off-white plantation shutters. An English countryside print hung to the right of the desk.

"I am Phoebe Fain, Miss Parrish. I have been employed by this bank as a loan officer, and your file has been assigned to me."

Ms. Fain settled in her chair and opened a thick manila folder.

"My file?" Leigh asked timidly, sliding to the edge of her chair.

"Your mortgage," Phoebe Fain explained impatiently. "Your house mortgage is past due. We need to discuss it and resolve the issue in some way."

Leigh took a deep breath. "I've been making payments, Ms. Fain, and I do understand the note is a little past due."

"*Seriously* past due. Seventy-six days, to be exact."

"But Mr. Crosley, the president, knew my situation and was allowing me to make smaller payments until I could go back to work fulltime."

"Where *have* you been?" Ms. Fain sputtered. "Mr. Crosley is no longer president since the bank is under new management." She paused. "You live in the vicinity, Miss Parrish. Surely you knew of this bank's merger."

Leigh swallowed. "I'm sure I probably heard about it, Ms. Fain, but my grandmother's illness and death have precluded everything else."

Phoebe Fain stared solemnly at Leigh, then spoke without a trace of compassion.

"Your loan has been reworked three times, and a fourth request was denied. It is the bank's intention to deal with our past due accounts in an expeditious manner."

Suddenly, the small office was very warm and close. "I'm not sure what you mean by an *expeditious manner*, Ms. Fain."

The loan officer rose from her chair and came to stand in front of the desk.

"Then let me clue you in. Unless the loan is up-to-date within ten days the property will be foreclosed." Ms. Fain considered her bright red nails. "I regret having to be this blunt, Miss Parrish, but loans just cannot be allowed to remain past due for an extended time. If you can clear the past due amount in ten days and keep it on a current basis, everything will be fine."

"I cannot get the note up-to-date in ten days, Ms. Fain. I'll be starting back to work next week and I'll begin to make payments. That's the best I can do."

"That's not good enough." There was a moment of awkward silence. "Good day, Miss Parrish. I'll expect to hear from you soon."

With a minimum of lost motion, Phoebe Fain crossed the office to open the door for Leigh.

"Please don't ignore what I've said, Miss Parrish. I'm sure you don't want a foreclosure on your credit records."

Leigh nodded but could find no appropriate words. The door closed behind her with a loud click, and she stumbled along the corridor, through the lobby, and out the door.

Once in her car, she glanced at the mirror, then tugged it to a better position before expressing her feelings to her reflection.

"Lose Carmela?" She thrust the keys into the ignition. "That won't happen!"

Traffic was light. Leigh slowed for a caution light, then turned into the parking lot at Spring Flowers Florist Shop, where a bright sign warned of fresh paint. She entered to the spicy aroma of potpourri and the pungent scent of narcissus. Even the bell's familiar jangle brought a surprising degree of comfort to her spirit.

"Leigh!" A slightly plump woman with round face and bright pink lips came around the counter and greeted Leigh with a hug.

"Hello, Eve. How good it is to see you again!"

Evangeline Holliday stepped back to look at Leigh.

"My favorite part-time helper. I've missed you, Leigh. And I'm so terribly sorry about Jeaneen."

"Thanks, Eve. I shall miss her very much."

"As will we all, Leigh. She was good for Crescent Orchard, what with her neighborliness and concern. I'd venture to say not a family in this town has been without her kindness—and her apple pies." She hugged Leigh again. "But you didn't come here to endure another funeral, I know."

Leigh smiled. "I'm always delighted to hear good things about Daddy's Mama. But actually, I came to talk to you about working fulltime."

Eve's face clouded. "I'm so sorry, Leigh. I've already hired someone fulltime. I had no idea you would want to work here. Aren't you almost through college? I thought you'd be looking for a job that pays better than this."

"I have one more semester, but it must wait. I need to go to work to meet some obligations at the bank."

"Oh, honey, I am *so* sorry. I had no idea…"

"Don't feel badly, Eve. You did the right thing to hire someone when you needed them. I'll look around town. There'll be something available."

Eve turned to answer the telephone, and Leigh waved good-bye. She closed the door and stood for a moment soaking up the March sunshine. It was the first day of spring, heralding a season of new beginnings. She turned and walked to her car, not noticing the van that stopped at the curb, or the driver who got out and watched her intently before he entered Eve's shop.

"Good morning," Eve greeted him. "May I help you?"

"Yes, as a matter of fact, you can. The blonde who just left your shop—would you know her name?"

"Half the folks in Crescent Orchard know Leigh Parrish." Eve was struck by her customer's good looks. Just *tall, dark, and handsome* wasn't sufficient, she decided, but it went a long way. Black hair and dark eyes emphasized his clean-cut features, but what really got her attention was his obviously expensive suit and the leather-cornered book tucked under his arm. "Why do you ask?"

He smiled. "I'm sure you've heard the explanation— she looks like someone I've seen before."

Eve returned the smile. "You're right. I have heard it." She picked up her order book and pulled a pen from the carnival ware dish that doubled as a pencil holder. "Is there something I can get for you?"

"An arrangement sent to the hospital."

"To whom?"

"Just to the ICU waiting room. I thought it might lift spirits for families who are waiting."

"What a lovely thing to do. They have such limited space there—I'll fix an arrangement for $31.80, and that includes the tax. No charge for the delivery."

"I appreciate that." He handed Eve a credit card, signed the sales slip, then stuffed the card back in his wallet. "Thanks for your help."

"No problem."

Eve watched as he left the shop, saw him pause and look down the street before getting in a blue van. She picked up the merchant receipt to file and glanced at the signature.

"Dear Gussie," she breathed softly. "That was Jason Trent!" She folded the paper carefully and tucked it away in a white plastic shoebox file, then looked out the front window of the shop as the blue van drove away. "Dear Gussie!"

§§§

March sunshine filtered through a canopy of branches bare of foliage. The road stretched ahead, a ribbon of asphalt edged in brown earth, winding into the mountains in a deliberate path. Terrence Elliott pulled to the shoulder of the road and switched off the ignition. He drew a cell phone from his coat pocket, punched in a series of numbers, and waited impatiently for an answer.

"You have reached Olnick. Please hold."

He held. For an interminably long time.

"Olnick, here."

"Yeah, Boss. Elliott reporting in."

"Where have you been? You're a week late. And why haven't you answered your phone?"

Elliott decided to ignore the last question. "Had a small problem."

"Get the payment?"

"No."

"You have a good reason, I hope."

"The old man was uncooperative. Refused to pay."

"So?"

"So I left him laying on the floor."

"Dead?"

"Don't think so."

"Anybody see you in the store?"

"No. A customer came in, but she didn't know I was there. Bought a magazine. Trent gave her a cassette tape and she left."

"Gave her *what*?"

"A cassette tape. Told her it was some kind of music. Big band, I think. She told him she would play it for her sick grandmother."

There was a very long pause before Olnick spoke again.

"You would be more properly named *Terror*. That's what you are to this profession. Suppose that tape *isn't* music. Suppose Trent did a neat little recording telling the whole world who *you* are. Would that be a good thing?"

"I think it's just music, Boss. Couldn't be anything more than that."

Terrence Elliott switched the phone to his left hand while he waited for Olnick's response. It came with frightening finality.

"If you value your future, find that tape and get it back. *Understand*?"

CHAPTER 4

RURAL CRESCENT ORCHARD
MARCH 25

He trudged along in the early morning light, shoulders stooped under some invisible weight, his black coat clutched tightly against the March chill. Melting patches of snow made the ground soggy and his rubber boots made squishing sounds as he made his way through the trees.

He stopped for a moment to rest, squinting at the rising sun. His gaze followed a graceful hawk in flight as it soared, then dipped toward the earth, disappearing from sight. As he followed the descent of the bird to the horizon, a fluttering movement on the ground drew his attention.

He blinked. Twice. And again. Stirred by the gentle breeze, money was wrapping around his muddy boots. Startled, he bent to examine it.

Cash. Hard, cold cash. Lots of it.

Chester Leveritt grabbed all he could find and stuffed it in his pockets.

§§§

The news reached Spring Flowers Florist just before five on Thursday afternoon. Eve Holliday gripped the telephone receiver and took several deep breaths to stall the panic attack she knew was coming.

"He wants the service at *what* time?" she asked the funeral director.

"At noon on Saturday," he replied patiently for the third time. "I know it doesn't give you much time, Eve, but just do what you can."

Eve pressed the button to get a new line and immediately dialed Leigh Parrish's number.

"Leigh, I need help! Are you available? Marcus Trent passed a short time ago, and Jason wants the funeral Saturday at noon and my new girl has gone out-of-town for the weekend. Can you come? *Like right now*?"

§§§

The lights stayed on at Spring Flowers Florist until one A.M. on Friday and were back on before seven. The Holliday-Parrish team worked non-stop until shortly after noon when they sank to the floor and indulged in a lunch of potato chips and Coke.

"There goes my resolve to cut calories," Eve remarked as they resumed work. "How are we on wreaths?"

Leigh conducted a quick count.

"Forty-seven. Plus six vases and twelve pot plants."

"Sixty-five total. Seems like I remember there were about seventy orders. We should be through in another three hours." Eve glanced toward the cooler. "Hope I don't run out of flowers."

"Do you want me to start delivering these arrangements to the funeral home?" Leigh asked.

"We don't have to do that. Morgan said he would be here at three o'clock for pickup…" Eve turned toward the door as the tinkling bell announced a customer.

"Joy!" she exclaimed. "Joy Bliss! What a surprise!"

"Hi, Eve," Joy greeted her. "I have some floral offerings from the Atlanta area for Mr. Trent's service and need direction to the funeral home."

"Just leave them here," Eve instructed. "They'll pick them up when they get these." She indicated the mass of arrangements with a sweep of her arm. "Let me help you bring them in."

As they unloaded the van, Joy complimented Eve. "You're unbelievable, Eve. I am impressed with all those arrangements you have assembled in your shop."

Eve laughed. "You're right—I'm good. But not *that* good. I had help. Wish I had a place for Leigh fulltime. She's been my part-time helper for several years."

Joy paused before closing the van door. "Are you saying she's not currently employed?"

"Exactly what I'm saying. She's looking for a job. Desperately."

"Has she experience with weddings?"

"She's directed at least a dozen for me." Eve slid a carnation wreath on her arm and picked up a pot of red tulips. "Do you have an opening?"

"Actually, two. A floral designer and a wedding coordinator."

"She'll be perfect for both," Eve said. "Can I send her for an interview?"

§§§

Joy Bliss had barely exited the parking lot when Eve grabbed Leigh and swung her around the limited space in the shop.

"Leigh, my friend, Joy Bliss, is desperate to find an experienced person for her shop in Atlanta. Are you interested?"

"I hadn't planned to relocate just yet. And where would I live?"

41

"That's not even a challenge. I have another friend who has a guest cottage that's vacant. I'll be glad to recommend you."

Leigh laughed. "I also have an *old* car. I can just see it leaving me stranded on some Atlanta street."

"Can't help you there," Eve said. "But I'm willing to do what I can any other way."

"Maybe I should give some thought to your suggestion. I need to work."

It was all the encouragement Eve Holliday needed. "Let me get Joy on her cell phone right now. Then, I'll call my house friend."

Eve dialed a number, chatted a moment, then turned to Leigh. "You *can* be in Atlanta at two on Monday, can't you?"

Leigh nodded. "Yes, of course, I can."

Eve completed her call and scribbled information on the back of an index card. "Here you are, Leigh."

Leigh tucked the card in her shoulder bag and turned her attention to the remaining wreaths. "Thanks, Eve, for your help. Maybe someday I can repay you."

"I'm not the least bit worried about repayment. I only wish I had a place for you." She smiled. "But Joy Bliss is getting great talent. I know, because I trained you myself."

§§§

Leigh stood for a moment watching a bird as it struggled to begin construction of a nest over the Spring Flowers door. Less than a week earlier, the first day of spring had come to Crescent Orchard. It was the season of the year that most reminded her of Daddy's Mama—the gentleness, the beauty, the brightness that had been reflected in her grandmother's life and transmitted to everything that was special in Jeaneen Bracken's life, particularly Carmela.

With a sudden lilt to her step, Leigh hurried to her car and drove to the Crescent Orchard bank. She completed her deposit slip for Eve's salary payment, then wrote her check to the bank for $700 and waited her turn for an available teller. A moment later, she had her receipts in hand, ready to leave, then turned back to speak to the teller.

"Would you please advise Ms. Fain that I have made this payment?"

The loan officer who was in charge of her file couldn't evict her yet.

§§§

MARCH 27

Warm sunshine filtered through the limbs of the oak trees as Marcus Trent was laid to rest by the side of his beloved Christine. Hundreds of mourners stood respectfully as Pastor Cavanaugh concluded the committal service with prayer.

Leigh waited quietly until the crowd moved away from Jason Trent.

"Jason, I'm Leigh Parrish. I wanted to offer condolence…"

"Leigh," Jason said as he shook her hand. "Thanks so much for being here." He paused. "The world has lost an incredible man. Uncle Marcus was unique."

"I couldn't agree more," Leigh said. "No one can count all the times he's helped the people in Crescent Orchard."

Jason released her hand and stepped back. "He loved his town and its people, and I'm sure they knew it." He looked past Leigh to a small group of men who waited by the hearse. "Would you excuse me, Leigh? I need to speak with Mr. Morgan before he leaves." Jason paused briefly. "I'd like to give you a call when I'll be back in town. Maybe we can have dinner."

Leigh walked slowly to her car. Just as she reached to open the door, a rough hand grasped her elbow. She turned to face a man dressed in rusty brown slacks and blue pullover sweater. A black overcoat was draped over his arm. His scuffed brown boots bore traces of dried mud across the toes.

"Chester, I'm so sorry about Marcus. He was a very special person."

Chester Leverett dropped his hand and muttered unintelligible sounds before stumbling away.

§§§

No one paid attention to Chester Leverett as he retrieved his bike and pedaled down the drive from the church.

Providence Church of Crescent Orchard was situated between Providence Hill and the thriving town of Crescent Orchard. Both locations were well-known to Chester. He had lived with Marcus and Christine at the edge of Crescent Orchard since he was almost five until four years ago when the disagreement with Marcus caused him to move out. Uncle Marcus was always a forgiving person and didn't want him to leave, but Chester made his decision and refused to return.

He had found the abandoned hunting cabin a few hundred feet up Providence Hill and decided to call it home. He grew to love the quiet and serenity and only left to travel the few miles into Crescent Orchard for supplies. His path went by Carmela, and Leigh and her grandmother often gave him fresh vegetables from their garden and fruit from the orchard. He was sure they were the only people who cared about him.

Chester constantly glanced behind him. When no vehicles followed from the church, he knew it was the right day, the right time, to get the picture from Marcus' house before Jason remembered it was there.

He pulled into the yard, jumped from the bike and let it fall to the ground near the bed of spring bulbs as he ran to the back entrance and located the key that was hidden under the chrysanthemum pot plant.

It wasn't necessary to be quiet since no one was around to hear, but he was careful not to disturb anything along the way to the den. Once there, he lost no time removing the picture of Marcus, Christine, and himself—in its walnut frame with the cracked glass—from the hook above the sofa.

The two-by-three foot frame would make it awkward to handle on the bike and would brand him as a thief if anyone saw him with it, but this picture was all he had to remind him he once had been part of a family.

§§§

ATLANTA
MARCH 29

Tabitha Parks gently caressed the white lace mantilla and noticed, not for the first time, the fraying edges. The delicate pattern of the lace was blurred—was it because of tears in her eyes, or because her eyes were weary with age?

She moved with painful steps to her dresser and surveyed her mirrored reflection. Slowly, she draped the mantilla over her silver white hair and let its edges flow gently down her back. What memories were evoked!

Today, March 29, marked her forty-fifth wedding anniversary, and today, like every March 29 for the last thirty years, she was remembering it alone. Widowhood had not made her bitter, thank goodness—just lonely. Pulling out the mantilla that had been her wedding veil only emphasized the loneliness. Yet, she found it impossible to discard it. Mrs. Carruthers down the street had suggested selling it in the church's antique auction. "It will fetch a hundred dollars easy," she had said. Tabitha could use the money, but she refused to sacrifice a sacred reminder for a mere pittance.

With trembling hands, she removed the veil and straightened her hair, then pulled the gold wire-rimmed glasses down just enough to wipe a tear. Each year, it took a little longer to go through the ritual, and each year it was harder on her emotions. But just as surely as rainbows followed rain, she would do it again next year if God allowed her to remain on earth.

After wrapping the mantilla in tissue paper and storing it in her cedar chest, Tabitha walked slowly back to her den and picked up the mail she had laid on the table the day before. The usual *Occupant* circulars, the utility bill, and the Wal-Mart sales sheet—it was all she got any more since the newspaper subscription had gone so high and she had cancelled. She opened the utility bill and gasped at the $137.57 charge. That was over a third of her social security check. And when her pharmacy bill came, that would be another $150.00. After food and clothing, hardly anything was left for the upkeep of her treasured old house, and absolutely nothing for the vacant caretaker's cottage. Times had always been hard, but now they bordered on disastrous.

Tabitha sank into a chair, still clutching the utility bill. She eventually dozed, and the ringing phone roused her several minutes later.

"Hello?"

"Tabby? It's Eve Holliday. Do you still have that little caretaker's cottage available? I have a friend who needs to rent a place—pronto!"

§§§

Leigh Parrish looked again at the index card on which Eve had written the address: 2451 Walnut Ridge. With a great deal of mental effort, she reminded herself that it was only a house without charm, but that could be fixed.

The only spot of beauty was a row of dogwood trees almost ready to burst into bloom. Leigh took hesitant steps along the uneven ground to the end of the row and saw the house on the hill, a two-story mildly Victorian, whose white paint had surrendered to the elements and left exposed huge patches of weather-darkened wood. The front lawn that sloped gently to the street was studded with forsaken shrubbery and neglected flowerbeds—a gardener's nightmare.

She turned her attention again to the small cottage. Like the big house, it needed paint. Decorative braces that trimmed the top of the wooden post supports at the roof line on the entry porch sagged badly. Several banister posts were completely gone. The porch and steps, however, appeared fairly sturdy.

"Here's the key, dear. I intended to be here when you arrived."

Leigh turned to see a silver-haired woman approaching from the left side of the house. Dressed in a blue chambray dress and plaid flannel jacket, she stopped at the steps and leaned heavily on her cane.

"I'm so sorry," she apologized. "I just let the time slip up on me."

"Mrs. Parks?" Leigh questioned.

"I am. And you must be Miss Parrish. Eve told me about your need for a place to live."

Leigh smiled. "Everything has happened so fast, and I hope I don't have the cart before the horse. Here I am looking at a place to live and I don't know if I'll get the job—my interview is at two this afternoon."

Tabitha climbed carefully the four steps to the porch. "When Eve called this morning about the cottage, she was sure you would be hired." She unlocked the door and pushed it open. "The cottage hasn't been cleaned in quite some time, but with some scrubbing and paint, it can be very charming. It's small, but completely furnished, and should be fine for one person. Come, let me show you the other rooms."

Leigh followed as Tabitha led her to the living-dining area with its vaulted ceiling. A compact, U-shaped kitchen was separated from that area with a bar that doubled as a casual eating area. The bedroom and bath were located at the back of the house.

"That's the whole tour, Miss Parrish. I hope you see some possibilities in it."

Leigh pushed the faded curtain aside. Something about the cottage now intrigued her—its compactness, its close proximity to the house on the hill, the endless possibilities with the yard.

"How much is the rent, Mrs. Parks?"

Tabitha hesitated. "I hope you'll not think me greedy for money, but I was thinking in the neighborhood of $400.00 a month."

Leigh turned from the window to face Tabitha Parks. "That sounds like a very fair price, Mrs. Parks. But not knowing about the job at Weddings of Bliss…"

Tabitha laughed and clicked her cane on the floor. "I do not have a list of prospective tenants. I can wait to hear from you."

Leigh considered her expenses: house rent, mortgage payment on Carmela, an ailing automobile, clothes, food, utilities, other routine monthly expenses. How could she do it? How could she *not* do it?

"I'll take it."

CHAPTER 5

When Murphy's Law was in effect at nine in the morning, it was a pretty good indication that *down* was the only direction for the rest of the day.

Terrence Elliott threw his burned toast in the garbage and poured the sour milk down the sink drain. The bacon was curling into a blackened glob over too-high heat while the percolator hissed and sputtered its contents onto the counter. He silently vowed that from now on, he would stay in a motel, not some cheap tourist park where the cabins were equipped with postage-stamp-size kitchens.

Terrence muttered his displeasure at the whole kitchen scene and picked up the newspaper. His cell phone jangled at the same moment.

"Elliott."

"Did you read the obits last week?"

Terrence groaned. *A call from Olnick is just the icing on the cake. It's going to be a very bad day.* "Not unless it was on the sports page."

"Trent's funeral was Saturday."

"What?" Terrence sank against the sink.

"It is vital that you get back up in the mountains and find that woman he gave the tape to and get it back."

"How am I supposed to do that?"

49

"That's not my problem. It's yours. You have 24 hours."

"Or what?"

"You don't want to know."

§§§

The BMW purred along the mountain highway, leaving Atlanta in the background. Terrence glanced at the speedometer, saw the needle waver around 80 and decided it would not be wise to call attention to himself by attracting the eye of the State Patrol. Accordingly, he slowed to 70 and attempted to concentrate on a plan of action.

His thoughts shifted to the night at Trent's Pharmacy when a late customer came in. He had heard her conversing with Marcus Trent, but she had been just out of his sight. He remembered her voice was soft and gentle when she thanked Marcus for the tape, but it seemed rather stupid of Olnick to think he could locate her when he didn't even know what the woman looked like, nor did he know her name.

Terrence swerved to avoid an apple crate at the edge of the road, and like a ton of bricks the thought hit him: she had told Marcus she would take the tape to the hospital and play it for her grandmother.

Suddenly, his job seemed easier. He would go to the hospital and inquire about the young woman who had a sick grandmother on March 16. Totally inspired with his plan, he turned the car around and retraced the route to the Crescent Orchard exit. An hour later, he pulled into the parking lot at Crescent Orchard Hospital, then briskly made his way to the patient information center.

"Good morning," he greeted the Pink Lady volunteer. "I'm trying to locate the daughter of an old friend. I understand her grandmother was a patient here around the middle of March."

"The name, please?"

"That is a problem. I don't know it."

"I'm sorry, sir. I can't help you without a name."

The desk phone rang and she reached to lift the receiver. "Patient Information Center. Mrs. Burkhalter."

There was a moment of silence, and Terrence propped against the desk.

"Mr. Trent was brought in *before* seven on March 16," Winifred Burkhalter continued her phone conversation. "I remember thinking how sad it was that he never knew about Jeaneen Bracken's passing—and their families had been such good friends for so many years."

Terrence Elliott perked up.

"I'm absolutely certain," Winifred reiterated to her caller. She paused, listening, then continued. "Why not check with housekeeping? Jason didn't get here until the next day and if he left a book in the ICU waiting room, they would have found it and put it in safekeeping."

She replaced the receiver, then turned to give her attention to the visitor at her desk—who had now disappeared.

§§§

Terrence ran his finger down the "B" listings in the local telephone directory, stopping on *Jeaneen Bracken*. He made a note of the address, 121 Providence Hill Road, then stepped from the hospital phone booth. He hurried to his car, pulled out a map, and located Providence Hill Road, then drove out-of-town in that direction. When he finally found 121, a Spring Flowers Florist van was pulling out of the drive. He continued down the road, deciding it would be a good time to retrieve the money he had stashed in a barn.

§§§

Leigh closed the back door at Tabitha's and wiped her forehead with a hand smudged with dirt.

"Through with your moving?" Tabitha asked from the kitchen.

"All completed," Leigh answered wearily. "I would still be riding between Crescent Orchard and Atlanta if Eve hadn't let me borrow the flower shop van for moving."

"And everything's in the cottage?"

"Everything. Which amounts to my clothes, a few recipe books, dishes, cookware, and some linens. And everything's in its proper place."

"And did the cleaning service get through? No cobwebs in the corners or dust bunnies under the bed?"

"Everything's fine. They dusted, vacuumed, mopped—even put in new shelf paper in the kitchen cabinets. Shall I just add the cost of cleaning to my first month's rent?"

"There's no charge, Leigh. My sister-in-law gave me a gift certificate for Christmas for a total housecleaning by Heidi's Cleaning." Tabitha chuckled. "I'm sure Heidi would much rather clean the little cottage than this monstrous house."

Leigh sighed in relief, then tried to conceal it with soft laughter. Four hundred dollars just for rent would severely fracture her bank balance at the moment, so she breathed a quick prayer of thanks for Heidi.

Tabitha lifted a lid from a pot on the stove. "I've got vegetable soup," she told Leigh. "If you want to shower and change, it will be ready in half an hour."

"I can make a sandwich…"

"There's enough for an army, Leigh. Don't you know one can't make a small amount of soup?"

"I'll be right back," Leigh promised.

§§§

CRESCENT ORCHARD

Terrence Elliott gripped the steering wheel to divert his attention from the incessant pounding in his head. The headache reminded him of a Morse code message that kept repeating *24 hours...24 hours...24 hours...*

From the grocery store parking lot where he sat, Terrence watched people hurrying about in the gathering twilight, laden with bags of groceries. Headed home, he guessed. To warm, comfortable homes and good hot meals.

He squeezed into traffic and headed out-of-town, determined to locate the barn and the stolen pharmacy money. Thanks to his non-existent sense of direction, he had no clue where to begin. He did, however, know where the house was located that just might have the cassette tape he needed to get. Maybe this would be a good night for a burglary at 121 Providence Hill Road.

§§§

"Leigh's moved to Atlanta, Brian. To take a job with my friend, Joy Bliss. She doesn't have her phone in yet, but you can call her at Tabitha Parks' house. I'm sure Tabitha won't mind getting her a message. In fact," Eve glanced at the clock that boasted green metal leaves for hands, "she should have gotten there by now. She used my van to do the moving, and she brought it back and got her car just before four."

Brian Porter grinned. "That car of hers is an accident waiting to happen."

Eve turned the sign on the door so that it read *Closed* from the outside.

"The engine for sure is in critical condition. It coughed and sneezed until she was out of sight. I hope she didn't have any problem on the interstate. As far as I know, she doesn't have a cell phone, so if anything happens—"

"Nothing will," Brian interrupted, wishing he felt as confident as he sounded.

"Hope you're right." Eve handed him a gift enclosure card that proclaimed *Happy Birthday*. "I've written Tabitha's number on the back of this card."

Brian thanked her and held the door open while Eve fumbled for her keys. "Why do they always wind up in the bottom of my purse?" she grumbled.

Brian watched her drive away, then got in his patrol car and headed for the station. For some reason, Carmela surfaced in his thoughts. It was vacant for the first time in many years, now that Leigh had moved to Atlanta. He hoped the county deputies would keep a vigilant eye on Jeaneen Bracken's cherished Carmela.

§§§

All was quiet in the country. Terrence had driven onto a dirt logging road and secluded the BMW in a grove of evergreen trees. He got his flashlight and gloves, climbed from the car, and took cautious steps across the ruts, then hurried several hundred yards along Providence Hill Road until he reached the graveled drive at the Bracken house. He kept in the grass, still lifeless and winter brown, until he reached the back porch. There were no vehicles in the yard, no lights on in the house. Quietly, he went up the porch steps to the door, pulled on his gloves and turned the knob.

Locked.

No sweat. There was always an alternative means of entry, in this case a small window to the right of the door.

He examined the screen, focusing his flashlight on the upper left corner. From the assorted collection of miniature tools on his key ring, he found one with a sharp point and proceeded to puncture the screen and slice it across the top and down the sides. He was relieved to find there was no lock on the window, and he cautiously lifted the lower sash enough to squeeze through and step into the kitchen sink.

Once on the floor, Terrence listened. Only the measured ticking of a clock somewhere in the house interrupted the silence. He switched his flashlight to dim with only enough light to illuminate a path ahead of him, and slowly made his way through the kitchen. Once in the den, he pulled the heavy draperies together, then turned his flashlight to bright and surveyed the room. Directly in front of him stood a maple entertainment center and on top were stacks of cassette tapes.

"Oh, yeah! Jackpot!"

With a vengeance he tore into the tapes, focusing the beam of his flashlight on the ones that fell to the floor, deciding to begin his search there. He looked at the titles, then hurriedly tossed them aside. Gospel readings, hymn instrumentals, sermons. But nothing about big band music. He turned his attention to the remaining tapes, reading each title, but finding nothing remotely connected to band music.

Disgusted, he returned to the kitchen and climbed through the window, trudging across the yard, down the edge of the highway to the logging road and his secluded car. Once on the road, he decided to look again for the barn and his hidden money.

A half-mile down the road from the Bracken house, he stopped at the barn. In the dusky light, he opened the door, appalled at the squeak of the hinges. With the door closed behind him, he switched on the flashlight and stopped, horrified. The barn was empty!

No tape. His money was now gone. And a horrible message started replaying in his mind. *24 hours…24 hours…*

§§§

ATLANTA

Leigh slid her chair from the table but made no effort to get up.

"Tabitha, that meal was so good it had character!"

Tabitha beamed. "It was only vegetable soup and corn-bread."

"Makes no difference. It was wonderful!"

"Well, thank you, dear. Until you've got everything settled in the cottage, you're welcome to eat with me. It won't be fancy, but you can get by on it."

"I've no doubt, Tabitha. But I'll stock my pantry tomorrow—"

Tabitha reached for the ringing telephone. "Hello," she said, then handed the receiver to Leigh. "For you," she whispered.

"Hello?" Leigh smiled. "Sgt. Hendley. How nice to hear from you."

Tabitha watched the smile disappear from Leigh's face as she replaced the receiver a moment later.

"How strange."

"What is it, Leigh?"

"That was Sgt. Hendley from the Crescent Orchard Police Department. He said I was the last person to see Marcus Trent on the night he was attacked and they want to talk to me!"

CHAPTER 6

Tabitha poured the leftover soup in a Tupperware bowl and sealed the lid.

"That's probably just standard procedure, don't you think? Surely you're not a suspect!" Tabitha shivered. "How do they know you were the last person to see Mr. Trent?"

Leigh put the tea in the refrigerator, closed the door and leaned against it.

"The night of the attack, I stopped at the pharmacy to get a magazine. When I left, I went to the hospital to be with my grandmother, and Brian Porter from Sgt. Hendley's office saw me drive by as he was walking his rounds."

"Was Mr. Trent injured during the attack?"

"Eve said when Brian found him, he was complaining about his chest. He did have a heart attack, but I haven't heard if there were any injuries related to the robbery. Marcus never regained consciousness." Leigh glanced toward her cottage. "I don't *know* anything, Tabitha. Why do they want to talk to me when I don't know anything?"

§§§

CRESCENT ORCHARD
MARCH 31

Terrence Elliott washed down the last of his too-done hamburger with a swallow of too-tart lemonade. He sat in a back booth of the Burger Palace in downtown Crescent

Orchard, slumped low, his face partially hidden behind the super-size napkin.

Failure. It was the only word that described him on this day. Finding no cassette tape spelled his doom with Olnick. For a brief moment, he wondered what would be his punishment when the 24 hours expired. It was getting close to midnight, so in a matter of hours he would find out.

He shifted slightly, propping against the wall of the booth. What he needed was an outstanding plan of action. It would not be to his advantage to report to Olnick that he had failed to get the tape, nor would it be wise to ask for more time.

Terrence glanced out the window at the traffic, and the idea was born. He would take the coward's way out. He would leave, simply disappear—even though he knew that, historically, people in his profession didn't disappear, unless it was permanently at the hands of the superiors in the organization. At this point, however, he was willing to be the exception to the rule, to prove that history did not always repeat itself.

Terrence laid the napkin aside and slid to the end of the booth just as the door opened. Startled, he sank back, thinking there was something familiar about the fellow's face. But how could it be when so much of it was covered with beard? He tried to hear the voice.

"Howdy, ya'll!"

It fell into place then. A lonely road outside of Crescent Orchard. The night of March 16. A faulty new car. Lights along the road.

And now here. Wrecker boy.

Terrence watched him weave his way through the crowded dining area and disappear on the far side. When he was out of sight, Terrence wasted no time leaving the booth.

A clock at the front door chimed midnight, and Terrence took a deep breath. It was now the tomorrow he had dreaded for hours. With his situation, it was most fitting.

April Fools Day.

§§§

When Terrence Elliott slipped from the Burger Palace shortly after midnight, he stumbled through the darkness and across a graveled area to his car, conveniently parked in the darkest spot. He crawled in, locked the door, and settled back against the headrest to consider his predicament.

He had not meant to kill Marcus Trent. Frighten him, psychologically rough him up a bit, yes…but not murder. He found a certain amount of satisfaction in subordinating people to his power, but it didn't go so far as taking the life of anyone.

A siren shrilled along the road, accompanied by flashing blue lights. Something about the sound brought to mind the tape he had not found at the Bracken house. With a jolt, he wondered if the break-in had been discovered, and if that was where the law was headed.

In a swift motion, he cranked the car, eased out of the parking area, and drove in the direction of Providence Hill. As he neared the familiar location, he saw additional blue lights scattered along the road and scores of people rushing frantically about.

He groaned. The break-in had been discovered, and like the proverbial crook, he was returning to the scene of the crime—riding right into it in the car that had been at the scene of his first crime. How much dumber could he get?

Just ahead, an officer was stopping traffic. Terrence slowed the BMW.

"Good evening, sir," the deputy said pleasantly enough.

"Officer," Terrence acknowledged. "What's the problem?"

"Bill Robbins' cows are out. All over the highway. We're trying to get them in the pasture across the road."

"What is this road?" Terrence asked innocently.

"Providence Hill. Robbins owns from the Bracken place on up to the county line, twenty miles or better, and we've got cows out half that distance."

"And you're just trying to get them across this road?"

"Right. Fences are better on the other side. If we can get them over there and past the barns, we'll have done a good night's work."

"Barns?"

"There're several in the area that are alike. Mostly storage buildings for feed."

Terrence eased his foot off the brake. "I wish you well."

The deputy stepped back. "Just watch for people and animals in the road. And keep your speed down."

Terrence nodded and drove slowly away, reflecting on the officer's reference to *barns*. Maybe he had been unable to find the stashed pharmacy money because he had looked in the wrong barn. He would come back and search each one.

He drove across the state line at four A.M. As dawn broke across the eastern sky over two hours later, he pulled the BMW into the compound that housed six other expensive, late-model cars, carefully wiped his fingerprints from the interior, left the cell phone on the seat, and climbed out.

All was quiet on the estate and no lights were on in the big house. With his overnight bag grasped in his hand, he hurried down the hill to the highway, keeping in the shadows of the early morning, and waited for a passing motorist to come his way. It would be difficult to explain his three-piece charcoal gray business suit to a potential ride. He tried his explanation on a squirrel rummaging for its breakfast: "My new car turned out to be a lemon. Could you give me a lift to town?" Terrence decided it sounded pitiful.

A vehicle was approaching and he stepped to the edge of the road. It had been a very long time since he had been reduced to hitching a ride.

§§§

ATLANTA
APRIL 1

Leigh Parrish studied her reflection in the mirror attached to the back of her bedroom door. A navy plaid skirt topped with a white long-sleeved blouse and navy blazer seemed to be a good choice for her first day on the job. Simple pearl earrings, a three-year-old leather-banded Timex watch, and her grandmother's open circle lapel pin of amethyst stones complimented her outfit. Blonde hair in a simple classic cut framed her face. Eyes just a shade lighter than cobalt were the perfect match for long brown lashes and slightly arched brows.

Satisfied with her appearance, she gathered her purse and lunch bag from the kitchen counter, and headed for her first day of work at Weddings of Bliss.

§§§

Challenge was definitely the proper word to describe the journey from Leigh's compact cottage on Walnut Ridge to the ultramodern building that housed Weddings of Bliss. She entered the spacious showroom inhabited by dozens of mannequins robed in wedding dresses, from chic sheaths to billowy formal gowns with trains curled gracefully on the floor.

61

The furnishings were elegant, mostly in polished cherry with seafoam green upholstery. Window treatments consisted of ivory brocade drapes held back with seafoam ropes ending with six-inch tassels. Three fine art pieces clustered on the wall directly behind the receptionist's desk.

"Good morning, Miss Parrish. Welcome to Weddings of Bliss. I'm glad you're here."

Leigh glanced at the brass nameplate on the desk. "Thank you, Mrs. Coleman. It's good to have a job."

The woman at the desk smiled pleasantly. "Mrs. Coleman hasn't arrived yet. Ten is her usual time. I'm Gillian Grayson, the human resources person." Gillian studied the appointment book briefly. "We don't have a client until 9:30. Want to look around a bit?"

"I'd like that," Leigh answered.

Gillian led the way from the showroom along a corridor lined with six small office areas. She stopped at the last one.

"This is yours."

"I get an office? The newest employee?"

"You came highly recommended by Evangeline Holliday, and since we're short on wedding coordinators and the busy season is about to begin, Mrs. Bliss wants you here." Gillian indicated the office with a sweep of her hand. "If you want to store your purse and come with me, I need to get your signature on some employment forms so I can get you set up for payroll and insurance coverage."

Leigh took a moment to admire the eggshell walls with deep gold trim, the walnut desk and matching file cabinets, the desk chair upholstered in brown and gold floral and the companion chair opposite the desk. This had to be a dream career.

"If this day goes anything like that stupid traffic this morning, I hope no customers come because I will not be very pleasant!"

Gillian took a deep breath. "Anna Gibbs, this is Leigh Parrish. Or did you meet her when she interviewed?"

Anna's glance at Leigh traveled from head to toe and back again. "I saw her. She's co-ordinating?"

"Of course," Gillian replied.

"Good. Then I'm bringing her the Kelly file. I've had it with that girl."

"Leigh's just beginning, Anna. Mrs. Bliss may have another assignment for her."

"Gillian." Anna folded her arms across her chest. "If Mrs. Bliss wants to keep the Kelly account, it's Leigh or you. You don't do weddings. That leaves Leigh. All of the other coordinators have had the opportunity to satisfy that brat, and no one can. Patti Kelly is an impossible bride." Anna paused a moment before continuing with her opinion. "I really feel sorry for Prince Alex and for the Isle of Windemere. A hurricane may be calm compared to the fury that girl has the potential for releasing!"

§§§

Leigh studied the open Kelly file on her desk, reading with considerable interest the multiple sticky notes that lined the inside of the manila folder. Dates, times, and places had been written, then crossed out. A bright yellow note boldly stated *She will call about appointment to visit church. A. Gibbs, March 19.* A second entry on the same note said *Have not heard from Her Highness. A.G. March 29.*

The official contract of Weddings of Bliss was attached to the next partition in the folder, indicating that Patrice Kathleen Kelly was to be married on Friday, October 29, to Alexander Gregory William Spencer, Prince of Windemere.

The place and time were *TBD*. The wedding gown was marked *Ordered,* but the invitations, flowers, and music were all blank lines.

Leigh thumbed through the remainder of the file, closing it just as Anna Gibbs came to her door.

"Your client will be here at two o'clock on April 5," she said. "Patti Kelly. But I wouldn't count on it. I doubt that she's been to an appointment on time in her life. And it'll be that way for her wedding. I guarantee it." Anna exhaled a long breath. "You know who her father is, don't you?"

Leigh shook her head. "Should I?"

"He's Creede Kelly."

"I'm sorry?"

Anna perched on the corner of Leigh's desk. "Creede Kelly, honey. Six feet two. Muscular. Thick wavy dark brown hair and brown eyes you could melt in they're so warm. The author of the Erin Wintergreen books. You do read, don't you?"

"Not that much."

"Read at least one," Anna suggested. "Then you'll have something to talk about when Miss High and Mighty can't make up her mind."

"Discuss the book with Miss Kelly?"

"With *Mr.* Kelly. Patti won't be eighteen until June. Since she's not of legal age, everything must be approved by Mr. Kelly. And based on the few things Patti has selected, she's definitely not opposed to separating Daddy from his money."

"Does she know about this?" Leigh asked. "I mean the legal part?"

"Sure. She was *told*, but whether she remembers...She's young and in love with getting married. It could have slipped her mind. But you can remind her when she comes Monday. And also, her father must come with her on the next appointment to review and sign the contract." Anna slid from the desk and started to the door. "And he needs to bring his checkbook."

"Anna, I noticed on the contract the wedding gown had been ordered. If her father has not yet signed the contract, why would we place an order for the gown?"

"*Ordered* on the contract simply means she's agreed to purchase her gown here. We've not actually submitted an order to the dressmaker. We require a deposit before doing that."

"Thanks for clarifying that. I guess I have a lot to learn."

Anna pointed to the Kelly file. "And you'll learn it all with this one."

§§§

CRESCENT ORCHARD

Burkhalter's Grocery had been a Crescent Orchard institution for more than a century. Situated just beyond Crescent Orchard proper, Burkhalter's had been witness to a hundred years of progress in the hills of North Georgia. The store's origin was preserved at the county courthouse in pictures that captured a ten-year-old entrepreneur with his lemonade stand under the shade of a sprawling white oak. Accompanying documents proclaimed an eight-ounce glass of lemonade was sold for a nickel, with one free refill. Horatio Burkhalter, at ten, had seen the wisdom of providing his customers with a complimentary drink. His mother, however, wasn't exactly impressed with his generosity when the lemon squeezing was her responsibility.

As the years passed and the summer lemonade industry flourished, Horatio expanded his business to include produce, meat, and dairy products, and Burkhalter's Grocery was born. When he began promoting soft drinks in glass bottles packed in wooden crates, future success was all but guaranteed. The old-timers discovered the crates made wonderful seats when turned on end, and many a winter afternoon was passed in pleasure as they gathered around a checkerboard, hugging the pot-bellied stove and downing partially frozen colas.

Succeeding generations witnessed few changes in the store. Horatio had insisted *"If it ain't broke, don't fix it."* It would be left to Horatio's descendants to decide when fixing was due. The store passed to each succeeding generation with silent fanfare and Horatio's instruction to "keep it in the family." His son, Herman, had done that for fifteen years and now the store belonged to Herman's son, Hannibal.

Hannibal knew his general store could not compete with the downtown Kroger in prices or merchandise, but he was overtly proud of his modernizing achievements. He had put in a frozen foods department, painted the interior, and installed fluorescent lighting. He had even updated the cash register to one of those snazzy machines that read bar codes. His most embarrassing moment had been his confession of ignorance about using the scanner, which led to the subsequent hiring of his daughter, Sue Ellen—fresh out of technical school the previous December—as cashier.

Sue Ellen was bright and highly capable. She could greet vendors and stock shelves. With her long black hair flowing down her back in a single braid, her huge brown eyes and olive skin, she was not bad looking. She was also Hannibal's only child and the future owner of Burkhalter's of Crescent Orchard. But it did try every ounce of Hannibal's patience and his very last nerve to endure her gum chewing and her incessant talking. Hannibal was sure both were inherited from her mother.

He heard the *ching* as the cash drawer opened but did not look up from stocking oatmeal just down the aisle. He did look up when Sue Ellen erupted.

"I'm not believing this!"

"What's up, Ellie?"

"Look at this money! We haven't taken in a hundred dollar bill in six weeks, and today I get two of them from the same customer!"

"What customer?"

"That one! I can't think of his name. Going toward the hardware store!"

Hannibal glanced out the window. "Guess I missed him."

"Counterfeit!" Sue Ellen exclaimed. "What if they're counterfeit? And we're stuck with them?"

"Can you recognize a counterfeit bill?"

"What do I look for? The picture's on here, there's a serial number, somebody's signed it. What else should there be?"

Sue Ellen blew three bubbles, popping each with the zing of a flying bullet. She raced to the window, glanced both ways, then blew another trio of bubbles.

There were times when Hannibal almost wished that Kroger had her.

"There!" she cried. "There he is! Coming across the street!"

Hannibal watched as the shabbily clad man stepped up on the curb, then continued down the sidewalk.

And suddenly, it clicked.

He reached for the phone and dialed, waited to be connected.

"Morning, Sergeant. This is Hannibal. Chester Leverett was just in the store with some mighty big money. Thought you might want to talk to him."

CHAPTER 7

Leigh Parrish drove through Crescent Orchard, past the landmarks so much a part of her memory of days gone by. Providence Hill was her favorite landmark. When it appeared, Carmela was just around the next bend.

She pulled into the yard, her thoughts momentarily flooded by a multitude of emotions: Daddy's Mama working in her flower garden, straw hat pulled low over her eyes; the rocking chairs and the deacon's bench on the front porch that could not keep a coat of paint…

Suddenly, something looked different. Leigh studied the scene before her for a moment before grasping the door handle and flinging it open.

"I don't remember closing the den drapes! Why would I have done that?" She hurried across the yard, up the steps, and inserted her key in the door. It opened noiselessly and she stepped inside, moving quickly to the den.

April sunshine made a brave effort to lighten the room through the heavy drapes but succeeded only in creating shadowy effects. Leigh flipped on the overhead light, then gasped in horror. Cassette tapes trailed across the entertainment center and onto the floor. Empty plastic tape holders were intermingled in the jumble.

She glanced about the den, then hurried to check other rooms. Nothing appeared disturbed. In the kitchen, a peculiar scratching sound came from the area around the sink. It was then Leigh discovered the loosened screen on the window was flapping in the gentle spring breeze.

With trembling hand, she reached for the phone and dialed the sheriff's office.

§§§

"It wasn't very smart of you to come in here by yourself," the deputy admonished after completing his initial survey of the house.

Leigh looked at him. "I didn't know anything was wrong until I came *inside*," she said.

He flipped back a couple of pages in his notepad, then drilled her with his stare. "You said you noticed the drapes were pulled when you drove up. I have that in my notes. Shouldn't that have alerted you to some possible danger?"

Leigh took a deep breath. "I did notice that, yes. And, no, I didn't have the forethought of impending danger."

Momentarily caught off guard by her unexpected confession, Deputy Blackburn shuffled his feet and groped for a suitable comment.

"I'll check for fingerprints and then be on my way. We'll check your place every day from now on."

"Thanks."

§§§

Leigh waited patiently in Sgt. Hendley's office as the sergeant and Brian Porter completed their whispered conversation just outside the open door. She turned as they entered.

"Leigh, I appreciate you coming by today. It shouldn't take but a few minutes to get your statement."

The sergeant indicated a chair for her, then turned on the video camcorder.

"Please state your name and today's date."

"My name is Leigh Parrish, and today is Saturday, April 3."

"Now, if you'll just state the events of March 16."

"I went to Trent's Pharmacy on my way to the hospital to visit my grandmother. It was approximately six P.M. I bought a magazine, chatted with Mr. Trent for a moment, then left."

"Did you see anyone other than Mr. Trent?"

"No one."

"And the magazine is all you bought at the pharmacy?"

"It's all I bought. Mr. Trent gave me a cassette tape."

"What was the tape?"

"Big band music, Mr. Trent said."

"Did you listen to it?"

"I have not. My grandmother passed away shortly after I reached the hospital. I had not thought of the tape since then."

Sgt. Hendley turned the recorder off.

"I understand from the sheriff's office you had a break-in at Carmela, and that only cassette tapes were disturbed." He paused. "Do you think there could be a connection?"

Leigh was stunned. "What sort of connection?"

"I have no idea. I think it might be wise to hear that tape. Can you drop it by this afternoon?"

"I'll do that. But what can be on a tape of music that makes it evidence?"

§§§

ATLANTA
APRIL 5

Leigh Parrish replaced the telephone receiver and laid her head on the desk. She had spent the weekend in Crescent Orchard searching for the missing tape. It was quite clear when she reported her lack of success to Sgt. Hendley that he was reluctant to accept it as her best effort.

"You okay?"

Leigh looked up.

"Fine, Anna. Thanks. Just an unexpected weekend of surprises I haven't recovered from."

"Sorry about that. But Patti Kelly is here." Anna glanced at her watch. "Exactly one hour and twenty-four minutes late, the little brat. Ready to see her?"

"Sure. Please ask her to come in."

Anna disappeared down the hall, and a moment later Leigh greeted her client.

"Miss Kelly? Please come in. I'm Leigh Parrish."

Patti blew in like a whirlwind, chestnut hair tossing around her shoulders, brown eyes flashing, her face slightly flushed. "I have one question," she sputtered.

"Of course," Leigh said with a smile. "What would you like to ask?"

For a split second, Patti Kelly was silent. Only a split second.

"How many more coordinators must I deal with?"

"Well, Miss Kelly, I would say that depends on you. Your file has been given to me, and I fully intend to help you plan your wedding so that your special day will be perfect. I will do everything I can to assure every detail is carefully

72

planned and carried out to your satisfaction. I will spend as much time with you as you need in the planning. But it is necessary that you keep all scheduled appointments, unless there is a major conflict, and then I expect you to give me 24 hours notice so that I may adjust my plans accordingly."

Patti dropped into the chair opposite the desk and focused on her clasped hands in her lap.

"I forgot the 2:00 appointment for today. I got involved in a TV movie."

"What is more important to you, Miss Kelly, planning your wedding or watching a movie? I understand your fiancé is a prince, which leads me to believe after your marriage you will have certain obligations that must take precedence over your personal wishes."

Patti did not look up.

Leigh opened her desk drawer, pulled out a purse-sized calendar, and slid it across to Patti.

"This is for you, Miss Kelly. You will need to record many dates and appointments over the next six months. You may begin by entering an appointment with me for tomorrow afternoon at 2:00."

"But what about today?" Patti asked, frowning. Can't we do something now?"

"I'm sorry. It will have to be tomorrow."

Patti reached for the pen on the desk and entered the information, then stood. "I'll—be here," she said, then turned and left.

Leigh entered the appointment on her calendar, glancing up as Anna entered.

"What happened?" she asked. "I just met Patti in the hall looking like her attitude's been lowered a notch or two. What did you do?"

Leigh smiled. "It's what Daddy's Mama would call a non-threatening lesson in old-fashioned, garden-variety manners."

§§§

APRIL 6

At ten minutes before two, the receptionist announced that Patti Kelly had arrived.

"I'll be with her shortly," Leigh replied.

She spread an October calendar on her desk and arranged a book of dress designs and one of invitations close to the calendar. A spiral bound picture book of flower designs completed the layout. She checked the supply of paper in the copying machine, opened the mini-blinds to let in more light, and laid her book of fabric swatches on the floor by the desk. Finally, she pressed the intercom switch to Mrs. Coleman's desk and asked that Patti Kelly come to her office.

Leigh greeted Patti at the door. The angry, blue-jean clad teenager of yesterday was today dressed in a trim green pantsuit, calm, just like any other bride planning her wedding.

"Miss Kelly, please come in."

"Thanks." Patti sat on the edge of her chair, gently twisting her engagement ring.

"I don't know anything about the Isle of Windemere, Miss Kelly. What is it like?"

"Beautiful," Patti answered without hesitation. "Absolutely beautiful. In the middle of the Caribbean, perfect climate, abundant sunshine, orchids grow as easily as kudzu does here. It's just unbelievable beauty!"

"What an atmosphere in which to live. And in the palace, I presume?"

"Right. Alex and I will have an apartment in Coventry Palace until we decide about building a house."

"Alex has brothers and sisters?"

"One of each—older brother, David, and younger sister, Camille. The family calls her Carrie."

"Interesting derivative of Camille."

Patti chuckled. "You know how royalty is—they never know when to stop tacking names on babies. Her official name is Camille Victoria Caroline, the family liked Caroline best, chopped it off to Carrie—and that's who she is."

"In the wedding party?"

"David is a groomsman and Carrie is my maid of honor." Patti slid to the back of her chair, caught a strand of hair and twisted it around her finger. "What do you think of brown dresses for my attendants?"

"Brown can be nice for an autumn wedding. Have you decided on the time?"

"In the evening. Six o'clock. At Redeemer Church. The reception will be at my house."

"Have you reserved the church? And asked the minister and organist?"

"Not yet. But I will do that by tomorrow." Patti glanced at her watch. "Do you have time to go see the church now?"

"Of course. We can get an idea about placing the flowers around the altar area and decide if the windows need anything. Let me get a sketch pad and we'll be on our way."

§§§

Patti Kelly had grown up in Atlanta and knew the back way to get everywhere. She maneuvered her red VW through the mid-afternoon traffic with the dexterity of a seasoned NASCAR driver.

"Here it is."

Leigh stepped from the car, immediately impressed with the exquisite lines of the church. The gleaming white structure was surrounded by stately oak trees, probably as old as the building and rising majestically through emerald grass. Brave bulbs had pushed tender leaves upward, surrounding stalks of buds ready to explode into bloom. It was spring beauty at its pristine best.

Patti pushed open the massive door and they stepped into the foyer.

"Over there," Patti pointed to the right, "is the bride's parlor."

She opened the door that led into the sanctuary. Leigh stood on the threshold, awed at the beauty before her. The walls were a cool refreshing green punctuated by huge stained glass windows along two opposite walls. The furniture was white with dark green upholstery. At the front of the church, hundreds of brass pipes formed the background for the choir loft. Leigh could only imagine the immensity of the organ. She took a deep breath.

"Decorations should be kept at a minimum," she said, opening the sketch pad and making several illustrations. "This will give me something to work with."

"Don't you just love the long aisle?" Patti asked. "It's the longest of any church in Atlanta. And the acoustics are a dream. Or so Daddy says. I don't know anything about that."

"I think you've made a good selection. Is this where you're a member?"

"Sort of."

Leigh hid a smile. "Exactly what is a 'sort of' member?"

"Oh, you know—I come Easter and Christmas, maybe a couple of other times during the year."

"I see." Leigh studied her illustrations for a moment. "What are your plans for the reception?"

"At the house? That's what you're supposed to tell me. We can drive by there on the way back to your office. Is that okay?"

"Fine."

Twenty minutes later, Patti pulled into the winding driveway at 9 Rockingham East. White dogwood trees were in bloom, forming a breathtaking focal point for a background of flowering fruit trees. Beyond the fruit trees a thick growth of maple, American beech, sweet gum, and sycamore provided a backdrop of deep green.

"How beautiful!" Leigh breathed softly. "And an excellent choice for the reception. The maples should be gorgeous at the end of October."

"Are you saying to have the reception in the yard?" Patti asked.

"That was not your plan?"

"Guess I hadn't thought about it."

"How many invitations are you sending?"

"Six hundred."

"And most of those will include two names, which gives 1200 people. You can probably plan on a little less than a thousand guests."

"There won't be near that many here, since a lot of people from Windemere won't come. There'll be several receptions on the Isle in November and early December that'll be almost like another wedding to go through." Patti glanced around the yard. "Outside sounds great to me. But suppose it rains?"

"We can rent tents."

"And the parking?"

"My suggestion would be to charter busses to shuttle the guests from the church and back again."

Patti smiled. *I think I'm gonna like her.* "Want to go inside?" She opened the door from the deck to the small foyer that opened into the breakfast area. "This way," she motioned.

The house was elegantly furnished, but the living room was a classic. Even with a baby grand piano, a three-piece damask-covered sofa, loveseat, and chair ensemble and several occasional chairs and tables, the area gave a feeling of spaciousness.

"What a wonderful large room," Leigh said.

"Twenty-one by thirty," Patti told her. "Daddy says this extravagance is wasted. We never use this room."

"Do you play the piano?"

"After six years of lessons—no. But the interior designer thought the piano would be useful in filling up space. Come this way and you can see the dining room."

Patti led the way into the adjoining room and dropped into a chair at the table.

"Can I get you a Coke?" she asked.

"Thanks, no. I'm fine." Leigh settled in a chair next to Patti and opened her sketch book.

"Where will you display your gifts?"

Patti frowned. "I've no idea. What do you think?"

"Perhaps the best idea would be to rent some folding tables and use pretty white covers. Maybe set them up along the wall in the living room. That way, they'll be out of the main traffic area. And if necessary, we could use some of the dining room area as well."

"Neat."

Leigh scribbled notes in the margin of her pad. "I really like the idea of the reception at your home, Miss Kelly—"

"Maybe it's time we quit being so formal," Patti interrupted. "Could you just call me Patti? And I'll call you Leigh. I don't think Weddings of Bliss has any more wedding coordinators, so I guess you're stuck with me."

Leigh smiled. "That's fine with me."

"You were saying something about the reception at the house," Patti prompted.

"Your home just seems to be a very appropriate place, Patti. It's beautiful, and I'm sure it holds a lot of happy memories of your growing-up years—Christmases, holidays, the birthdays in your family." Leigh snapped her finger. "You might even want to have a picture gallery and display family photographs at the reception."

"I'll—have to think about that," Patti said hesitantly.

"That's fine. But anything related to home and family would give a nice touch."

Patti frowned. "Seems like pictures would be sort of out-of-place at a reception."

"Perhaps they would be if the reception was not at your home. But here, it gives your guests an opportunity to see your family and Alex's family—if only in pictures—in the special setting of home. And perhaps the minister will include a part in the service about the sacredness of home since home is the first institution God established."

"I'm—sure he can." Patti looked at her watch. "I didn't mean to keep you tied up all afternoon. If you're ready, I'll drive you back and look at those dress designs and invitation samples."

§§§

From his study that joined the dining room, Creede Kelly had listened intently to the conversation between his daughter and the wedding coordinator. He hadn't meant to eavesdrop, but it had been a rather interesting few minutes. He had not seen them, but he would bet his next Erin Wintergreen royalty check that the wedding coordinator was fifty-something with gray hair pulled into a tight bun at the back of her head, wire-rimmed glasses, a classic black suit with white blouse, and utilitarian shoes with square heels.

Only a middle-age individual had enough wisdom to define *home* the way he had just heard.

§§§

In his Washington office, Jason Trent laid his uncle's abbreviated will to one side and rubbed his chin. Marcus' will consisted of a brief, handwritten document, dated more than twenty years prior, and named his wife, Christine, as the executor. Jason frowned. Aunt Christine was in the nursing home for years and even after her death a couple months ago, Uncle Marcus had failed to make a new will and name a new executor. Since Jason was the only remaining relative, it should be only a small technicality to have himself appointed as the replacement.

Only five items, added by codicil the previous year, were specifically listed: an antique boudoir chair and crystal cake plate were to go to Evangeline Holliday, and an oak washstand with accompanying bowl and pitcher, a hand-decorated walnut keepsake box, and a walnut picture frame were for Leigh Parrish. A sentence had been included in parenthesis by the items for Leigh: *They're not valuable, but Leigh's Grandfather Bracken made the wood items and I want her to have them.*" All other property was to be sold and the money put in a trust fund for the benefit of Christine and Chester.

Jason smiled. By administering the wishes of his uncle in regard to the mentally challenged Chester Leverett, it would be a feather in Jason's future political cap if the constituents in his state perceived him to be vitally interested in the welfare of those who could not successfully fend for themselves.

Jason folded the document and stuffed it in a blue envelope. He pulled the phone to him and dialed the number for Spring Flowers Florist, feeling confident that Eve and Leigh would be overwhelmed to know they had been included as beneficiaries in Marcus Trent's will.

CHAPTER 8

"I honestly don't know what you've done to that girl, but she's almost pleasant now. What's it been—a week you've been working on the Kelly wedding? She's not been late for an appointment, she waits patiently when she comes in, she even speaks to all the employees. I don't understand it." Anna Gibbs shoved a spool of iridescent ribbon to one side, then pulled it back. "What do you think? Is this good with blue hydrangea?"

Leigh nodded. "Outstanding."

"Wouldn't you hate to get a pot plant for your twelfth wedding anniversary? Twelve years, and the romance is gone. Tragic, isn't it?" Anna frowned at the bow she had fashioned, let the loops drop out, and started again. "Twelve years and only a pot plant. *My* pre-nup agreement is going to include a provision about anniversary gifts. An *elaborate* provision. Jewelry…furniture…a cruise. But *no pot plant*."

"Maybe hydrangea was used in their wedding and giving a pot plant makes the anniversary that much more significant," Leigh reminded Anna. "Different people have different tastes about gifts."

"I won't argue that. It's just—"

Anna was interrupted by the loud speaker paging Leigh from the floral design studio.

"Leigh, Miss Kelly and her father are here. They're waiting in your office."

"Miss Kelly *and* her father. Hmm-m." Anna laid the ribbon on the work table. "Did you read that Erin Wintergreen book yet? When you tell Daddy the amount of the down payment, it might be good to have something pleasant to talk with him about when he regains consciousness."

Leigh chuckled. "I expect he's already aware that the wedding is going to be pricey. Patti said he pretty much told her to get what she wanted."

"I'll bet *she* never gets a pot plant for an anniversary gift," Anna said dryly. "Check your horoscope tonight for accuracy, Leigh. I just bet it says this is the day you'll meet somebody extraordinary. Like the incredibly famous, incredibly handsome, incredibly unattached Creede Kelly!"

§§§

From where he stood in the office, Creede Kelly saw her before she entered. She walked gracefully with top-model poise. Her lavender suit was accessorized with a delicate floral print scarf at the neck, which emphasized the amethyst circle pin that she wore on her lapel. The pin intrigued him.

"Leigh, this is my dad, Creede Kelly. Daddy, this is Leigh Parrish."

Creede Kelly mumbled a short "Good afternoon." In the deep recesses of his analytical mind was the description of wedding coordinators he had planted there a few days earlier. That description fell considerably short of the young woman he had just met. She definitely was not within decades of fifty, classic black suits definitely were not her taste, and square-heel shoes definitely were not her style. Character description was not his weak point in the Wintergreen novels, but in the present situation he had failed miserably. *Analyze that, Kelly.*

Once past the formality of introductions, Leigh opened her file and her October calendar.

"Patti, we need to get some dates confirmed—your bridesmaids' luncheon, the rehearsal dinner, any other special time."

"The luncheon will be at the house on Thursday. And the rehearsal will be on Wednesday evening at Misty Lake Country Club." Patti turned to her father. "What time did you decide on, Daddy?"

"Rehearsal at the church at seven, dinner at the club at eight-thirty," he answered in clipped words.

"There'll just be those two events," Patti explained. "The rehearsal is on Wednesday because it's a tradition on Windemere that the evening preceding the wedding is reserved for the families of the bride and groom to be together."

"That's an interesting tradition," Leigh remarked as she made notations on her calendar. "So, for the luncheon and the dinner, we'll need floral arrangements and corsages. You can let me know the exact number when that's determined." She sifted through the papers in her file, finally pulling out one.

"Mr. Kelly, since Patti is not of legal age, I will need your signature on this contract and a check for the deposit, if that's convenient."

Creede signed the contract, then gasped at the deposit required. *Convenient? Spending this kind of money is never convenient.*

He slid the check and contract across the desk to Leigh with no comment, then stood.

"Need me for anything else, Patti?"

"No, Daddy. I'll be here for a little while, but I'll be home for supper. Are you going out?"

"I'll be home. Thanks for your help, Miss Parrish. Let me know what I'm supposed to do."

"Certainly, Mr. Kelly. Thank you for coming today."

Creede nodded politely, trying to decide if his nerves or his bank account would be the first to expire.

He left the building, climbed into his truck and sat for several minutes. When his thoughts would not budge from the deposit he had just paid, he pulled his checkbook register from his coat pocket and looked at the amount again. A check with that many zeroes should pay for a new truck, not a wedding. Why couldn't Patti have fallen in love with a commoner and eloped, as her mother and he had done?

He stuffed the checkbook back in his pocket and realized he did not have a copy of the contract. Patti's Miss Parrish was a poor businesswoman to have overlooked that important step in dealing with her customer—with him. After all, he knew contracts and he should have a copy. Come to think of it, he had signed his name on that piece of paper Leigh Parrish had handed him without reading the first word. Suppose he had written a check for the entire amount rather than the deposit?

He would have a serious talk with Patti tonight about the financial side of a wedding. And she could pass his choice words on to that lady in the lavender suit.

§§§

"Oh, Patti, your dad left his copy of the contract. Do you mind taking it to him?"

"I don't mind," Patti answered.

Leigh folded the paper and placed it in an envelope. "There," she said, handing it to Patti. "I know there are a few blank spaces, but until you decide on the bridal bouquet and the flowers for the rehearsal dinner, I can't complete that portion. If he has questions, just ask him to call me."

"He will, believe me."

"I understand he's an author."

"Right. The Erin Wintergreen books are his brainchild."

"It must be an exciting life for you being the daughter of a celebrity."

"My dad really doesn't think of himself as a celebrity, so life is pretty normal for me. I went to a year-round private school and spent Christmas vacations with Daddy at his cousin's place in England."

Leigh smiled. "Of course, that's very normal."

Patti tucked the contract in her purse. "It's been Daddy and me for as long as I can remember. I never knew my mother. She abandoned us before I was two years old."

Impulsively, Leigh went to Patti and hugged her. "Forgive me, Patti. It wasn't my intention to pry into your private life."

"That's okay. My mother got bit by the acting bug after she won an amateur talent contest and decided she should follow her dreams. Daddy didn't hear from her for four months, had no idea which direction she went, and then the NYPD called that she'd been in an automobile accident. Daddy went right away. She never regained consciousness."

"I'm so sorry," Leigh whispered sympathetically.

Patti continued her story. "Daddy's writing took off about that time. Not with Erin, that came later, but with a children's book and lots of short stories for magazines. Aunt Jan came to live with us and we got Polly—Pauline Barnes—as housekeeper. Aunt Jan was a high school history teacher and Polly was a former store clerk who decided she'd rather cook and garden than sell ladies' ready-to-wear. Aunt Jan and Polly didn't exactly see eye-to-eye on raising kids. Neither of them had any, so they thought they were experts in early childhood development, and that's why I've grown up with this warped personality." She smiled at Leigh. "Now, you know my story."

"Not the best part. How'd you meet Alex?"

Patti brightened. "In England, Christmas almost four years ago. The Spencers were visiting relatives who live close to Daddy's cousin, and all of us happened to be at the same Christmas Eve dinner."

"You were only thirteen at the time?"

"Thirteen *and a half*. Exactly. My birthday is June 24. But we didn't date until I was fifteen, and then with the strictest supervision. Daddy and I went to Windemere for Easter two years ago, and we were there for New Year's this year. That's when Alex and I got engaged." Patti smiled all the way to her eyes. "And now I'm here planning the wedding. All of a sudden, it's real. Maybe I needed to say all of that out loud. What do you think?"

"I think we need to get you to Jessica's office for measuring for your wedding dress. The New York dressmakers like at least six months and we're running out of time. Formals don't get made overnight. If you'll just follow me—" The ringing telephone interrupted Leigh. "Excuse me, please, Patti."

Patti noticed the smile that curved Leigh's mouth as she spoke.

"Jason Trent! Of course, I remember you!...Yes, I moved to Atlanta almost a month ago...Spring has arrived here beautifully...And in Washington?...You're coming to Crescent Orchard?...No, I don't work on Saturdays unless there is a wedding...This Saturday, the seventeenth? Yes, I'm free...I'll meet you there...Thanks, Jason. I look forward to seeing you."

§§§

"Let me guess," Patti said through laughter. "I know it's Polly's night off and you're cooking. But what is it?"

"Thought you were guessing," Creede Kelly said as he settled into the chair opposite his daughter.

"Well, it kind of resembles broccoli—something."

"I was aiming for soup, but I forgot to puree the broccoli. That's why it's lumpy."

"Erin on your mind?"

"Not exactly. It's more like that check I wrote to Weddings of Bliss. And that I have nothing to show for it."

"You forgot your copy of the contract. Leigh asked me to bring it and tell you the blank spaces are because I haven't decided on my bouquet and some other flowers."

"How much will that change the price? Any idea?"

"If I use calla lilies instead of roses, it'll be just a tad more. Not much. And I think I've already decided for the attendants to carry those fuzzy-looking mums, which will be cheaper than roses, so it should pretty well even out. And I think we're going to use those same kinds of mums in the reception arrangements here at the house. Leigh said it would give a nice touch of similarity—you know, tie everything together. And, Daddy, Leigh suggested maybe having family photographs of birthdays and Christmases sitting around at the reception. What do you think?"

Creede took a long swallow of iced tea. "Why ask me?"

"Because I want your opinion."

"More than my money?"

"As much as." Patti stirred her soup. "I told Leigh about my mother."

For a moment, Creede said nothing. "Was that necessary?" he asked quietly.

88

"It just sort of spilled out. How else was she to know why I couldn't give her an answer about having a family gallery at the reception?" Patti hesitated a moment. "Was it wrong for me to tell her, Daddy?"

"We've talked about this before, Patti. Some family situations are better not being discussed with other people. Our situation is one of them."

"But that doesn't *change* it, Daddy. It's not any better or any worse because I told Leigh. And she was so understanding. She hugged me." Patti studied her soup. "That meant a lot," she finished softly.

Father and daughter did not look at each other but concentrated on their meal. It was Patti who broke the silence.

"Ever hear of Jason Trent from Washington, D.C.?"

"Can't say that I have. Should I?"

"Leigh has a date with him Saturday."

"That's breaking news?"

Patti turned in her chair to answer the wall phone, chatted a minute, then handed the receiver to her father.

"Max Benedict," she whispered.

"What's up, buddy?" Creede asked his friend. When he heard the sigh echo along the telephone line, it provided an answer he really didn't want to hear.

Max coughed. "Roxanne's in town."

§§§

The house was quiet except for the ticking of the grandfather clock in Creede's study. He sat at his computer, stuck for the fourth time on page 117 and expecting inspiration to strike him at any moment. When it failed to happen again, he got up and paced the floor.

He told himself it wasn't Erin Wintergreen who was creating this dilemma. It was that wretched phone call from Max Benedict. At least half of Max's calls were like the one tonight—the simple message that Roxanne was in town. It meant that Max and Julia Benedict needed a fourth body for the bridge table on Saturday evening.

Roxanne was not a thing of beauty, but she knew how to play bridge. It was as though she had a sixth sense that was programmed exclusively for the game, and she knew how to use every ounce of her knowledge to a winning advantage. With Roxanne at the table, playing bridge became a world summit.

Creede had been introduced to Roxanne some five years earlier during one of her impromptu visits to Atlanta. As he recalled, she was the kind neighbor who befriended Julia Benedict's cousin's mother-in-law in Memphis, looking in on the partially disabled woman a couple of times a day. Roxanne's interests gravitated between bridge and baking coconut cream pies, neither of which particularly interested him. He regretted having told Max that he knew a little about bridge, but Max was Patti's godfather, so the family connection kept him going back to the bridge table. He had long ago given up coconut cream pies, deciding he would round out the foursome simply because of Julia.

Creede returned to his computer, staring at the bulletin board covered with the Erin dust jackets. *Murder in the Mountains* needed a spark of interest. Maybe Erin should get kidnapped, or be a hostage, or suddenly meet the man of her dreams and disappear into oblivion.

He cleared the screen saver and exhaled a heavy sign. Something needed to happen soon, or Zachary Bennett would be reading him the editor's riot act, enforcing Zachary's strong feeling about deadlines.

Then, suddenly, without warning, the inspiration came. Creede attacked the keyboard with determination. *Erin strode into the room, the very essence of confidence. Her pencil-slim lavender suit was immaculate, a perfect compliment to her glowing look. The casual observer would be hard-pressed to determine if she was a detective in disguise—or Millie the Model ready for the Easter Parade.*

Creede read the paragraph, scowled, and hit the delete button. It was happening again. His writing was getting twisted around a single, insignificant, non-event that had been mixed into his day. *Lavender. Amethyst. Blonde.*

The business of good writing was complex, indeed.

§§§

CRESCENT ORCHARD
APRIL 17

Leigh angled her car between the Spring Flowers van and Eve's fiberglass greenhouse. She ran a comb through her hair, checking her efforts in the rear view mirror, pulled on her suit jacket, and made her way to Trent's Pharmacy.

Jason Trent was seated at the last booth, engrossed in a sports magazine.

"Jason."

He looked up, pushing his magazine aside and standing to greet her.

"Hello, Leigh. Thanks for coming. I hope it wasn't an inconvenience for you to make the trip to Crescent Orchard today."

"Not at all. It's always great to come back home."

Jason caught her elbow and directed her to the door. "Eve Holliday is going with us to Uncle Marcus' house." At Leigh's look of surprise, he continued. "The will states a couple of things go to you and Eve. I had to be in Atlanta this weekend—don't know if you knew Aunt Christine was

91

executor of the will, which Uncle Marcus had never changed. My attorney is going through the legal process to have me appointed. Uncle Marcus didn't have a large estate, but there were a couple of items for you and for Eve that my attorney says we can dispose of now. There's a donation to the church and a provision for Chester."

"Who will look after Chester?" Leigh asked.

"I will."

"Jason, what a wonderfully unselfish thing for you to do!"

He shrugged. "I won't be seeing much of Chester. Washington's keeping me busy, but I will be back a couple of times a month. There's a ton of papers to sort through, get the pharmacy business settled, see if there may be family business to deal with, get the house ready for sale. And most important, claim some of your time. You're free on weekends, right?"

"Unless there's a wedding."

"I'll check well in advance."

Jason opened the door at Spring Flowers just as Eve came from the back of the shop holding an arrangement of tulips.

"Pitiful, huh? Sometimes, tulips can be very uncooperative. This one stands up and that one's limp as a dishrag." She placed the bowl on the counter. "Are we ready to go to Marcus' house?"

"When you are," Jason answered. "We need to go in your van, Eve. There's not room in a sports car to accommodate three people very comfortably."

"No problem," Eve answered. "I'll get the key."

§§§

"This way, ladies," Jason invited, leading the way down the hall to the den. He stood in the middle of the room, then pointed to a piece of furniture by the fireplace.

"Leigh, Uncle Marcus wanted you to have a washstand—whatever that is—a bowl and pitcher he kept on top of it, a keepsake box, and—of all things—a picture frame. And, Eve, the boudoir chair and a crystal cake plate are for you."

Leigh gently rubbed the top of the pitcher, letting her fingers caress the edges, pausing on the chips in the porcelain. "It's so beautiful, Jason. I don't know what to say, or how to thank you."

"Don't worry about it. I don't know any background on the bowl and pitcher, but the washstand—what is it, by the way?"

"Just a small chest," Leigh replied.

"Okay. The washstand was made by your Grandfather Bracken. And the keepsake box and picture frame were, too." He smiled. "A washstand is a chest. Who'd have thought it? Anyway, you can leave the items here for awhile, if you like. I'll get everything that remains organized for an estate sale in July, so if you can make arrangements to move these items by then, that will be fine."

"Are you sure they won't be in the way, Jason?" Eve asked. "I don't want my chair and cake plate getting sold."

"They'll be fine." As Jason turned from the fireplace, it occurred to him that there was an unusually large vacant space on the wall above the sofa. "Funny. I thought there was a picture there." He took a step closer. "The one Uncle Marcus wanted you to have, Leigh. Maybe it's in another room."

CHAPTER 9

Creede Kelly said a silent prayer of thanks and vowed that one day he would do something extremely nice for Julia Benedict. She was the ultimate gracious hostess, always doing exactly the proper thing to make her guests feel comfortable, so he knew it had been no breach of etiquette that Julia suggested bringing the evening to a close at ten o'clock. *Maybe she noticed me yawning.*

He glanced at his watch. "It's been fun, as always, Julia. Thanks for the invitation." He turned his attention to the guest of honor. "Roxanne, great game. Your skills continue to amaze me."

Roxanne beamed. "I'll be back in a couple of months. Perhaps you'll come then."

"Perhaps," Creede responded absently. "But I doubt that my game will be improved."

Max followed Creede to his truck.

"Do me a favor, Max? Don't call me in a couple of months when Roxanne comes."

"Wouldn't have called you this time if you had gone to the mountains last month like you *promised*!"

Creede stopped abruptly. "So that's it. You did this for revenge?"

"You got it, buddy."

"I wouldn't do that to you."

"You did already. Remember? For a month—a *whole* month—I looked forward to that mountain trip and what did I get? A parade of blue lights in a two-bit town, a pharmacy holdup, and *you* get sidetracked by a blonde who can't watch where she's going! You sent me back home disappointed to a disappointed Julia because she had looked forward to a weekend by herself!"

"Are you through?"

"With what?" Max asked.

"Your tirade."

"Yeah."

"Good. We'll go camping the week after Patti's wedding. How's that?"

"If that's the best you can do, guess I have no other choice."

"I'm scheduled to go to Nance's Crossing in July to meet with Zachary Bennett about the book, and since I'm about two months behind schedule now, any kind of vacation is on hold."

Max slapped his friend on the shoulder. "I accept that explanation. However," he tightened his grip, "just remember that Roxanne *does* come on a regular basis. And I *won't* forget to call you."

§§§

VIRGINIA
APRIL 19

Olnick turned from the window, carefully folding the morning paper with each section in order. He placed it precisely in the center of his desk and moved his wife's photograph an inch before pulling out his chair. With his left hand remaining on the back of the chair, he pointed his right index finger at the man opposite the desk.

"If you were reading the story I have just told you," Olnick said evenly, "would you believe it?" He waited a moment. "Would you, Tamplin?"

Tamplin shook his head.

"And neither do I." Olnick dropped into his chair. "We've heard nothing from Terrence since March 31—three weeks ago. Yet, the car was returned to the compound, the cell phone left in it, but Terrence is nowhere to be found. There's no record of calls made anywhere but here, so we can't track him that way. He closed his bank account, but left no forwarding address." Olnick selected a cigar from the box on his desk, unwrapped it, and placed it on the ashtray.

"I suppose he's not much of a menace. He was never given any privileged information about the organization. But if he told anyone about the location of his assignments, it's possible we could be traced."

Tamplin moved closer to the desk. "You don't think he would do that, do you? Tell anyone about his assignments?"

"Terrence is not the brightest individual in this organization, which means he might not have been as careful as he should have. If he was seen leaving a location, or if he said too much—do I need to elaborate further?"

Tamplin didn't reply as Olnick retrieved the cigar and rolled it between his fingers.

"Check his file, Tamplin. I think he was from Virginia." Olnick smiled. "Terrence wasn't very astute. Perhaps he has gone back home. That would save us the trouble of an extensive search."

§§§

96

"I didn't dream they would be so pretty."

Patti Kelly held her wedding invitation and read the engraved words aloud: "The honor of your presence is requested at the service of marriage uniting Patrice Kathleen Kelly and Prince Alexander Gregory William Spencer on Friday, the twenty-ninth of October at six o'clock in the evening. Redeemer Church, Atlanta, Georgia. Reception to follow at 9 Rockingham East, Atlanta."

She laid the invitation on Leigh's desk. "This makes it seem so real. Like once the invitations are printed, there's no turning back."

Leigh smiled. "And when your bridal gown comes, you'll say *that* makes it official."

Patti walked to the window, turned, and came back to the desk. "Three-and-a-half months and I'll be leaving Atlanta. Leaving Daddy." She laughed. "I really wonder how he's going to adjust when I leave. He says he'll be fine, but I'm not sure."

"He has his writing to keep him occupied, but even with that, it may be a difficult transition for him," Leigh said.

"Writing hasn't been so great the last few months," Patti said. "In fact, he's in Nance's Crossing now for a heavy conference with his editor. Did I tell you it was Louisa Bennett, Daddy's editor's wife, who found the jewelry that had been stolen from Alex's family?"

Leigh shook her head. "I've not heard about that."

"Over three years ago, Alex's family was visiting in Nance's Crossing when the jewelry disappeared. Louisa— this was before she married Zachary Bennett—was researching old houses on the coast last year and stumbled on the jewels hidden in one of the houses. It was quite an adventure, as I understand it. The Spencers want to meet Louisa and reward her in some way. She and Zachary are invited to the rehearsal dinner, the family evening on Thursday, and to the wedding. Daddy met Louisa just before Christmas last year. The Bennetts have adopted three children—actually, Louisa's nieces and nephew—and they have a baby daughter, just a few months old."

Patti read the wedding invitation again. "Did we talk about addressing these? The proper form to use and all that?"

"Addressing the invitations can be included in the wedding package for an additional fee," Leigh answered.

"How much?"

"One dollar each—so, six hundred dollars. That amount must be paid in full before the addressing begins."

Patti opened her purse and searched for her checkbook. "I'll write my check for this. When should they be mailed?"

"About six weeks prior to the wedding, which would make it about the middle of September."

Patti signed her check and slid it across the desk to Leigh. "There. Now you can get started with the addressing. I conveniently brought the list with me." She opened a manila folder, gave a quick review to the list, and laid it on the desk. "Do you write in that pretty calligraphy, Leigh?"

"I do. It takes time, so don't get impatient."

Patti laughed. "I don't do patience well. I make no promises. See you later."

Leigh accompanied Patti through the showroom and to the door, then stopped at the receptionist's desk to pick up mail, thumbing through it as she returned to her office. An envelope with the Providence Church of Crescent Orchard return address caught her attention, and she read the enclosed letter with much interest. *Dear Member, Sunday July 18 will mark a very special day in the life of your church. Jason*

Trent has donated a new piano in memory of his uncle, Marcus Trent, and it will be dedicated at the eleven o'clock service. Pack your picnic basket and join us for dinner on the grounds after the service. Sincerely, James C. Cavanaugh, Pastor.

A postscript had been added in longhand: *Leigh, sorry this is such short notice, but the 18th is the only Sunday Jason has available until the end of the year. Selfishly speaking, I didn't want to wait four months to have a new piano, and the Memorial Committee wouldn't let it be placed in the sanctuary for use until it was dedicated—hence, the compromise. Hope you can make it. JCC.*

Leigh pulled her personal calendar from her purse, made a notation on the July 18 block, and put the letter inside. She reached for the manila folder containing Patti's invitation list and uncovered Patti's checkbook.

"I'll take this by her house on my way home."

"Who're you talking to?" Anna Gibbs asked from the hall.

Leigh laughed. "Patti left her checkbook on my desk. I'll drop it off on my way home."

"Never would I go to that trouble. She left it—let her come get it." Anna snapped her fingers. "Surely, you don't think Daddy's going to reward you."

"He's out-of-town," Leigh said and instantly wished she hadn't.

"How *interesting* you should know that," Anna said, and disappeared down the hall.

§§§

Leigh pulled into the drive at 9 Rockingham East, followed the curving asphalt to the side of the house and parked parallel to Patti's red VW. Bright summer flowers nodded lazily in the late afternoon sun as Leigh walked to the door and touched the bell. The chime barely ended its melody when the door was flung open by Patti, her face stained with tears.

"Oh, Leigh!" she wailed, and a fresh barrage of tears began.

"Patti? What's wrong?"

Patti turned and Leigh followed her inside.

"Patti?"

Patti turned to face Leigh. "It's Alex!" she sobbed.

"What's happened?"

Patti wiped her eyes with a soggy tissue. "David called. Alex is very ill—a ruptured appendix. And I can't find Daddy!" Exasperation emphasized each word. "There's bad weather, a hurricane or something, along the Georgia coast and phone service is out! He should be on his way home, but his cell phone won't ring!" She caught Leigh's arms. "I *have* to go to Windemere, Leigh!"

"Of course, you do. Would you like me to drive you to the airport?"

"Would you? I can get a flight out at 8:30 tonight."

"Are you packed?"

"Almost."

"I'll write a note to leave for your father while you finish packing."

Leigh fished a pencil and an index card from her purse and wrote a brief note: *Mr. Kelly, Patti received word that Alex is very ill—a ruptured appendix. I am driving her to Hartsfield-Jackson for an 8:30 flight to Windemere. Leigh Parrish.*

CHAPTER 10

Creede Kelly locked his truck, then remembered he had left his Erin Wintergreen file laying on the seat and angrily jabbed the key into the lock. He jerked the door open, retrieved the file, and slammed the door with vengeance.

Creede walked toward his house, his footsteps echoing eerily on the flagstone path to the back entrance. He inserted his key, gave it a twist, and nothing happened. Another try. And yet another. With an angry stomp of his foot, he yanked the key out, realizing the deadbolt lock was turned and he didn't have that key.

In silence ripe with anger, Creede turned and headed to the front door. Halfway there, he saw Patti's car and heaved a sigh of relief. Patti was home. That explained why the deadbolt was on. At last his instructions of a thousand times had registered with her—*keep the door locked, especially when you're home by yourself.*

Once inside, he reset the alarm, tossed the Wintergreen file folder on the table, and watched it promptly slide to the floor. He dropped into a chair, weary from an unproductive trip to Nance's Crossing. Zachary Bennett had been understanding about the delay in the progress of the manuscript, but his patience was wearing thin. That much was evident to Creede. On the way home from Nance's Crossing, he resolved to have the first draft of the manuscript to his editor by September 1.

Adding to the dismal failure of his weekend trip had been the atrocious weather. Never had he seen so much rain fall in two days. Surely, there was no deficit now. The fringes of a hurricane downgraded to tropical storm had flirted with the coast, depositing an abundant supply of moisture as far inland as Nance's Crossing. Power lines snapped in the turbulent wind, plunging the town into darkness. Lightning severed the phone service, and even cell phone signals bounced helplessly back to earth. It had been a grueling trip, all things considered.

He closed his eyes for a moment, resting his head on the back of the chair. The silence was deafening. That's the way it was with a big house. No matter how much furniture was in it, it still echoed. Sounds became ominous, magnified a hundred times. And the upkeep was enormous. With a big house, there was that much more to break down, to go wrong, to require maintenance. Maybe he should give serious consideration to getting a smaller place after Patti married.

Patti. With a start, he came back to reality and forced himself from the chair and up the stairs to her room. The door was open, as was the closet, and an assortment of clothes littered her bed.

"Patti?"

No answer came. He called again, looked on her desk for any messages, then wearily descended the stairs and retraced his steps to the entrance hall. He bent to retrieve the file folder that had slid to the floor and placed it on the table by the telephone.

It was then that he saw the index card propped neatly between the phone and the lamp. He pulled it out, read the message—and allowed his anger to overrule his common sense.

"Leigh Parrish took my daughter to the airport? Who does she think she *is*? And Patti—why didn't she call *me*?"

With the card still in his hand, he stormed to the kitchen, poured a glass of iced tea, and drank it in giant gulps. When his anger had cooled, he went to his study, flipped on the computer, and punched the keys unmercifully as he produced his masterpiece—the letter to Joy Bliss requesting that Leigh Parrish be dismissed as the wedding coordinator for his daughter. He proofed it hastily, then pulled out his checkbook and wrote a check for $500.00 to Miss Parrish. Surely that was an acceptable amount for severance pay.

By 11:45 p.m. the letter was in the mailbox on the front porch for the morning pickup. Creede Kelly crawled into bed, depleted of mental and physical energy, but gloating with satisfaction.

Three hours later, however, he was still staring at the ceiling.

§§§

JULY 13

"Good grief, Mr. Kelly! You look worse than yesterday's news!"

Creede Kelly reached for the sugar dish as Pauline Barnes filled his coffee cup.

"It's yesterday's news that makes me look this way, Polly," he said dully.

She set the coffee pot on the sink and turned to face him. "Mr. Kelly, no news could be that bad. Look at you—"

"I'd rather not," he interrupted, and decided in the interest of time and his nerves, Polly should know at least part of what he knew.

"Patti's at the palace. Alex is very ill—appendicitis. She flew to Windemere last night, called me at four this morning."

"Oh, Mr. Kelly!" Polly exclaimed. "I didn't know—I'm so sorry—I didn't mean to be—"

Creede waved her apology aside. "Forget it, Polly. We'll get through it."

"But the prince—"

"Patti will call when she knows something."

Polly Barnes left the kitchen, her sniffles somewhat muffled by a paper towel she jerked from the holder on her way out.

Creede stirred his coffee, tasted it, pushed it aside. He unrolled the morning newspaper, glanced at the headlines, and sent it to join the cup of cold coffee.

His thoughts went back four hours earlier to his conversation with his daughter. Patti was crying softly, every other word punctuated with a sob. Alex had been in surgery when she arrived after midnight. The previous 24 hours had been critical, according to the palace physician, and recovery was still uncertain. The report was less than encouraging.

But then her question unnerved him more than anything ever had.

"Daddy, can you tell me how to pray?"

Her voice sounded so small, so scared.

"Daddy?"

"I'm here, baby." He took a deep breath. *Prayer was almost a stranger to him; he did believe in it and practiced his belief on an irregular basis, but to tell someone how to pray was quite beyond his power.* *"Baby, I think—just—say what's on your mind. That seems to have worked for me."*

"Thanks, Daddy. I'll try. Please call Leigh and tell her about Alex and that I can't keep my appointment for Wednesday." *She coughed.* *"I'll call you later, Daddy. Love you."*

"Love you, baby."

He poured a fresh cup of coffee and took a deep breath, remembering the conversation. Perhaps it would be beneficial now if he said a prayer—actually, two: one for Alex, and one for himself when Patti found out he had fired her incredible Miss Parrish.

§§§

JULY 14

Leigh balanced a binder of fabric swatches as she reached to punch the speakerphone button.

"Yes, Mrs. Coleman?"

"There's a gentleman here to see you."

"I'll be right out."

Leigh placed the binder on her desk and hurried down the hall to the reception area, stopping at Esther Coleman's desk.

"Over there," Esther whispered. "By the Layla Lang rack."

Leigh walked slowly toward the visitor, who turned just before she reached him.

"Jason!" she exclaimed. "What a surprise!"

"Don't you like surprises, Leigh?" he asked with a charming smile.

"Well, yes, of course, I do. It's just that I didn't expect to see you here today."

"You just never can tell when Jason Trent will show up," he said. "Could you get off work and ride to Crescent Orchard with me?"

Leigh shook her head. "Not until four o'clock."

"Not even if you told them you would be with me?"

"I won't even ask, Jason. I've only been working here for three months. Not long enough to have any special privileges."

Jason heaved an impatient sigh. "Then I suppose I'll need to occupy myself for—" he glanced at his gold watch "—for one hour and thirty-seven minutes. What do you suggest I do?"

"The mini-mall is just down the road."

Jason bowed low. "Suggestion well taken. I'll go to the mall and be back here promptly at four."

"Jason, why do you want me to go to Crescent Orchard today?"

"It was to be a surprise. However, I'm having the estate sale at Uncle Marcus' house Friday and Saturday, and I wanted to be sure you got the bowl and pitcher out before then. We can bring it back to Atlanta tonight."

"How thoughtful, Jason. I'll be ready at four."

Leigh watched as Jason drove off, then turned toward her office.

"New beau, Leigh?" Anna Gibbs joined her.

Leigh laughed. "He's hardly a beau, Anna. I've known him for some time."

"Does he have a name?" Anna persisted.

"He's Jason Trent—"

"I *know* that name," Anna interrupted. "He's on TV a lot—from Washington."

"He's an aide to a senator."

"And you have a date with him tonight?"

"I do not. His uncle very kindly remembered me in his will, and Jason asked me to go to Crescent Orchard later today to get my bowl and pitcher from the house before the estate sale this weekend."

"That's it?"

"All of it."

§§§

Joy Bliss finally got to her mail at five that Wednesday afternoon. At mid-week, the stack was enormous; she said a prayer of thanks for Esther Coleman's efficient manner of sorting and rubber banding correspondence before it reached Joy's private office.

The envelope with Creede Kelly's return address caught her attention and she slid the brass letter opener under the flap and removed the letter, silently reading the brief message as she poured a glass of water: *Dear Mrs. Bliss: I will thank you to see that Miss Parrish receives the enclosed check and my thanks for her past assistance with my daughter's wedding plans. We will make different arrangements next week. Sincerely, Creede Kelly.*

Joy read the letter again. With less than 40 words, Creede Kelly had fired the only coordinator at Weddings of Bliss who had been able to work with his demanding daughter. For someone who required a 600-page novel to effectively get his story across, that must have been a major accomplishment.

§§§

CRESCENT ORCHARD

Leigh Parrish stepped from Jason's black Porsche and followed him inside Marcus Trent's house. The furniture had been rearranged to allow easy access through the house for the sale. The lemony smell of furniture polish did not completely mask the musty aroma of a house that had been denied fresh air for three months.

"This must be difficult for you, Jason. I'm sure you have fond memories of this place."

"Memories, Leigh, but not all of them fond. Chester made things difficult, so I mostly stayed away."

"The people of Crescent Orchard thought your aunt and uncle were very special to look after Chester."

"I agree with that. But Chester caused them some problems. I'm probably asking for trouble by agreeing to be his guardian, but he's not capable of making wise decisions about his welfare. He needs me for that. You know he's got that shack up the mountain, and I guess as long as he stays up there, he's not creating problems in town."

Jason wrapped the bowl and pitcher in separate terry-cloth towels and laid them on the sofa.

"What shall we do about Eve's boudoir chair?" Leigh asked, "and my washstand?"

"They've been tagged not for sale and stored in the dining room, away from the sale area. I'm hoping your picture frame shows up; I've been searching for it."

Leigh walked slowly about the room, pausing to examine a collection of books. Jason watched her for a moment as she studied the titles.

"See anything you'd like to get?" he asked.

"This is a fine collection of classics," she answered. "I would be interested, except I have stacks of books waiting to be read. That's the bad result of joining two book clubs and no time to read."

Jason laughed. "I know the experience."

"I'll get Bo Patton to help me move the washstand, probably Sunday afternoon," Leigh said, examining the piece of furniture. "You've no idea how delighted I am to have this, Jason—something that my grandfather made."

"I'm glad Uncle Marcus thought of you." Jason made a final appraisal of the room. "We probably should get started back to Atlanta. I've a late flight to Washington for a meeting, then fly back tomorrow night for the sale on Friday."

"Do you ever slow down?"

"Not until I retire. Another 35 years."

"At the pace you're going you won't make it to retire."

"Leigh." Jason stopped on the porch, locked the door and turned to face her. "I've set this pace because I thrive on activity. I stay busy because I expect that of myself. Anything less, and I won't be able to keep up with the political crowd."

"Is that important?"

"Without a doubt, the most important thing in my life, now or ever."

§§§

ATLANTA
JULY 15

Leigh flipped the page on her daily calendar Thursday morning and noticed the hot pink sticky note with a message from Joy Bliss. *Leigh, the attached check is yours. Mr. Kelly is making other arrangements about Patti's wedding. J.B.*

Leigh peeled the note away to reveal a $500.00 check payable to her from Creede Kelly. Anger melted into hurt and rekindled to anger. *What have I done?* One thing she could say for Mr. Kelly was his generosity overwhelmed her. It would make a small dent in her financial obligation at the Crescent Orchard Bank.

She pulled a sheet of stationery from her desk drawer and wrote a crisp message. Dissatisfied, she ran the letter through the desk shredder and started over. After the third attempt with the letter and a terrific battle with her conscience about the $500.00, she slid the letter and the Kelly check into an envelope addressed to him. She then walked the half block to the postal pickup station and deposited the letter in the in-town box.

Before nine o'clock she had e-mailed a request for the most recent Layla Lang catalog, sharpened every pencil on her desk, and fed plant food to her African violets. Patti Kelly's file had been returned to Central Records, and Leigh Parrish's first coordinator's job at Weddings of Bliss—uncompleted—was now merely a memory.

§§§

JULY 17

Patti had arrived home shortly before midnight on Friday. Exhausted from the stressful week and the plane trip to Atlanta, she had fallen asleep shortly after her father met her at Hartsfield-Jackson Airport. Wearily, she had climbed the stairs to her room and collapsed in bed, where she stayed until eleven o'clock on Saturday morning. Upon arising, she had showered, dressed, and called the palace. The report on Alex was excellent, and the prognosis was very favorable.

Patti skipped down the stairs, humming a lilting tune. The rich aroma of hazelnut cream coffee greeted her, the prelude to finding her father in the kitchen.

"Good morning, Daddy. Or is it still morning?"

"Barely. It's three minutes away from noon."

"What are you having—breakfast or lunch?"

He looked at the container in his hand. "I suppose it's a toss-up. Which meal does cottage cheese go better with?"

110

"Neither, as far as I'm concerned." Patti shuffled through the mail on the kitchen counter as her father reached to answer the phone. She winked at him when he acknowledged the caller's greeting.

"Yeah, Max, she got in last night...Alex is doing well, thanks for asking...Tonight?...Can't make it, buddy. I've got a week to get the next three chapters to Zach or else...Thanks, anyway. Enjoy the evening."

"Roxanne must be in town," Patti guessed.

"Been with Max and Julia all week. Max said the house is shrinking by the minute."

"Why don't they just gently suggest to Roxanne that she go home? I can't imagine—" Patti's voice trailed off.

"Can't imagine what?" Creede asked as he poured coffee.

"Daddy, what does this mean?" Patti read from a sheet of paper: "Dear Mr. Kelly, I regret having offended you and Patti. Obviously, I don't understand what may have happened. I am returning your check. It was my pleasure working with your daughter. Sincerely, Leigh Parrish."

Patti waited for her father's response. "Daddy?"

He stirred two spoons of sugar in his coffee before answering.

"How would you feel if you came home and found a note that an *unknown* had assumed the responsibility of granting permission for your *only child* to go out of the country? Not only that—the same *unknown* takes it upon herself to drive that *only child* to the airport. And to top it off, neither the *unknown* nor the *only child* bothers to call the parent. Really, Patti. Is *that* too much to ask?"

Patti circled the table, stood behind her father and wrapped her arms around his neck.

"Two things, Daddy. I—the *only child*—didn't ask Leigh—the *unknown*—for permission to do *anything*. She offered to drive me to the airport. I didn't know where you—the *parent*—was, and I couldn't get your phone to answer. I had to go to Alex. And, Daddy, don't forget I'm 18, since June 24, legal age. I don't have to have your permission now."

Creede pushed his cup aside. "For a conversation that was intended to be the severe admonition of a father, this dialogue somehow did a one-eighty. And it wasn't supposed to be so brief. I had more ammo in the arsenal, but now it doesn't even sound convincing to me."

Patti kissed him on the top of his head and pushed the cottage cheese across the table. "Take me out to lunch?"

§§§

Leigh Parrish settled in the corner of the sofa and adjusted the volume as the video rolled, bringing to life the several years of Christmas and birthday celebrations in the extended Bracken family. Her mother and stepfather, on one of their rare visits to the States, had begun the video journal. Special occasions had been compiled into one tape, and it was a source of family comfort to Leigh to watch it often, especially when her spirit needed a lift.

She set her half-filled coffee cup on the floor and pulled her bare feet under her. Jeans that had assumed the stone-washed appearance through many launderings were fringed on the edges where the hem had raveled. Her shirt, floral printed with yellow tulips, had inched out from the belt and bloused gently over the top of the jeans.

Leigh smiled at the video scene before her. It was Daddy's Mama's birthday, four years earlier, and the party was enormous. The lawn at Carmela, freshly mowed and resembling green velvet, was dotted with hundreds of people talking and laughing. There was the mayor of Crescent

Orchard pulling hard on the dinner bell cord, sending the summons across the yard and beyond to come to the feast. He continued to ring the bell—ring—ring—

Startled, Leigh realized the ringing was her doorbell. She scrambled to her feet and made her way to the door, opening it, and faltering a moment as she struggled to maintain her composure.

"Patti! What a surprise!"

And then she saw Creede Kelly.

CHAPTER 11

"What is it that smells so wonderful?" Patti asked as she settled beside her father on the sofa.

Leigh stood by the only chair in her living room, thoroughly self-conscious. "Probably apple pie."

It seemed such a short sentence. Maybe it needed some clarification.

"For church tomorrow."

That certainly didn't clarify much.

She retrieved her coffee cup from the floor, set it on the table, and apologized for her motions.

"Tomorrow," she started again, "is a special day at the Crescent Orchard church. Jason Trent is giving a new piano in memory of his uncle, and after the dedication and worship service, there will be a fellowship dinner."

Patti stretched her arm across the back of the sofa. "Well, if it's half as good as it smells, you'll have the best dessert there."

Leigh mumbled her thanks and reached for the remote.

"Don't turn it off," Patti said. "It looks interesting."

"A video of family occasions," Leigh explained. "This is my grandmother's birthday, four years ago."

"Which is she?" Patti asked.

"At the table—blue dress, white hair."

"Who is the cute little lady with the sunglasses shaped like butterflies?" Patti prompted.

"My Aunt Hazel. Actually, my great-aunt."

"Is she saying something about a house?" Patti asked.

Leigh adjusted the volume. "She is."

Patti listened attentively as Aunt Hazel spoke.

"Just remember, Leigh. Anyone can build a *house* because it only requires wood and stone and money to make it happen. A *home*, on the other hand, doesn't happen until love surrounds it." Aunt Hazel whispered behind her hand.

"I didn't hear what she said," Patti remarked. "It must have been important. Or scandalous."

Leigh eased into the chair. "She was —providing me with one of her lectures."

"About what?" Patti questioned.

Creede Kelly would have pinched his daughter but she was just out of reach. He crossed his leg, surveyed the scuff on the toe of his loafer, and waited for Leigh's answer, sure it would be the gem of the day.

"Aunt Hazel was saying that a woman should never marry a man who didn't share her feelings of home and family, and that she should know his thoughts about it before they were married because just getting married wouldn't change him."

Creede turned his attention to his other shoe. *Gem of the day, all right. Let me tell you, Aunt Hazel, that philosophy is supposed to work the other way, too, but it doesn't always happen. I could write a book about that. Maybe I will someday.*

"I suppose she's right," Patti said. "Oh, by the way, Leigh, Daddy has something to tell you."

Creede Kelly was uncomfortable. His glance at Leigh suggested to him that she was bordering on being embarrassed. He coughed, wishing a severe case of laryngitis would instantly descend on him but just until he got Patti home and then he wanted a very clear voice, which he fully intended to unleash on her in well-chosen words.

He coughed again. "Miss Parrish." It closely resembled a squeak and he started over. "Miss Parrish, it seems I acted rather hastily earlier this week. I apparently was not fully aware of all the facts when I wrote Joy Bliss." He took a deep breath. This confession was mortifying. "Will you accept my apology and continue with Patti's wedding?"

Somehow, he knew—he just *knew*—that Patti was thoroughly enjoying his misery. He didn't dare look in her direction as he waited for Leigh's acceptance speech.

"Mr. Kelly—"

The phone buzzed loudly. Leigh looked unnerved. "Excuse me," she said and went to the kitchen to answer.

Creede turned toward his daughter. "Happy now that you've succeeded in wringing a confession out of me?"

"Oh, Daddy, it wasn't meant to be that."

"Then what?"

"It's just reality, Daddy. We need her—what's that word?"

"Expertise," he answered without thinking.

"That's it! She knows what she's doing. And let's face it—we need somebody like that. I don't have a clue about pulling off a big wedding. Do you?"

"It's not something I know a lot about."

"Thought so. The matter is closed. Leigh's coming."

Leigh sat on the edge of her chair. "I'm sorry for the interruption. It was my friend from Crescent Orchard."

"Not bad news, I hope," Patti said.

"Not—all of it. A dear friend of ours was robbed in March and suffered a heart attack. He died several days later. His nephew by marriage is now considered the prime suspect in the robbery."

"Are you from Crescent Orchard?" Creede asked.

"I lived near there, in a little community near Providence Hill."

"Was your friend the pharmacist?" he questioned.

"Why, yes. Did you know him?"

"No, I didn't. A buddy and I were there the night of the robbery, on our way to the mountains for a few days. Max—my buddy—knew the officer who found the pharmacist and we drove to the hospital for Max to see him."

"I was at the hospital that night. Daddy's Mama passed away. I had stopped by the drug store before going to the hospital and talked with Mr. Trent, but I didn't know about the robbery until a couple of days later."

Creede suddenly shuddered. *It was Leigh I almost hit on the hospital parking lot that night.* The events of that March evening stirred in his thoughts as each segment played out.

"Daddy? Where are you? I called twice."

"Sorry, Patti. What were you saying?"

"Leigh's agreed to come back as the coordinator. Aren't we glad?"

"Very glad," he answered, somewhat surprised by the sincerity of his reply.

"The apple pie is ready. Would you like a slice?" Leigh asked.

"Absolutely," Patti answered without hesitation.

117

Leigh led the way to the kitchen and indicated chairs for her guests. She placed dishes and utensils at the three places and pulled napkins from a holder on the cabinet. Tiny spirals of steam crept upward from the slices of pie as the brisk aroma of coffee mingled with spicy cinnamon.

Creede took a bite of pie, and another. "Very good pie. Family recipe?" he asked.

"It's the recipe Daddy's Mama always used."

"There's something different—not like other apple pie I've eaten," Creede persisted.

"A little grated cheese and a touch of cayenne pepper in the crust," Leigh explained.

"It's the best I ever tasted," Patti complimented. "Whose recipe?"

"My grandmother—Daddy's Mama. My father—her son—died when I was very young. My mother remarried and my stepfather adopted me, so to keep two paternal grandmothers separated, I had Daddy's Mama and Mother Parrish. I lived with Daddy's Mama for many years."

"No wonder she's special," Patti said softly. "And such a special name for her."

"Thanks. She—" The ringing telephone interrupted Leigh. "I'm sorry. It seldom rings, and today it's gone into overtime."

Between bites of pie, Creede watched as a troubled expression clouded Leigh's face. She returned to the table but did not immediately sit down.

"Problem?" he asked, then wondered why he was concerned.

"I'm—not sure. Just something garbled and then they hung up, just like two other times this week."

"Maybe it's a wrong number," Patti suggested. "From a rude caller."

"Could be," Leigh agreed.

"Well, we ate your pie for the church fellowship dinner tomorrow," Creede said without apology.

"I always bake two," Leigh replied. "It's just as easy."

And for the life of him, Creede couldn't help thinking about that other pie and the beneficent piano donor who would be enjoying it tomorrow. He even wondered if it would be too un-Christian to wish that Jason Trent would get a severe case of indigestion from eating it.

§§§

CRESCENT ORCHARD
JULY 18

More than a few parishioners dabbed gently at their eyes, and a hush of quietness settled over the sanctuary as the strains of "Fairest Lord Jesus" hung pleasantly in the quaint Providence Church. The walnut piano stood grandly in the corner of the church, a perfect memorial to Marcus Trent. Emma Durbin, the pianist/choir director, had a unique ability for coaxing the sweetest sounds from an instrument, and today her talent had touched the congregation and brought them to their feet in reverent approval.

Following the benediction, Jason caught Leigh's elbow and guided her toward the door as the aisles became flooded with people eager to dig into their collective lunch basket and feast through part of the afternoon. They crossed the lawn and made their way to the picnic tables that had been built between tall oak trees. A gentle breeze stirred the leaves with welcome mountain coolness. After the blessing, lines formed along both sides of the table. Eager hands reached for servings of ham and fried chicken and home-baked biscuits. Bowls of potato salad were kept cool in the eighty-plus degree temperature by nesting in metal containers filled with crushed ice. By the time Leigh and Jason made it to the dessert table, all of Leigh's apple pie was gone, and by mid-afternoon most of the crowd had gone.

"It's been a wonderful day, Jason. The piano is magnificent. It's a grand addition to the church and a beautiful memorial to Marcus."

"Thanks," he acknowledged rather absently. "Leigh, I hate to eat and run, but I have a long drive ahead."

She looked surprised. "I thought you flew."

"I drove, but I did fly to Washington on Thursday and back that night. I have some stops to make during next week, so it was best to have my own car."

"It's an elegant one. We don't often see a Porsche around Crescent Orchard."

"You could have ridden in it with me today," he chided.

She laughed. "I appreciate that, but I plan to spend tonight with Eve and drive back to Atlanta in the morning."

"Eve has the key to Uncle Marcus' house, if you have an opportunity to get your washstand." He paused. "Tell me one more time what in the world is a washstand?"

"Just a small chest. And I will get it today."

"It's always good being with you, Leigh. I'll give you a call when I head this way again. Maybe we can get together for dinner." He leaned over and kissed her on the cheek. "Take care." And then he was gone.

§§§

Leigh gathered her empty pie plate and the Tupperware pitcher from which the last drop of tea had been drained. Just at the corner of the parking lot, she met Bo Patton.

"Need a hand, Leigh?" he asked.

"Actually, Bo, I need to borrow you and your truck for a few minutes, if you have the time."

"Rest of the afternoon. What can I do for you?"

Leigh stored her empty containers in the trunk of the Toyota, then slammed the lid.

"Wouldn't do that too often if I was you," Bo warned.

"Do what?"

"Slam the lid like that. As old as this car is, it could collapse with many jolts like that." His serious expression broke into a broad grin. "Now, what can me and my truck do for you?"

"Jason Trent very kindly gave me an old washstand from his uncle's house and I need to move it to the barn for storage."

"No problem. I'll run home and get on my work clothes and meet you at Marcus' house in 20 minutes. You got a key?"

"Eve Holliday has one. I'll get it before she leaves the church."

In a matter of minutes, Leigh arrived at Marcus' house, followed shortly by Bo Patton.

The estate sale had gone well on Saturday and the house was now basically empty, stripped of all the appointments that had made it uniquely Marcus Trent's. A faint musty aroma still lingered, wrapping around the drapes that hung close to the windows. Only the ticking of a quartz clock disturbed the quietness within the house.

Bo followed Leigh to the dining room where the washstand had been shoved against the wall.

"This it?" he asked.

"It is." Leigh winked at him. "Try not to scratch it, okay?"

Bo surveyed the piece with a critical eye. "One more won't make any difference, I'd say. You gonna refinish it?"

"Someday. My grandfather Bracken made it for Marcus and Christine, and Marcus wanted me to have it. For the time being, I'll store it in the barn until I decide about moving it to Atlanta."

Bo pulled the washstand to the middle of the floor, checked the casters, then guided it across the room and out the door to the porch and his waiting truck.

"If you don't mind dropping me back here for my car, I'll just ride to the barn with you," Leigh told him.

"Don't mind at all. Seat's clean, too. Washed the whole truck yesterday. Didn't want Sue Ellen to think ill of me for drivin' a dirty truck."

Leigh climbed in and settled on the Scotch plaid seat. "Nice interior," she commented.

"Thanks," he beamed. "Sue Ellen's crazy about red."

"And you must be crazy about Sue Ellen."

"Yeah. She's all right. She graduated from the vo-tech school, you know. Workin' at her dad's grocery store, now. Boy, can she tell some wild stories about the customers. Take Miz. Plymale. Sue Ellen says she buys three-day-old bread, makes toast, then crushes it to feed the birds. Why not just buy bird seed? I bet the birds would like it better."

"Could be it gives her something to do."

"I guess. And Sue Ellen said Chester Leverett was in the store with some big money. Could be from Marcus' holdup."

"Oh, Bo, you don't really think Chester did that, do you?" She caught the edge of the seat as Bo slowed to turn in the drive leading to the barn. "Surely, he wouldn't have harmed Marcus, not after all Marcus and Christine did for him."

"But it is suspicious, don't you think?" Bo killed the engine and opened the door to get out. "Where else would Chester get money? Big money?"

Leigh joined him at the rear of the truck. "What concerns me is who will look after Chester. Jason said he will become the guardian, but he'll be in Washington. Chester needs someone here who can give him stability."

"Guess it'll all work out. It usually does."

They placed the washstand in the barn beside a broken captain's chair. Something scurried beyond them and Leigh made a hasty exit.

"Don't you lock it?" Bo asked as she closed the door.

"There's no lock on it. And nothing of value in it. I really need to sort out everything and get rid of a lot of it, but there's so much sentiment attached, even to the old barn."

"Major decision category, huh?" Bo turned the truck onto Northern Boundary Road. A half-mile down the road, a metallic bouncing interrupted him. "There it goes, again," he said, pulling to the side of the road and stopping. "The hubcap flew off. Take me a minute to find it."

"I'll help you look," Leigh offered.

Bo backtracked, searching the grass at the edge of the road. "I know this is where it came off," he yelled to Leigh. "I'm goin' a little piece into the trees."

Leigh walked slowly, canvassing the area where Bo had just been. The grass at the side of the road was brown and brittle from the summer heat. No shiny reflection caught her attention and she started back to the truck just as Bo called to her.

"Found it! Rolled up against a tree and lodged!"

A moment latter he was jogging to the truck, the hubcap held high.

Leigh kicked at a stone on the edge of the road, watched it skip along the pavement and disappear into the grass. Its journey disturbed a scrap of paper that fluttered slightly in the breeze. She went a step closer to investigate.

"Bo?" she called. "Look at this. A fifty-dollar bill! I wonder who lost it."

"Could've blown out of somebody's car," he said.

"But you don't really think so, do you?"

Bo studied the area carefully. "It was just up the road a piece I picked up a man and further on, his car. He thought he had a major malfunction, but it was only out of gas. Expensive car. Had all sorts of aerials on the back."

"Recently?"

"Last winter. I remember there was still some snow around—" He left the sentence hanging. "It was about the time of the drug store robbery—in fact, it was the same night, 'cause I called Sue Ellen when I got home and she told me about it."

"Bo, I went by the drug store that night before going to the hospital to visit Daddy's Mama. A car was parked in the lot adjacent to the pharmacy, with a lot of aerials about the back window."

"Could be more than a coincidence. See anybody around it?"

"No. And Marcus had no customer. Except—"

"Except what?" Bo prompted.

"Except Marcus came out of his office. Do you suppose someone was in there?"

§§§

The porch swing glided gently as Leigh sipped lemonade. Late summer dusk crept in, a prelude to an evening sky

124

sprinkled with twinkling stars and highlighted with a huge golden moon.

"This is the perfect ending to a perfect day," she said quietly.

"Tell me about it," Eve Holliday responded. "I just want it to go on like this and not turn into Monday."

Leigh laughed. "At least, I hope next week isn't like last week. I got fired—then un-fired—"

"You *what*?" Eve exploded.

"My bride's father dismissed me, then had a change of heart."

"Who is the jerk?"

"Creede Kelly."

Eve strangled on her lemonade. "*The* Creede Kelly?"

"There's more than one?"

"Not that I'm aware of." Eve coughed. "The one who writes the mystery stories?"

"Um-hum."

"What did you do to upset *him*?"

Leigh set her glass on the floor. "I drove his daughter to the airport for an emergency flight while he was out-of-town. He misinterpreted and thought I had given her permission to go. But Patti is an adult, and she didn't need his permission. Anyway, they came to my house yesterday to reinstate me."

"You must be really good with this wedding and they can't do without you."

"It's not that exactly. Every wedding coordinator at Weddings of Bliss has had the opportunity to work with Patti. I was the only one left. But so far, we've managed to have a fairly good relationship."

Eve yawned. "I've got to get some sleep after I walk out to the box and get the mail. Forgot it all day yesterday—is that my phone ringing?"

Leigh got up from the swing. "It is. Go ahead, I'll get the mail for you."

"Thanks," Eve said as she disappeared into the house.

Leigh walked slowly to the mailbox, enjoying the beauty of the summer evening. She opened the door and reached inside, pulling out several pieces of mail.

Suddenly, she sensed someone behind her. Before she could turn, a hand was clasped over her mouth. She struggled, kicking the shin of her assailant and freeing herself from his grasp, in the same instant turning enough to see who was there.

"Chester!" she exclaimed.

He mumbled incoherently, turned, and faded into the shadows.

CHAPTER 12

"I have someone for you to meet."

Leigh turned from the bridal parlor closet. Patti Kelly stood at the doorway of the bride's parlor accompanied by a tall, brunette woman dressed in a floor-length moss green outfit. Except for tiny lines at her eyes and a single frown line across her forehead, there was a striking, although mature, resemblance to Patti.

"Leigh, this is my Aunt Jan Kelly. Daddy's favorite sister."

Jan hugged her niece. "His *only* sister." She turned to Leigh. "And you must be Leigh Parrish. What Pat hasn't told me about you on the phone, she's e-mailed. I'm very pleased to meet you."

"Thank you, Miss Kelly. I've been looking forward to getting acquainted with you," Leigh smiled.

"Aunt Jan got in from Oregon this morning," Patti said, "and left 182 Western Civilization students sobbing."

"More like jumping for joy," Jan said. "They don't care if I stay away a month, which is what I plan to do."

"After the wedding, Aunt Jan is going to Florida to visit until Thanksgiving," Patti explained.

127

Leigh cleared a chair laden with her wedding files. "Could I get you a glass of water while we're waiting to get started? It's almost seven so it shouldn't be more than a few minutes."

Jan shook her head. "Nothing for me, thanks."

"Then if you will excuse me, I'll check with the minister and the organist," Leigh said as she left the room.

Jan Kelly opened her evening bag and pulled out a miniature bottle of perfume, unscrewed the top, and dabbed fragrance behind her ears.

"Your coordinator is quite lovely and she certainly seems professional," she commented to Patti. "Weddings of Bliss—is that the company's name? And is their work expensive?"

"Expensive enough, I guess. Daddy almost had a stroke when he made the down payment, but Weddings of Bliss is well-known around here. They're good and work hard to make everything perfect." Patti chuckled. "Daddy fired Leigh when she drove me to the airport to fly to Alex when he was so sick."

"Fired her for what reason?"

"You know Daddy. He jumped to a conclusion— thought Leigh had given me *permission* to go. He didn't wait to ask any questions or listen to any reasons."

"He's not known for that," Jan said. "Never has been. But you surely know by now that when you make your own decisions, you also have to assume the responsibility of the consequences of those decisions, like incurring the wrath of your over-protective father."

"There were no consequences for me, but they were pretty strong for Leigh. I found the note she wrote Daddy when she returned his check. She wasn't mad or bitter, but I know she must have been hurt."

"So what did you do?"

"Daddy and I went to her house the next day and re-hired her."

"Well, I'm glad she came back." Jan laughed. "I'd like to see your father get this wedding accomplished without the help of a professional."

"Not I. Daddy's so mired up in Erin Wintergreen right now he doesn't think about how important wedding coordinators are in the total scheme of things."

"To not be angry with your father for firing her, she must have the disposition of an angel," Jan said. "Hasn't he noticed she's beautiful? Intelligent? Gracious? Your father needs to get his interest growing in something other than Erin Wintergreen. There is another side of life beyond writing novels." Jan winked at Patti. "Think we may be able to motivate him?"

"Aunt Jan! Are you and I going to play matchmaker for Daddy and Leigh? That is *really* cool!"

§§§

From her vantage point halfway up the aisle, Leigh sur-veyed the wedding party gathered at the altar, then walked slowly toward them.

"I think the only adjustment we need to make is for Princess Camille to move in a step toward Patti. Any questions about the logistics? No? Then we're ready for the rehearsal. If the king and Prince Alex will go with Rev. Harrison, and the rest will come with me to the back of the sanctuary, we'll get started."

As the wedding party gathered at the altar, Creede Kelly tucked his daughter's hand in his elbow and prepared to follow.

Leigh laid a restraining hand gently on his arm. "Wait just a minute, until Princess Camille turns and looks this way," she whispered.

With Camille at the altar, the organist began the introduction to *Trumpet Voluntary*.

"Now," Leigh said softly. "But not too fast. Enjoy this walk with your daughter."

Not at all sure what prompted him, Creede smiled warmly at Leigh, adding a wink as he and Patti began their procession.

"How can I?" he whispered to Leigh. "I'm losing my tax deduction."

"Tough," she whispered back.

He wasn't convinced she was really sympathetic, but somehow that whispered exchange had been uncommonly meaningful. Deep wine dress, he remembered, floor length, long sleeves. Blonde hair with gentle, natural curls flowing below her shoulders. Intriguing amethyst pin that she had on every time he saw her.

Over and over the description played in his mind, even after he had gone to sit beside his sister and wait for instructions from Leigh to escort Jan at the conclusion of the rehearsal.

Jan stole a glance at her brother, who obviously was not objecting to being told what to do and when to do it. Perhaps wedding rehearsals were quite the proper place for a romance to begin, she decided. Playing matchmaker might be easier than she had thought.

§§§

REHEARSAL DINNER
MISTY LAKE COUNTRY CLUB

Leigh parked her Toyota at the end of the circular drive and walked briskly toward the entrance of Misty Lake Country Club. She had been there earlier in the day to deliver gifts from Patti and Alex for their attendants, and now stood, awed at the transformation in the building and grounds. Inside, autumn floral arrangements graced every empty spot. The main dining room held tables and chairs for 100 guests, each table complete with flowers, candles, and place cards. Sparkling white linen coverings under silver-bordered white china set the stage for an elegant wedding party. Papier-mache bells were suspended from the ceiling and swayed gently.

Creede stood with his sister near the fireplace, warming before a lazy fire.

"Well, Leigh, you were outstanding. Your efforts got everybody in the right place at the right time. Quite an accomplishment with the Kelly clan," Jan complimented.

"Thank you, Miss Kelly. Everything went well."

"The third time through it. Don't they always say—bad rehearsal, perfect wedding?" Jan asked.

"Who says?" Creede asked. "I've never heard that."

"It's a platitude that's been around for eons." Jan caught his arm. "Can we sit down? These shoes are killing me."

"I think we're supposed to greet the guests and introduce Alex's family," Creede answered. "Which we can begin doing now. The king and queen have just arrived." He turned to Leigh. "Do Camille and David have dates?"

"Camille is with a friend of Patti's, but I understand David is alone."

§§§

131

Leigh watched as the last guest drove from the parking area and traveled down the long drive at Misty Lake before turning onto the road leading to Atlanta. It had been an exhausting evening, but one wrapped in family warmth as special memories had been shared of two children growing up in vastly different worlds, falling in love, and uniting those two worlds with their marriage. Leigh had listened as Peyton Spencer told of Alex growing up as a normal boy who played T-ball, ran away from home, and failed math tests in school. Lorraine remembered her son's handmade valentines, juvenile culinary excursions, and college graduation.

Creede had devoted his words to memories of Patti wobbling in her first high heels, getting her driver's license and wrecking the car the same day, and convincing him she could survive on a Caribbean island without her father.

Leigh turned from the door, shaking her head. She had grown close to Patti during the preceding six months and marveled at the maturity Patti now displayed. With Alex's help, she would make a fine princess for Windemere.

One final glance around the room convinced Leigh that nothing had been left behind by any of the guests. The tables had been stripped of dishes, decorations, and coverings, their polished oak finish sparkling in the dim light. The fire had been reduced to a mound of smoldering coals with an occasional wisp of smoke spiraling lazily up the chimney.

"Is everything all right, Miss Parrish?"

Leigh turned to find the head waiter standing within a couple of feet. She smiled warmly.

"It was absolutely perfect, Thomas. I'm sure Mr. Kelly was pleased. And it looks as though none of the guests left coats or purses."

"None except Mr. Kelly," Thomas said. "He left his gift from the groom."

"That's a custom new to me," Leigh remarked.

Thomas shrugged. "Royalty always does things a bit different, I guess. It was a book of some kind. Anyway, it's locked in the safe now. He'll probably come back tomorrow for it. If you think about it, mention it to him."

"I won't be seeing him tomorrow, but I'll see that he does know about it." Leigh snapped her purse, then held her key ring to the light. "There's the right one. It's easier to find in here where there's some degree of illumination."

"Want me to walk you to the car?" Thomas offered.

"That's kind of you, but I'll be fine. Thank you, Thomas, for all you and Misty Lake did to make this a perfect evening."

"Our pleasure," Thomas said, bowing from the waist.

§§§

Leigh walked hastily down the Misty Lake drive, wishing she had accepted Thomas' offer to accompany her to the car. Her high heels clicked in perfect rhythm on the asphalt. The night was still, pleasantly warm for the end of October, with only a hint of moonlight. An out-of-season mockingbird chirped somewhere close, chanting a melody that somehow kept time with Leigh's beating heart.

She rounded the last bend, welcoming the sight of her car at the same time the country club disappeared from view. A sigh of relief started, hovered, but was never completed as approaching headlights came into focus.

Leigh stepped to the side of the drive, seeking cover in the shadows of tall camellia bushes. The lights drew nearer, as did the noisy rattle of a vehicle that probably had seen better days, accompanied by the thunderous vibrations from the radio. Raucous laughter and coarse vocabulary added to the tension of the moment.

Leigh slid further behind the bush, scarcely daring to breathe. And then she heard bits of conversation as the old truck sputtered along.

"…piece o' junk…old car?…lift hubcaps…"

Then came a different voice with a more complete sentence. "Check it out on the way back. Let's cruise by the back o' the club and see if anybody left a boat tied up with keys handy. Never hurts to check out the lake."

When the truck was lost from sight, Leigh crept from her hiding place and dashed to her car. She locked the door, turning the ignition in the same motion. There was a spasmodic cough and then the engine died. Frantically, she turned the key again, only to have the scenario repeated. The darkness of the night and the shadowy silhouettes of the trees stirred melodramatic thoughts into action.

"Calm down!" she whispered hoarsely. "Try the key again."

Slowly, she tried and was rewarded when the engine began to purr smoothly. She sent a prayer of thanks heavenward.

Inching the Toyota from the parking space, she turned on the lights and drove toward the exit. Less than five minutes later, she was on the road to Atlanta.

As she drove, Leigh struggled to secure the seatbelt over her shoulder, drifting unnoticeably to the road's center line. She jerked the steering wheel and automatically checked the rear view mirror. Some distance behind, Leigh saw the unmistakable reflection of headlights.

Her speedometer showed 50. She pressed the accelerator and saw the needle climb to 55, then just shy of 60. Bo had warned her of an alignment problem, that speeds over 55 could cause the car to vibrate. His prediction proved accurate and she slowed to 50.

The other vehicle was quickly closing the distance between them. Leigh was startled when it pulled out to pass and she recognized the dilapidated truck that she had seen at the country club.

The truck slowed a bit, allowing the passenger to shout through his open window.

"Well, as I live and breathe! It's the limousine we saw at the country club. But now, there's a driver. Hey, got an idea! Let's race! Can you get it up to 60? My driver'll give you a head start. Right, Coco?"

Leigh looked straight ahead, never altering her speed, as laughter erupted from the truck's driver and passenger.

"Hey!" the passenger yelled. "Coco says we should give you a push."

The truck slowed, dropping back of Leigh. Almost instantly, her car was bumped from the rear, then a second and a third time. She glanced in the mirror as the truck pulled out, momentarily slowing alongside.

"Company's coming!" the passenger yelled to Leigh, and she saw blue lights some distance behind. "Gotta leave now, but we'll be back to finish the race! Don't go anywhere!"

The truck pulled ahead in a burst of speed, disappearing into the night. A moment later, a deputy car roared past her.

She drove slowly, still shaken from the experience of the last few minutes, her hands unconsciously gripping the wheel.

The road was empty, the night dark and lonely. Without warning, Leigh's car sputtered mournfully and she guided it to the edge of the road. Headlights were visible in the darkness, moving toward her. Hastily, she loosened her seatbelt, opened the door, and slid out. She ran, intent on seeking cover in the dense forest that bordered the road.

Progress was impeded as her high heels snagged the grass and her long dress twisted around her ankles.

The lights were so close they illuminated a path behind her. She moved further into the grass, and with growing fear realized the vehicle had stopped. The door opened and suddenly footprints were pounding the pavement.

As Leigh ran faster, her heel abruptly turned and she sprawled to the ground. Darkness swirled about her, then eerie silence as consciousness surrendered to oblivion.

CHAPTER 13

Darkness began to fade as Leigh slowly drifted back to reality. Events became focused, and she remembered trying to run, only to find her progress considerably slowed by the flapping skirt. Eventually, the tangled fabric had contributed to her fall.

Suddenly, Leigh was aware of a silhouette towering above her and moving closer. Groping for something to assist her in getting to her feet, she lost her balance and fell face forward on the grassy edge of the road as the silhouette continued to move toward her. With one final push, she heaved herself to her feet and started to run, only to stumble again.

Powerful hands grabbed her arms.

"Leigh, what's wrong?"

"Mr. Kelly!"

And without a clue as to why, she collapsed against him, not even embarrassed at the tears that spilled over.

For a long moment, he held her and let her cry.

"I'm—so—sorry," she sobbed.

Creede pulled his handkerchief from his coat pocket. "Here," he said.

She blotted her eyes and began to back away. "I'm sorry," she apologized again. "My car stalled—a truck had been following me—and when I saw the lights of your truck, I thought they were coming back—" Her voice trailed off as she fought to regain composure.

"I'll drive you home," Creede said. "Need to get anything from your car?"

"Only the key and my purse."

He caught her elbow and guided her toward his truck. When she was inside, he went to retrieve her belongings from the car.

Several minutes into the drive to Atlanta, Creede spoke. "Want to talk about it?"

She waited a moment, organizing her thoughts.

"As I walked to my car, a truck came up the drive toward Misty Lake. They were talking loudly, above the radio. One of them mentioned something about an old car and stealing hubcaps—*my* car, since it was the only one in the parking lot. The other person said they would do that later, after they checked for a boat with keys. I had trouble with my car. First, it wouldn't crank, then it stalled, then it sputtered along. The truck pulled beside me and the passenger asked if I wanted to race. Then, they suddenly dropped back and hit my rear bumper, I think three times. They sped away when blue lights appeared, but said they'd be back. When I saw the lights from your truck, I thought they were coming back. I decided I would be safer outside the car, but I stumbled and fell, about the time you got there."

"Ever seen the truck before?" Creede asked.

"Never."

"No ex-boyfriend?"

"None."

"No irate father of the bride who thinks he's been overcharged?"

"Patti's wedding is my first since coming to Atlanta."

"Ouch." Creede slowed the truck for a deer at the side of the road. Perhaps this was a good time to add a light

138

comment. "Well, Patti's father may have to mortgage the family home for her wedding, but he can't complain—much. After all, this isn't the year for a new truck, but he was planning to upgrade his computer."

His nonsense drew the tiniest giggle from Leigh, but she said nothing. He let the subject drop.

"I'll get a towing service to take your car in tomorrow for an estimate on the repairs."

"I appreciate your help, Mr. Kelly, but I don't want you to be bothered with that—especially tomorrow when your family and the Spencers are planning to be together."

"That's not until evening. I need something to occupy me during the day." He turned at the corner of Walnut Ridge, stopping in front of the cottage. "Will you have a vehicle? I could see about getting a rental for you."

"That's very kind, but I can use one of the business cars."

As Creede opened the door for Leigh, she thanked him again for the rescue.

"Chalk that up to my failing memory," he grinned. "Alex gave me a book, which I forgot and left at the club. Got halfway home when I remembered and started back to get it."

"Thomas said it was locked in the safe."

"Good. I'll get it tomorrow. By the way, I should have your phone number to give the garage so they can call you when they have the estimate ready."

Leigh pulled a business card from her purse and scribbled her home number on the back.

"On second thought, Mr. Kelly, just ask them to call me at work."

"Still getting anonymous calls?"

"On a regular basis."

"Have caller ID?"

"No," she said slowly. "No, I don't."

"How long has this been going on?"

"About a month after I got my phone. There's occasionally noise, but most often just a sound I can't identify."

"What kind of sound, Leigh?"

"I'm—not really sure. First, there's a grating noise, then it's like someone who's been running hard and their breathing is more like panting. It's strange. Why do you ask?"

"Call it technical research. I'm always on the lookout for a new twist for Erin Wintergreen."

She laughed softly, the most relaxed sound he'd heard from her in the last 20 minutes.

Creede walked her to the door and in the glow of the porch light saw blood near her chin. "You got a scratch on your face when you fell," he said. "Can I get you anything for it?"

Instinctively, her hand went to her face. "I appreciate that, Mr. Kelly, but I have something in the medicine cabinet that will work."

He waited until she had locked the door and turned on the inside lights. When he returned to the truck, he pulled out his cell phone and punched in Max's number. Six rings later, a sleepy voice answered.

"Benedict."

"It's me, Max."

"I'm impressed, buddy. Especially at midnight. What's up?"

"I need your professional help."

"I'm listening."

"It's Leigh Parrish, Patti's wedding coordinator."

"Yeah?"

"She's been getting anonymous phone calls, then had a problem on the road with a couple of creeps as she was coming from the rehearsal dinner tonight."

"So you want me to keep an eye on her?"

"That's the general idea. But quietly."

"I'm on it myself."

"Thanks, Max."

"Hey, no problem. You promised me next week in the mountains, remember?"

§§§

Max Benedict replaced the telephone receiver and smiled in the darkness. This new assignment was too good to keep to himself.

He nudged his wife.

"You'll never guess, Julia, so I'll tell you. I think Creede's got a girlfriend. Won't that break Roxanne's heart?"

§§§

"Gotcha ya!"

Max Benedict risked one eye to peep around the corner of the Thursday sports section to see his wife. She stood by the counter balancing a plate of toast in one hand and a percolator in the other.

"Something wrong, hon?"

Julia set the plate on the table and tipped the percolator toward Max's cup.

"Oh, no. Not now. We have the only toaster in Atlanta that ejects like it's powered by jet fuel, and since I've learned the precise moment it's gonna happen, I know right where to be to capture the toast before it goes into orbit."

Max put the paper aside. After 13 years of marriage, Julia was developing a sense of humor with a touch of sarcasm. With pink foam curlers in her hair and her red chenille robe, she made an interesting sight across the breakfast table. He smiled. After all these years they had settled into a comfortable marriage, just like their friends.

"So the toaster's a big problem, hon?"

"Like it's been since your Aunt Penelope gave it to us for a wedding present."

"Thirteen years." Max waited a moment. "But I never saw you catch the toast before today."

"Max." She laid her knife neatly across the edge of her plate, pushed her coffee mug aside, and propped both elbows on the table. "You've not even seen *me*. Once you get immersed in that paper, nothing gets your attention. Do you think I look like this every morning at breakfast?"

"Don't you?"

It slipped out before he could stop it. "I mean—red's a lovely shade on you. I like it. Maybe curlers of a different color would be better."

"Oh, Max! You're going to hang yourself with excuses." Julia pulled her mug back and stirred a spoon of sugar in the coffee. "I had the craziest dream last night."

His hand was inching toward the paper.

"What sort of dream?"

"Just crazy. Weird." She sipped coffee. "I dreamed you told me something about Creede breaking Roxanne's heart. Isn't that ridiculous?"

Max laughed. "Not at all. But it wasn't a dream. I told you that."

"Meaning?"

"Meaning I think Creede may be developing an interest in Patti's wedding coordinator. He called last night—seems she's been getting anonymous phone calls and last night ran into some trouble on the road, so he wants a shadow for her."

"You?"

"Between me and Tyler Simmons, we'll keep her in sight."

"Well, I guess we'll have to find a new bridge partner for Roxanne."

"Or Roxanne can find new friends to provide a free motel for her."

"Max!"

He grabbed the paper and hid behind it. "Hon, look at this. They've got toasters on sale at Lenox Square. Maybe you should check on one."

§§§

KELLY HOME
OCTOBER 28

They began to arrive at 9 Rockingham East shortly after six on Thursday evening—king, queen, two princes, and a princess. Creede assumed the other official half of the party was Patti, Jan, and himself. Unofficially, as far as this event was concerned, there would be Zachary Bennett and his wife, Louisa. As far as the records of Windemere indicated, it was the first time outsiders had been included in the family

143

evening that traditionally preceded the wedding day of a member of Windemere royalty.

The Isle of Windemere would be forever indebted to Louisa Bennett. It was she who had stumbled onto the royal family's jewels, valued in the hundreds of millions of dollars. Stolen by a trusted valet and transported to America by an unsuspecting Princess Camille, the theft had fueled gossip that Prince David had been involved. For three years, the Spencers had struggled to rise above the devastation created by the suspicion, and only when the jewelry was found by Louisa and returned to Windemere did a degree of normalcy return to the Caribbean island.

Creede stood at the entrance to the dining room watching his guests as they chatted amiably in the living room. Lorraine Spencer had given Louisa a bracelet with a charm engraved with an *L*, the small disc encircled with sparkling diamonds. It was one of the pieces Louisa had found and when she protested the extravagance of the reward, Lorraine smiled.

"Nonsense, Louisa. You earned it. And it's very little for the Spencers to do in the way of thanking you."

Creede glanced toward Jan as she ignited the last candle on the dining table, then gave him a thumbs up that everything was ready.

He invited his guests to join him and Jan for a catered dinner of standing rib roast and asparagus casserole.

§§§

They had lingered at the table until nearly nine, sipping coffee and indulging in caramel butter pecan trifle, the caterer's personal dessert creation for the evening. Small talk drifted back and forth, with advice being given as to the best route for getting the newlyweds to the airport, only to be rejected in favor of an alternate plan.

Creede walked with Louisa and Zachary to their car. "Any chance of getting with you on Saturday about the book?" he asked Zachary.

"If it's early. I don't think I can keep Louisa away from the children much longer. We drove from Nance's Crossing this morning and she's already called home four times."

"I can make it as early as you want."

"Breakfast at the hotel? About seven?" Zachary asked.

"I'll be there."

"Any problems with the story?"

"No problems. Just want to run a couple of ideas by you. A few changes here and there, maybe delete some things."

Zachary sighed. "No problem, huh? Sounds like we may be dealing with an entirely new book."

Creede leaned against the car. "Part of it is based on fact. Or an incident that happened several months ago. At present, that incident remains unsolved."

Zachary opened the door and slid in. "The flip side of that is you may solve the crime, fictionally speaking, and provide the answer that will assist the law in concluding their investigation."

"That would be a first," Creede said dryly.

"But a sure way to make the best seller list."

"I hear you." Creede shook hands with Zachary. "Glad you and Louisa could be here tonight. See you tomorrow at the wedding."

Before he could get back to the house, Jan met him, pulling on her coat.

"Good-night, Creede. You did good with dinner. The Spencers were favorably impressed. Did you hear all those nice compliments from Lorraine as they were leaving?"

"She has an awesome way with words," Creede agreed. "I thought you would spend the night here."

"I thought about it, but no. I need my beauty sleep in the morning and there'll be way too much activity here for snoozing." She kissed him on the cheek. "Call me if you need me. Otherwise, I'll be at the church around four."

Creede waited until her rental car disappeared down the drive before he went inside. Patti was waiting at the foot of the stairs. She came to him, her arms outstretched.

"Thank you, Daddy. It was a wonderful evening."

He hugged her tightly, burying his face in her hair.

"You're welcome, baby."

They stood for several minutes until Creede felt a little sob break against his chest.

"Baby?" he whispered.

"Sorry," she sniffed. "I've no idea where that came from." She paused briefly. "It's just that *tonight* makes everything seem so final. Even the rehearsal last night didn't affect me the way this has. Maybe it was the two families together, at *home*, the things we talked about—"

"I could tell you it's not too late to change your mind, but you wouldn't hear me."

Patti pulled away to look at her father. "I don't *want* to change my mind. I love Alex and I want to be married to him. The problem is I also want you close by. You represent *home* to me. It'll take a long time for the palace to feel like home."

Creede smiled at his daughter, who, this moment, appeared no more than a child, his little girl.

"If my mind is working like it should, didn't someone say, once upon a time, that home is where the heart is?"

Patti wrinkled her nose. "*You* said that every time I went to spend the night with friends." She sighed. "My friends' fathers would tell them to have a good time. You always said *home is where the heart is*."

"That's because you're my heart." Creede laughed. "It's time to confess. I borrowed that line. I forget what highly intelligent person said it, but I think there's a lot of truth in it." He paused. "Remember when you brought Leigh by the house, April I think it was—"

"To talk about the reception?"

"Right. She said something about *home* I had not thought of in years."

"Like what?"

"That it was the first institution God established. Your grandparents must have said that to me dozens of times as I was growing up." His expression became serious. "I've not done a very good job of teaching you that, Patti, so I just resorted to borrowing a cliché, hoping you would get the message. I also hope you will recognize long before I did that God deserves a place in your home. And you'll be happy in Windemere because you're becoming a part of an extraordinary family. *Home* is important to them because their family has lived in the same house for many generations, and you will help carry on the tradition."

Patti kissed her father. "Maybe we should conclude this conversation now, before I get weepy again. 'Night, Daddy. And thanks for everything."

She was up the stairs and out of sight before Creede could respond. He set the alarm, turned out the lights, and made his way through the dining room and down the hall to his room.

Snatches of the conversation with Patti replayed in his mind, especially their shared thoughts about home. All things considered, he felt he had done an acceptable job as a single parent. He had certainly tried to instill values and understanding as prerequisites to a satisfying life. Only time would tell if he had been successful.

He laid his watch on top of the chest of drawers and saw Leigh's business card. The family gathering tonight was the first nuptial event she had not been part of. For some reason, he had sincerely missed her.

CHAPTER 14

OCTOBER 29

Silvery, misty fog clothed the trees in a veil, hung in the air like a whisper, and attached itself to the ground with tentacles of determination.

At Weddings of Bliss, Leigh Parrish groaned.

At Rockingham East, Patrice Kathleen Kelly cried.

On I-20 West, inbound to Atlanta, Max Benedict fumed to his recently hired investigator partner, Tyler Simmons.

"What's a man to do with weather like this, Ty? I can't fish or hunt. Reading puts me to sleep. If I stay home, Julia's got a list of honey-dos a mile long and this is not house repair weather."

"Downright frustrating, isn't it? But I grew up in the northwest so this looks like an ordinary day to me."

"How'd you wind up in Atlanta?"

"Actually, I got here by degrees. My parents retired to Florida, my sister and her husband use Atlanta as home base when they're on missionary furlough, so I thought I'd try the South when I got out of college."

Max slowed for bottlenecking traffic, casting a side glance at his new partner. Tyler had earned a degree in criminal justice, then decided to try investigative work before applying for law school. He had come to Max from an agency in Tennessee, highly recommended, motivated and energized by his youth and a desire to walk with success. He

149

had told Max there was no romantic involvement, but Max knew with his tall, muscular frame and clean-cut good looks, sparkling blue eyes and wheat-colored hair, he probably wouldn't escape for long. Maybe, Max thought, he should warn Tyler of some of the pitfalls of their career, but that would be sometime in the future if things got serious between Tyler and a young lady. For right now, he had a good partner in Tyler Simmons and that made him happy.

"Ever been to a royal wedding, Tyler?"

"No, sir. Have you?"

"I don't make a habit of going to weddings of *any* kind," Max answered. "The one tonight I have an obligation for. Patti's my godchild."

Tyler chuckled. "Are you going in your official capacity, or the family connection?"

"Both. Our subject is the wedding coordinator. She's been getting anonymous phone calls and had some trouble on the road Wednesday night. Patti's dad thinks someone is out to harm her, so that's where we come in."

Tyler pulled a small notebook from his inside jacket pocket and scribbled a few notes.

"What's her name? And description?"

"Name's Leigh Parrish. At this point, that's all the information I know."

Tyler smiled. "She must be outstanding as a wedding coordinator for Mr. Kelly to be so concerned about her safety."

"Don't quote me on this, but I'd say it's ten percent professional concern and ninety percent personal interest."

§§§

"I have to hand it to you, Leigh," Anna Gibbs said as she worked with a white satin bow to mark the family pew at

150

Redeemer Church. She tucked tiny vials of water containing tuberoses and fern into the middle of the bow, secured the ribbon, and fastened it to the pew. "Not only did you get the year's most difficult bride, you got the weather of the century for a big wedding and outdoor reception."

Leigh forced a smile. "Think positive, Anna. It's only nine o'clock. The sun may shine."

"The fog may also turn to rain."

"If it does, it does. I can put the wedding together, but I can't do anything about the weather."

"How are you planning to handle the reception?" Anna asked, standing back to look critically at her work.

"I spoke with Mrs. Bliss about that. We'll wait until noon to make the decision. If the weather clears, she'll get everything set up for me outside; otherwise, the reception will be in the house."

"The Kelly house is big enough to accommodate hundreds of guests?"

"Not all at once. But everything will work out," Leigh said confidently. *It has to work out.*

§§§

Patti Kelly snapped the lock on her maroon overnight bag, pulled it from the bed, and set it on the floor by two other suitcases. She took a blue denim, button-front dress from the closet to wear to the church and reached to the back of the closet to get her shoes. She dug into the manicure case for her file to smooth a rough nail and made a mental note to change her engagement ring to her right hand when she got to the church.

She sat on the edge of her bed, staring out the window at the fog, the leaden sky, the gray day. From the time she awoke at seven to a similar scene that had brought tears, until now, eleven fifteen, she had trudged through one useless task after another, determined not to cry again. Her resolve was wearing perilously thin.

§§§

As though orchestrated by a well-planned synchronization, at precisely noon the sun broke through, burning away the fog to reveal a glorious day, canopied with a brilliant blue sky that was cloudless. Autumn leaves captured the glow of the sun, returning unparalleled beauty. Atlanta was aglow.

Redeemer Church was aglow as well. The sanctuary, which would be filled to capacity for the city's wedding of the year, was dimly lit by crystal chandeliers, which would be extinguished fifteen minutes before the service when dozens of white tapers across the altar area and along the windows would be lit. A background of ferns and arrangements of white roses completed the altar decorations.

From the foyer, Leigh gave one final glance to the sanctuary, then made her way to the bride's parlor. Pale pink walls were accented with cherry furniture. The opaque windows—one single, one double—were covered with white damask draperies. A row of closets along one wall had folding doors, all open, and a high shelf covered with white linen edged with Battenberg lace. A vase of pink roses and wall sconces holding small pots of trailing English ivy added a touch of magnificence to the parlor, dazzled by the light of a chandelier and table lamps. Full-length mirrors lined opposite walls.

"Patti?" Leigh called from the door. "I'm here to help if you need me." She looked around. "Where are the girls?"

"Down the hall. The pastor's wife said we could use a couple of other rooms for dressing. This one got kind of small when six other girls got in here with me." Patti laid her lipstick on the dressing table. "What time is it?"

"Five-fifteen."

"Does my hair look okay? I wanted to do it before I put on my bridal gown."

"It looks fine. I'll get your dress."

"Thanks." Patti moved toward the mirrors and Leigh removed the gown from its hanger. The ivory satin gown was bordered with lace inserts at the hem, and identical designs of lace cutwork delicately accented the skirt. The satin bodice had a jewel neckline that framed a pearl and diamond necklace, Alex's gift to Patti, and was completed with long lace sleeves ending in points over the hands. Dozens of tiny satin-covered buttons marched up the back of the bodice. A detachable 25-foot train with the identical lace inserts along the edge hung on a separate hanger. Classic lines with romantic styling, the dress was royalty in fabric.

"Oo—oh," Patti shivered as the dress slid over her head. "This is *so beautiful*!"

"It is exquisite," Leigh agreed. "And you wear it like a princess."

Patti laughed. "Almost. I can hardly believe it. Who would have ever dreamed little Patti Kelly would marry a real, live prince? I certainly didn't."

Leigh fastened the last button that attached the train to the dress and Patti turned slowly. "You know my dad hasn't seen my dress. I didn't want him to until today. Maybe when he sees how pretty it is, he'll recover from the shock of what he paid for it." She turned carefully in the opposite direction. "I just can't believe this is actually happening to *me*! Ten years ago I dreamed about it after I saw Cinderella, but who would have *ever* thought it would happen? And to *me*?"

Leigh smiled at Patti's reflection in the mirror. "God sometimes works out His plans for us in mysterious ways that we don't understand."

Patti turned again to face Leigh, her expression sober and just a hint of moisture in her brown eyes. "Last July, there wasn't much hope that today would happen. When Alex was so sick, the doctors didn't think he would survive, and neither did his family. But when he was better, I think on Thursday before I came home on Friday, he said God was working on a plan for us." Patti dabbed at the corner of her right eye. "I'd never heard Alex say anything like that, and it kinda frightened me. I mean—what kind of *plans* are there except what you make for yourself? And I certainly couldn't understand why God would choose to work on a plan while Alex was so ill. Is there logic in that?"

"It's called God's logic, Patti. We aren't meant to understand it all at once. But I do know that when we are down, whether it's because of illness or some catastrophe of our own making, we are in an excellent position to look up. For some of us, it's the first realization of our need for God. The need has always been there, we just sometimes don't realize that the emptiness in life is a longing for God, not more things to own or places to go."

"I hope Alex and I don't mess up God's plans. Wouldn't that be scary? And I don't think we will if we can just know—"

A gentle tap on the door interrupted Patti.

"That may be your Aunt Jan. I left word that her corsage would be in here," Leigh said as she crossed the room and opened the door.

"I came to check on the bride—" And rather suddenly, Creede Kelly forgot the rest of his sentence.

Leigh Parrish stood before him, framed in the doorway. Dressed in long-sleeved deep turquoise satin that reached to the floor and topped with matching lace-overlaid bodice, a corsage of white roses, and a three-strand pearl choker, she might have been Miss America at her coronation.

"Leigh." It was all he could say, and even then he felt he had stumbled over her one-syllable name.

"Good evening, Mr. Kelly. Everything's ready, I believe, except for your sister getting her corsage."

"She's—in the foyer—I think."

Leigh picked up the corsage box. "Thanks. I'll be back shortly."

Creede stepped back to let her pass. For several minutes, he stood there, waiting until Leigh disappeared from sight.

"Daddy," Patti called softly. "I'm over here."

"Sure, baby." He entered the bride's parlor, and for the second time that evening, he was speechless. He shook his head to clear the confusion.

"Do you like my dress, Daddy?"

He could only stare. His daughter—a beautiful bride. And on the threshold of becoming a princess.

"Do you?"

Creede coughed to clear a tightening in his throat. "Honey, I'm speechless."

"Twice in one day. That's a record for you."

Patti took tiny steps toward him. "Isn't it elegant? And this gorgeous train detaches so I can dance with my father at the reception without him stepping on it."

Leigh spoke softly from the doorway. "Mr. Kelly. Patti. It's time to get to the entrance."

Moments later, the musicians began Pachelbel's *Canon in D* for the wedding party processional and Patti and her father moved toward the sanctuary entrance as Leigh knelt to arrange Patti's train. She handed Patti the bridal bouquet of white roses and Windemere's specially cultivated bronzethroated orchids as the organist played the fanfare for *Trumpet Voluntary.*

"That's your cue," Leigh whispered.

Creede Kelly tucked his daughter's arm in his and began the slow procession down the long aisle of Redeemer Church. He glanced at Patti.

"You're beautiful, little girl," he whispered to her. "Even under that veil."

"You haven't called me that since I was ten."

"You objected."

"I don't now."

"Good. You'll always be my little girl, you know."

Creede knew this little whispered exchange of short sentences with Patti probably would be the one thing he would remember most vividly about her wedding. They were halfway to the altar, faces were a blur around him, but this would be his cherished memory. Until—

"Isn't she lovely tonight, Daddy?" Patti whispered

"Who?"

"Leigh."

"I hadn't noticed." *Whatever was wrong with Patti?*

"You should take time to do so."

"Patti—"

"You really should ask her for a date."

Creede stopped, causing Patti to halt. The congregation was instantly caught up in what they perceived to be a carefully rehearsed segment of the processional. For a moment, father and daughter simply looked at each other and smiled; he patted her hand as it rested on his arm, then they continued down the aisle as Creede struggled to translate and interpret Patti's words. Patrice Kathleen Kelly could make the strangest—*delete that*—most unusual—*wipe that out, too*—most pleasant—*ah, that was the word*—comments at the most inappropriate times.

Creede stood at the altar, listening to the ritual but not really hearing it. At some point, he presented Patti's hand in marriage to Alex and went to sit with his sister, who, in all probability would eventually let him know if he had carried out the official duties of the father of the bride according to the published rules of etiquette.

§§§

From the back of the sanctuary, Leigh viewed the wedding party gathered at the altar. As royal weddings go, it was small and simple—five bridesmaids, five groomsmen, a maid of honor, and a best man. Patti's attendants wore gowns featuring long-sleeve brown velvet bodices topping long ivory satin skirts. They carried bouquets of mixed seasonal flowers interspersed with autumn leaves. The groomsmen wore brown tuxedos. Alex wore his dress military uniform, barely a shade darker than Patti's ivory bridal gown.

Leigh smiled with satisfaction. Her first client for Weddings of Bliss, a perfect wedding, a perfect autumn evening. It just couldn't get any better.

§§§

The ceremony was lengthy, incorporating vows, music, and readings from the wedding rituals of two nations. It was almost seven o'clock when the organist began the recessional, Beethoven's *Ode to Joy*. Following Windemere tradition, the bride and groom descended the steps of historic Redeemer Church under an arch of crossed sabers. Church bells chimed the good news that Patti and Alex had been united with the vows of marriage according to God's holy ordinance. A dozen pairs of white doves were released, symbolizing the purity of love.

§§§

A harvest moon smiled brightly as wedding guests mingled, danced, sipped punch and enjoyed conversation. Joy Bliss had transformed the Kelly back yard into a wonderland. Autumn leaves and flowers had been used in profusion. The swimming pool was aglow with floating tea candles; hurricane lamps were placed strategically to cast warm reflections. A string ensemble filled the night air with music. As Patti and her father danced one last waltz, the crowd became quiet, respecting this time that Creede shared with his daughter.

Too soon, it was over. Patti slipped away to change, and Creede sought support from anyone who would offer advice on dealing with this new phase in his life.

"She's the one?"

Creede whipped around at the whispered question to confront Max Benedict.

"What?" he asked absently.

"The beautiful woman in turquoise."

"Leigh Parrish, the wedding coordinator."

"The one I'm supposed to keep an eye on. Buddy, you've done a better job of that than I have tonight. You haven't taken your eyes off her this entire evening. Even the bride hasn't received such rapt attention from you."

"No comment."

"No need." Max grinned. "But as your best friend, shouldn't I be entitled to know some background on this lady in your life?"

"Remember the Crescent Orchard hospital parking lot last March?"

"Oh, don't tell me she's the one who walked in front of your truck."

"She is."

"And it just *happens* she gets to be Patti's wedding co-ordinator? Come on, Creede. You write better fiction than that. You think I'm about to believe this?"

"I hope so. I'll tell you all the details one day."

Max shook his head. "I'll be waiting." He helped himself to another cup of punch. "I introduced Tyler Simmons to Princess Camille during the dance. Know what he said, first thing? 'What do I call you? Princess? Your Majesty?' Know what she said?"

"No idea."

"She says, 'You can call me Carrie. My family does.' Won't it be something if Patti's wedding sparks another royal romance?"

§§§

"This is the most special day of my life, Leigh. Thank you for making it that way."

Patti pulled on the orange coat that matched her dress and turned for Leigh to secure the cymbidium corsage.

"*You* made it, Patti. You knew how you wanted everything to be and we went from there. You were a wonderful bride with whom to work."

"Not so," Patti smiled. "If I have any glowing character traits, being cooperative is not one of them." She picked up her bridal bouquet. "Daddy was very pleased, Leigh. *Very* pleased."

§§§

159

Patti joined her husband on the deck overlooking the yard.

"Sometimes, Alex, parents don't know what's best for them when it comes to matters of the heart, even when it's right under their nose. In America, children must sometimes take the initiative to show them."

"You would exert authority over your father?" Alex was horrified.

"Only in a subtle way, darling. *Very* subtle."

"And how do you propose to make this happen?"

"Watch me."

Patti caught his hand and drew him toward the railing. She held her bouquet high, found Leigh as she paused to speak to Creede and his sister, then sent the bouquet sailing through the air. It landed at Leigh's feet.

Patti studied the amazed expression on Alex's face.

"That, my sweet husband, is an example of American subtlety."

§§§

Leigh Parrish backed through the swinging door separating the kitchen from the back foyer—and into Creede Kelly.

"Being a maid at the reception was not in your contract," he said, taking the tray of empty punch cups from her and setting it on the counter. For a long moment, he just looked at her.

"Your scratch is all gone. Must've been powerful antiseptic you used."

"Plus makeup. That covers a multitude of imperfections."

He smiled as the music drifted inside.

"They're playing our song, Leigh. *Now That It's Over*."

She laughed, a light lilting sound that spread joy over him like a mantle. "Wrong song. *We've Only Just Begun*."

"Whatever."

The orchestra could have been playing the entire score from *Oklahoma!* for all he cared. He had gotten his daughter married and in the process had discovered wedding coordinators were wonderful people, witty and wise, courageous, smart, and talented.

And beautiful, too.

CHAPTER 15

Max Benedict's exit from I-85 was heralded with more than a mild complaint

"You can't get there from here," he said emphatically.

"Where?" Creede asked through a grin.

"That hunting lodge I like near the Tennessee line."

"You should be on 129."

"I *know* that. I made a wrong turn and just realized it. Gimme a minute—I'll get it straightened out. As many times as I've made this trip, I should be able to do it blindfolded." Max ran his fingers through his salt-and-pepper crew cut. "If you had been driving, I could put a reason to being on the wrong road."

"Erin Wintergreen," Creede said. "I had a meeting with Zachary Bennett Saturday morning and he wants a completed manuscript by January 1."

"Not exactly the woman I had in mind," Max muttered. "You never did tell me what this book is about."

"Remember when we were in Crescent Orchard in the spring and the pharmacy had been robbed?"

Max nodded. "And the pharmacist was in the hospital."

"Right. I took some of that background and used it for the book."

"Case ever solved in Crescent Orchard?"

162

"Not yet."

"Too bad. You gonna dream up an ending, or wait for the real one to get solved?"

"I'm not particularly pleased with the way the real one is progressing." Creede fished his sunglasses from his shirt pocket and slid them on. "Leigh was the last person in the drug store before Marcus Trent was found. Since other suspects are minimal, where do you think that places her?"

§§§

ATLANTA
NOVEMBER 5

Tabitha Parks rocked gently back and forth, the familiar squeak of her chair providing a comfortable assurance of peace.

"This reminds me of something, but I don't know just what."

Leigh looked up from the newspaper. "Maybe another squeaky chair?"

Tabitha smiled. "I'm not sure. Have you ever looked at the clouds, or smelled flowers, or walked somewhere, and felt you were living that same experience from a previous time?"

"I don't think so."

"You will, when you've lived as long as I have. At my age, memories are very dear friends."

"So is the present a dear friend, Tabitha." Leigh glanced at her watch. "Eight-thirty. I must get down the hill. Thanks for supper, Tabitha. It was delicious, as always. If you need anything during the night, just call me."

"I will, dear, and thanks."

As Leigh unlocked the door to her cottage, the telephone rang. She pushed the door to close it and snapped the deadbolt lock.

"Hello?"

There was no response.

"Hello?" she repeated.

For several seconds she waited. Then came the scratchy garbled background sounds and a low moan that had characterized the similar calls over the last few months.

"Who is this?" she demanded as frustration crept into her voice.

The phone went dead.

Leigh replaced her receiver and turned to close the mini-blind above the sink. The phone chimed again.

"Hello?"

It was a repeat performance of the first call. She hung up and continued closing the blinds in the house. When the phone rang a third time, she ignored it for several rings, and when she did answer she made no attempt to conceal her irritation.

"Hello!"

"Leigh?"

"Yes?"

"It's Creede Kelly, Leigh. Did I call at a bad time?"

"I'm so sorry for the way I spoke, Mr. Kelly. I had just had two anonymous phone calls. I thought this was going to be the third."

"Are you okay?"

"I'm fine. Just a little angry."

"I called to let you know your car is ready."

"Ready? But I never heard from the garage."

"Wasn't a major problem. Some wires needed replacing. The mechanic lost your phone number, forgot where you worked, so he just called me. I'll get the car to you sometime tomorrow."

"Oh, Mr. Kelly, I do appreciate all the trouble you went to and I apologize for inconveniencing you."

"No trouble, Leigh." He paused. "That was only part of the reason for my call. You did a great job with Patti's wedding. I have tickets for the symphony tomorrow evening. Are you free?"

"You don't have to do that, Mr. Kelly. Patti's wedding was my job and I enjoyed doing it."

"And I would enjoy taking you to the symphony."

"I can't think of anything I would like more."

§§§

NOVEMBER 6

Creede Kelly considered himself proficient in plotting a story with twists and turns, but he discovered a major obstacle loomed in getting Leigh's car from the garage and to her house.

The shrill of the doorbell broke into the silence of his house. Creede pushed the study drape aside and saw Max Benedict's SUV parked in the drive.

"My answer," he said. A moment later, he opened the door, stepped outside, and pulled the door closed behind him.

"Max. Just who I wanted to see." Creede grabbed his friend's arm, urging him back to his vehicle. "I'm in desperate need of a taxi."

"What's the problem?"

165

"I need a ride to the garage to pick up Leigh's car, drop it by her house, and then come back home." Creede snapped his seatbelt. "Can you handle it?"

"Not a problem," Max replied as he shifted from reverse and eased into the street. "Looking after her car—is this getting to be a personal thing?"

"Working at it. We're going to the symphony tonight."

Max screeched to a stop as the traffic light changed to amber. "Well, congrats, buddy. You put me in a predicament. Roxanne's coming in today. I don't suppose you and Miss Parrish would like to skip the symphony and come play bridge."

"I don't suppose we would."

Max's expression became grim. "Creede, your friend may have a problem."

Creede turned toward Max. "Leigh? What sort of problem?"

"I assumed you wanted me to handle this case as I would any other, so I did my usual background check."

"So?"

"Remember the pharmacy caper?"

Creede nodded.

"Money was stolen—lots of money. It hasn't been recovered. Chester Leverett, Marcus' nephew, has been flashing fifties and hundreds at the grocery store—"

"Chester's a suspect?"

"Unofficially. Not yet charged with anything. He had a disagreement with Marcus a few weeks prior to the robbery and Chester wasn't seen in town for several weeks."

"What's his story?"

"Hasn't got one—or not one he can tell. Chester can't talk." Max flashed a grin. "If he could, Crescent Orchard would probably be Scandal City, U.S.A. Story goes that Chester always hung around town listening to everybody's conversations, but nobody worried, they knew he couldn't repeat anything."

"Can he write?"

"Negative."

"I don't understand how this involves Leigh."

"Remember you told me she was the last person in the drug store, the last to talk to Marcus?"

Creede nodded. "Are you suggesting somebody may have seen her there and drew the wrong conclusion—think she got the money?" Creede shook his head. "I don't buy that, Max. She's not the type."

"Careful, Creede. You can't be very objective when you have a personal interest. And there is another small matter you don't know about."

"And that is?"

"She owes money, Creede. Big money. The bank in Crescent Orchard is threatening foreclosure on her property near Providence Hill."

§§§

Creede Kelly knotted his tie and reached to the top of the chest of drawers for his cufflinks. When they were secure, he picked up the loose change and the encased four-leaf clover—a gift from Patti on his twenty-eighth birthday—dropping everything in his pocket. He checked his wallet for cash and a credit card, then picked up the key to Leigh's Toyota. She had not been home when he left the car earlier.

The key chain caught his attention. Only half of a charm was attached to the chain, broken in a ragged line almost down the middle. The initial *P* was engraved on the half-charm.

Suddenly, something clicked. Creede glanced again at the top of the chest, then reached into his pocket and pulled out the handful of change. And then he found it—the other half of the charm, the one he had picked up in front of Trent's Pharmacy in March. He put the two pieces together in a perfect match. What was puzzling was the *HJP*. The *P* could stand for Parrish, but what about the *HJ*? He turned the charm over and there were numbers: *191271*. Complete mystery.

In his writing career, he had invented codes to stump Erin Wintergreen. Hundreds of hours of research had convinced him there was not a code he could not master, but now he held one in his hand—alphabet letters and a numerical sequence that made no sense, all engraved on a silver charm that apparently belonged to someone who was getting to be special to him.

§§§

"What a fabulous evening! I can't remember enjoying music more than I have tonight." Leigh unlocked the cottage door and pushed it open.

"The Atlanta Symphony is an extraordinary experience," Creede said. "They do a summer program at Chastain Park that's incredible."

"Do you go often during the season?"

"Patti and I had season tickets every year. I guess we made it to half of the concerts."

Creede pulled the key chain and broken charm from his pocket.

"You weren't here when I left your car earlier and I didn't want to leave the key. Did you know your charm was broken?" *Stupid question, Kelly. Of course, she knew.*

"I did. When I stopped at the pharmacy the night of the robbery, I dropped my purse as I got out of the car and spilled everything. I had kept the piece of the charm in my purse and I suppose I missed seeing it when I picked up everything else." She looked questioningly at Creede. "Where did you get it?"

"My friend Max and I were in Crescent Orchard just after the robbery. I picked up the charm and dropped it in my pocket. Forgot about it until I saw your keychain. I wouldn't have thought about it being yours until I saw the part that had a *P* engraved on it."

Leigh smiled. "It is mine. The *P* is for Parrish, the *HJ* for Heathersleigh Jeaneen, for my two grandmothers. Leigh for short. My maternal grandmother was Scotch and her name came from the heather that grows in Scotland. Daddy's Mama was Jeaneen."

"Complete explanation, almost. What about the numbers?"

"Daddy's Mama gave me the keychain for my twenty-first birthday, the same time she deeded Carmela to me. The numbers refer to the nineteenth book of the Bible, Psalms, chapter 127, verse 1."

"Which says?"

"'Unless the Lord builds the house, its builders labor in vain.'"

§§§

Creede parked his truck in the garage and slowly made his way to the house. The ringing telephone welcomed him inside; the caller ID revealed Max Benedict.

"What's up, Max?"

"Not a lot. Have a nice evening?"

"We did." Creede stifled a laugh. "Did you enjoy the symphony?"

Max stuttered. "I—I—"

"Everywhere I looked you were there."

Max recovered. "Just doing my job."

"I thought Roxanne was in town."

"Oh, good news there. She didn't come. She's got a boyfriend. The justice of the peace in her hometown."

"So you were at the symphony to celebrate?"

"Tyler and I were on duty, keeping an eye on Miss Parrish."

"Am I paying two people to do the job of one?"

Max ignored the question. "We didn't see anything suspicious tonight, except a rattletrap truck that parked two spaces over from you when you stopped to get coffee. They watched you and Miss Parrish go from the truck to the restaurant, waited 'til you came out, watched you leave, then followed, maybe four cars behind."

Creede groaned. "I led them right to her doorstep," he said hoarsely. "How dumb is that?"

"We did get a tag number on the truck if that helps your feelings any," Max offered, "but I think they were more interested in your truck than your passenger."

"Get an ID on the tag?"

"Not yet, but soon."

"Call me when you know something."

"I will. When's the next date?"

"What?"

"The next date with Miss Parrish. And the time. I need to get my schedule arranged."

"Next Saturday. All day. We're going to Crescent Orchard to bring back a couple of pieces of furniture." Creede paused. "You and Tyler can have the day off. I'll watch after Leigh myself."

CHAPTER 16

"I'll have to admit something," Creede said to Leigh as he drove toward Crescent Orchard. "There are not many Saturdays with an eight o'clock in the morning that I know about, but here I am fifty-plus miles out of Atlanta at eight-thirty."

"Early morning is the best part of the day," she replied. "The world is waking up, we have a fresh, new start—"

"*Our* world is waking up," he reminded her. "What about England or France?"

"Same for them. They just woke up earlier than we did." Leigh included the foothills of the Blue Ridge mountains in the sweeping gesture of her hand. "Out there. Isn't it beautiful in autumn?"

"Magnificent."

She looked at him, a twinkle in her eye. "I never would have labeled you as one who would use that word."

"Magnificent?"

She nodded.

"Not the right word to use?"

"Oh, it's the right word, all right. It's just with your writing experience, I suppose I was expecting a whole string of words to describe this instead of just one."

"Words are only a vehicle for thoughts. I think simply and concisely. If you can say something in five words, why use ten?"

"Then why do you write two-hundred-thousand-word books?"

Creede flinched at the challenge. "Actually, it's my characters. They're such wordy people. Their personalities develop, they talk a lot. Dialogue moves the story along, and first thing I know, they've become mega-size in their vocabulary. They wouldn't be content to call this view simply magnificent. Three long paragraphs at a minimum to adequately describe this little portion of the Blue Ridge."

Leigh laughed. "No wonder you're on the best seller list."

Creede adjusted the heater. "It's just a bonus for doing something I thoroughly enjoy. I don't know if I write to live, or live to write."

§§§

Scores of vehicles lined the shoulders of the two-lane road in a makeshift parking area. Overhead banners proclaimed November 13 and 14 as Apple Festival Weekend, and throngs of people made their way along the streets of the courthouse square, transformed into a marketplace where vendors presented their items in neatly arranged booths.

"This is fantastic!" Creede said. "I've never been to anything like this."

"You've never been to a hometown festival? It's the most exciting time—almost equals Christmas. In fact, Daddy's Mama and I came every year and started our Christmas shopping, then spent Thanksgiving afternoon wrapping and tagging."

They browsed at a booth offering homemade jams and jellies, apple butter, and confections with an apple base.

Farther down the way, the sweet aroma of caramelized sugar and spicy cinnamon produced an intoxicating blend with an end result of apple pies baked in wood-burning ovens.

Creede looked at the ready-for-sale pies that lined the shelf at the back of the booth. "Ever bake your apple pie for the festival?"

"I'm not that good a cook," Leigh smiled. "These vendors have gone through a series of competitions to be eligible to participate in the festival."

"The best-of-the-best."

"Exactly. And this festival is so much a part of Crescent Orchard life the participants are constantly creating new recipes and improving old ones. As their apple pie fame spreads, the crowd gets larger. The festival brings in a lot of money for the town."

Arts and crafts dominated the next venue, featuring everything from dried apple slice wreaths to handmade doll clothes and crocheted afghans. Blue grass music drifted from another locale as smoke curled skyward from improvised barbeque grills.

Shortly before noon, Leigh led the way to a red and white striped tent that provided shelter for the cafeteria-style meal, and folks settled into almost comfortable folding metal chairs surrounding a long oak table and feasted on hearty beef stew, jalapeno cornbread, and Crescent Orchard's version of Waldorf salad.

Following lunch, Leigh and Creede strolled through the area, finally pausing at a place cordoned off for the bonfire. Several men were working hard to stack the wood in just the right way to insure a roaring fire for roasting hotdogs and marshmallows.

"Over there," she said to Creede, "the man standing by the woman with the red coat. That's Chester Leverett. Excuse me a minute, Creede, while I go speak to him."

Leigh maneuvered through the crowd, finally reaching Chester just as he turned to face her.

"Hello, Chester. Isn't this a wonderful festival? Even better than last year."

His piercing black eyes looked beyond her for a moment. Then, as the fire began to blaze, Chester flung his arms outward, then drew them back sharply, covering his eyes with his hands momentarily before shaking them helplessly.

"Chester, is something wrong? Do you feel ill?"

He took a step closer to Leigh, his eyes searching her face in a silent appeal for her understanding of his attempts at communication.

"I'm so sorry, Chester. I know you want to tell me something important, and I want to understand what it is. Please be patient with me. Will you try again?"

In response, he turned and disappeared into the gathering crowd.

§§§

Providence Hill had kept a vigilant watch over Carmela for years. With each changing season, the Bracken homeplace offered a new panorama of the wonders of nature, lovingly cultivated. Now, however, grass that had turned to autumn brown was in need of mowing. Early leaves had drifted to earth from chestnut and maple trees that formed a semi-circle around the front and north side of the house.

Creede parked the truck at the back of the house where the yard flowed gracefully to the apple orchard with hundreds of trees, still sparsely dotted with red fruit.

"You have an orchard?" he asked.

"Beautiful, isn't it?"

Creede turned to look at Leigh, surprised that the lilt in her voice a few hours earlier had now disappeared.

"The orchard has been here for many years, since shortly after the house was built, I think. My great-great-great grandfather and a friend developed the Crescent apple, planted some trees, and then succeeding generations have added more." Leigh paused. "We can walk through the orchard, if you'd like."

"Thought you would never suggest it."

A well-worn path that persistent weeds had failed to obliterate meandered determinedly through the orchard. The earth around the trees was immaculately clean; in contrast to the yard, the area had been recently mowed.

"Do you harvest the apples, Leigh?"

"Hannibal Burkhalter does it for me, on halves. He sells them in his store and also ships to other states. The ones still on the trees are too small. I usually freeze some and give some away. I'll take some back for Tabitha Parks and for the girls at work. And you are welcome to get as many as you like."

"I've never had an apple straight from the tree," Creede said, opening one of the plastic bags that Leigh had brought. "Polly will be happy with these. She says the grocery stores shouldn't advertise *fresh fruit*, because if you don't pick it just when you're ready to use it, it isn't fresh."

"Then get her a good supply."

"And these were developed by your family?"

"With a lot of help from Philip Patton many years ago. The Crescents became so famous the town was named for them. The Patton family said they're a happy combination of the best apples on the market."

"The Pattons live here?"

"Only one. Bo. He works at the garage and has absolutely no interest in making it big as the heir of the Crescent apple fortune. As Bo tells it, the fortune is gone, so if he must work, it will be at something he enjoys. And Bo enjoys working on cars."

"I ran into him while you were talking with Chester. He's quite a character. He told me a good bit about this area."

"Bo is the town historian by his own admission. I've never known anyone with so much interest in small-town history—he's a walking fact sheet of dates and places and events."

Creede pulled two apples from a low-lying limb and dropped them in his bag. "I'm about to believe that you and Bo belong to the same local historical society. His information says *you* are the favorite daughter of Crescent Orchard, that you've researched the history of your house and the surrounding area."

Leigh laughed. "That's Bo. Overly generous in his comments. But Carmela does have a wonderful history; the lumber that was used to construct the house came from this property. The floors were stained with walnuts from the trees growing along the creek that separates this land from the Patton land. There's so much richness in the traditions—my goal is to one day write it down."

"I must agree that's a worthy ambition," Creede said. "Plan on coming back here to live?"

She took a deep breath, waited a moment before answering. "I probably won't." Another deep breath. "I borrowed money to pay on Daddy's Mama's medical bills and used the house and land as collateral. I have not been able to make the required payments on the mortgage and the bank periodically threatens foreclosure."

"What about the income from the apples?"

"Hannibal has already paid that to the bank. There's no other source of income, except my salary." Leigh dropped an apple in Creede's bag. "So now you know why I asked if I could take a couple of small pieces of furniture back today. They're stored in the barn down the road."

An hour later, Creede drove down the narrow lane and parked at the barn.

"No lock on the door?" he questioned.

"No need," Leigh answered. "Everybody here is trustworthy."

"What about transients?"

"We've had no problem with transients." Leigh paused to get accustomed to the near darkness, then walked slowly among the assorted items in the barn, finally stopping at the chest from Marcus Trent. "This goes—and—there should be a trunk—there it is by the rocking chair."

"Here, let me get that." Creede caught hold of the chest and pulled it to the door. He returned and helped Leigh move the trunk.

"Both must be empty," he remarked.

"Basically. I just have an attachment to some things. The chest belonged to Marcus Trent, and the trunk has been in the Bracken family for three generations. Daddy's Mama loved keeping newspapers with historical articles. That's what she used the trunk for."

"What about everything else in here?"

Leigh sighed. "I'll have to do something with it when the property is sold. Just what, I don't know. And some things in here aren't worth moving." She pulled the barn door closed, then helped Creede lift the furniture onto the truck.

"Let me just look around the corner, please," she said. "Aren't these short-needle pines impressive? Daddy's Mama and I always had a pine Christmas tree—what's this?"

Leigh dislodged something with the toe of her shoe, then bent to pick it up. She shook it several times until the

178

folds opened. "I suppose we do have transients around here. It's a handkerchief—looks like it's been here for quite some time there's so much dirt on it."

Creede caught a corner and opened it out to full size. "Not left by a transient, Leigh. This is an expensive handkerchief—it's even monogrammed. *T.H.E.* Know anyone with those initials?"

"I don't think so." She rolled it into a ball and tossed it into the bed of the truck. "If we don't lose it between here and Atlanta, I'll launder it and take it to the Clothes Closet at the church the next time I come to Crescent Orchard."

They climbed into the truck and Creede turned around. "We have space if you want to get anything from the house," he said.

"Are you sure you wouldn't mind? I have some linens in plastic garbage bags, and some pillows and my comforter."

When they returned to the house, Creede parked the truck and they entered at the back entrance.

"Why the duck tape on the kitchen window screen?" he asked.

"There was a break-in and this is the way the damage got repaired."

"Anything missing?"

"Nothing was bothered except my cassette tape collection."

"That's unusual."

"Marcus Trent gave me a tape the night of the robbery and Sgt. Hendley thinks it may have some bearing on the case, if I could locate it."

"What's the tape about?"

"Big band music. I didn't have a chance to listen to it, but Marcus said is was very good."

"Could it hide a clue?"

"If it did have some kind of clue, that would mean the person who broke in knew about it and needed to get it for some reason. But what?"

Creede shook his head. "How did we get off on this tangent? Erin Wintergreen would accuse us of borrowing trouble."

"I certainly don't need to *borrow* any." Leigh sorted through several pillows on the den sofa. "I think I'll take these three, the two bags over there, and my comforter and drapes. Is there room for all this in the truck?"

He nodded and proceeded to pick up the bags and pillows she indicated.

Leigh gathered the comforter and matching drapes, pausing at the door for one final nostalgic glance around the room.

"I must stop this," she said softly. "I'm sure people get over foreclosures and life goes on." She locked the door and walked silently to the truck.

Smokey gray clouds scudded across the evening sky, bringing premature darkness over Providence Hill. Creede covered the furniture with a tarp, then wedged one plastic bag on the floor of the cab, settling the other on the seat and placing the comforter and drapes on top.

"Imagine that," he said. "No space for a passenger on this side." He caught Leigh's elbow and guided her around the front of the truck to the driver's side, opened the door, and bowed with southern charm. "Your carriage awaits, m'lady. Front row center."

"What a wonderful day," Leigh said softly as she settled in and shifted the comforter a bit. "The festival was even better than last year, if that's possible. Everybody works so hard to make it a success."

"Proof that hard work pays off."

"Of course, it does." Leigh was silent for a moment. "I wish I knew how to help Chester. He was trying so hard to tell me something today."

"About the robbery?"

"I have no idea. When I came for the piano dedication in July, I spent the night with Eve Holliday. I walked out to get her mail after nine o'clock, and Chester surprised me. He had such a look of fear. I've thought about it so often. It was just like today. He wanted so badly to say something and it was so frustrating for him."

"And you. Know what I suspect about you, Leigh? You take on everybody's problems, and you can't solve all of them. Not alone."

"I know," she said stifling a yawn, "but I just can't help being concerned." She paused a moment as a new idea dawned. "Creede, do you suppose Chester knows who stole the money and he's trying to make somebody understand?"

"It's possible, I guess. How many times has he approached you?"

"Three, counting the day of Marcus' funeral."

A gentle rain began to fall slowly, glistening on the road.

"How long have you owned Carmela?" Creede asked.

"Seven years. The house has been in the Bracken family for five generations, and I have the infamous honor of letting it get out of the Bracken family."

"An important place to you?"

"Very important. My father grew up there and our family lived there until his death and my mother remarried. Then, we lived all over for a few years until I finally went back to live with Daddy's Mama when I was 15." She paused. "Do you know what an awful age 15 is?"

Creede chuckled. "It's been so long since I was there I have absolutely no recollection."

"Well, it's very bad. Especially if you don't have lots of friends. And I didn't. We moved a lot as my stepfather made a name for himself and constantly got offers of better jobs. I had a hard time adjusting to these moves, so finally my mother suggested I live with Daddy's Mama. It wasn't what I wanted, but it was better than what I had. At least, Carmela seemed more like home, and eventually Daddy's Mama and I became very good friends. We would pass the long, cold winter evenings making plans to improve the house."

"How?"

"Oh, we talked about enlarging it, maybe add a huge front porch, asphalt the driveway, install storm windows, put in central heat, maybe vinyl siding on the exterior walls. It was all a pipe dream, and we knew it. But it was such fun." Leigh's voice trailed off in a long sigh.

"Sort of a prodigal son experience."

She turned slightly to look at Creede. "Where do you get that?"

"Remember Jesus' parable in Luke? The two brothers?"

"I remember. I just don't get the connection."

"What does the parable say to you, Leigh?"

"Well, the younger brother goes his own way and when things get really bad, he comes back home to his father."

"And father does what?"

"Has a party."

"Who's missing from the party?"

"The older son."

"Why?"

"Jealousy, I suppose. He spent his life doing what he was supposed to, staying home and looking after his job of running the family business, but got no reward."

"And when kid brother arrives, something snapped. Rational thoughts went out the window. Big brother felt he never got anything for his family loyalty, no party, no sit-down dinner. All his life, he did what he was supposed to do, but he didn't get what he thought he should have gotten. And remember what his final comment to daddy was? 'You spared no expense in welcoming home one who has literally thrown his life away and smudged the family name.'"

"What do you think he should have done?"

"Worked out the differences."

"So why do you think Jesus didn't tell us that the older brother forgave and was reconciled to his family?"

"This is only my theory, but I think it's valid. The older brother had within his power the ability to write a happy ending to the story and he blew it. He just didn't choose to reconcile."

Leigh sorted through Creede's remarks before answering. "Interesting. So you think this is a parable about choices?"

"Somewhat. The younger son made a bad choice in the beginning and paid the consequences of a nearly ruined life, but he also made another choice that turned his life around. *He came home.* The parable is 99 percent about coming home. Little else matters in the story if we miss that point." Creede slowed the windshield wipers a notch. "Take your situation, for example. Even if you didn't especially like the idea of coming to live with your grandmother years ago, at some point you *chose* to be happy at Carmela. Look at the plans you two made. Carmela became *home.* You *chose* to come back, just like the younger son in the parable." He adjusted the wipers again. "And that's my theological take on the prodigal son parable."

"I—had no idea—you—"

Creede slowed for a truck ahead. "Just because I don't go to church every Sunday doesn't mean I'm totally ignorant about the Bible."

He caught her hand, and experiencing a special joy in doing so, held it until they reached her house.

§§§

ATLANTA

The rain was beginning to fall in earnest just as the trunk and chest were settled in Leigh's kitchen.

"Everything got in just in time," Creede said as he picked up a pillow that slid from the sofa. "Rain sounds like it may continue for a while."

Leigh followed him to the door. "It's been the most extraordinary day, Creede. I can't begin to thank you for everything."

He turned to face her. "My pleasure, Leigh. Okay if I give you a call in a couple of days?"

She nodded.

He caught her hands. "Will I completely destroy this wonderful day if I kiss you good-night?"

CHAPTER 17

Creede Kelly finished a bowl of canned clam chowder and half a stack of saltine crackers that, with multiple misgivings, he called lunch.

He had gone to church that morning. He thought it was the first time since Easter, not counting Patti's wedding. Redeemer Church had placed his name on the membership roll when he joined at age 14. Through the years, the church had faithfully mailed him a weekly bulletin, and the succession of new ministers had made the obligatory pastoral call "to get to know you." He was sure the fame he had achieved as a writer had nothing to do with his lack of interest in attending church, but when Patti was his sole responsibility, he would drop her off for Sunday School, go walk in Piedmont Park, and pick her up an hour later. They never attended worship service.

So how in the world did he get inspired to deliver an expository account on the prodigal son yesterday? And to Leigh Parrish, of all people. She didn't say much about her faith, but it must be strong to keep her from surrendering to worry about her financial situation. And facing the future without the grandmother she dearly loved must be devastating. She did have rock-solid opinions about home, however, and that spoke volumes.

Faith?

That wasn't what saved a person's home. The formula for that was to work hard, earn the money, make the payments.

Leigh was doing all that. Heaven knows she put in untold hours of hard work on Patti's wedding. But the wages she earned were not enough to pay a mortgage, rent, car repairs, and day-to-day living expenses.

And then it hit him. *Faith* may not save a person's home, but faith saved a *person*. Faith was why Leigh could face each new day with integrity and get up one more time than she fell down. Faith made her strong for adversity, and adversity—well, it would just have to look for another victim.

Creede took his half-filled coffee cup to the study and set it on the desk. He waited while the computer ground into action, went where he told it to, and Erin Wintergreen bubbled to life on the screen. He read the last couple of paragraphs, focused his thought, and proceeded to pound the keys to bring Chapter 21 to a suitable close.

Before that happened, the phone rang.

"Hello?"

"Hi, Daddy! It's me!"

"Baby!"

She's not a child. She's a married woman.

"Hey, baby!"

She's still my baby.

"How are you, Daddy? Seems like *forever* since I've seen you!"

"I warned you about moving so far away! Gave you plenty of time to change your mind."

"I know—I know. I wouldn't listen. But I retained my visiting privileges and fully intend to use them on a regular basis."

"So how was Nova Scotia?"

"Wonderful! We did some skiing, some sightseeing, and lots of shopping! Ever been there, Daddy?"

"Never have."

"You should go. You'd love it. And I bet you could get some fabulous research done for a future Erin book."

"That's possible. She's never been there, either."

"Have you seen Leigh, Daddy?"

Uh-oh.

"As a matter of fact, I have. Twice."

"Cool! Did you go to the florist shop?"

"No. I invited her to the symphony a week ago. And yesterday, we went to the festival in Crescent Orchard—hold on a minute, Patti, while I check call waiting." It was the briefest of moments. "Let me call you back, baby. Leigh's calling."

"That's okay, Daddy. You don't have to call back. I just wanted to let you know we'd gotten home and to tell you I love you."

"I really don't mind calling—"

"I know. But Alex and I are going for a long walk, and then we're reading a book together before dinner each evening, and this is my turn to read."

"What are you reading?"

"The Bible," Patti answered.

§§§

"Sorry to keep you waiting, Leigh. I was talking with Patti. They've gotten back to Windemere and she called to check on me. For eighteen years, I kept check on her. Now, we have a role reversal."

"I'm sorry I interrupted the call, Creede."

"No interruption at all, Leigh."

"Thanks." She paused. "I don't know if I should even mention this, but a car has been by several times today. I ate lunch with Tabitha and when I came back to the cottage, it had parked down the street."

"Ever seen it before?"

"I don't think so."

"I'll be right over."

"I wouldn't have mentioned it except I opened the trunk we brought yesterday to see what historical events Daddy's Mama had saved."

"The newspapers?"

"Right. And you won't believe this, but I found money hidden in the papers!"

§§§

"Okay. What's your explanation?"

Creede stood by the driver's window of the car parked a short distance from Leigh's house.

Max Benedict pushed his hat back. "I'm on the job," he pointed out. "Have been since seven this morning. Want to check my logbook?"

"No. And I don't pay overtime for Sunday work." Creede slapped the top of the car. "You're losing your touch at being discreet, Benedict. Leigh saw you every time you drove past." He pulled the door open. "Come on to the house. She's got a bigger problem."

Max got out and followed Creede to the house. He stepped to one side as Leigh opened the door, not missing the delighted expression that settled on Creede's face as they entered.

"Leigh, I want you to meet my good friend, Max Benedict. Max is a private investigator and I asked him to—"

"Keep an eye on you," Max finished. "Creede was concerned after your little problem on the road the night of the wedding rehearsal."

Leigh looked from Max to Creede. "I'm not in any danger."

"I also understand you've been getting some undesirable phone calls, and until we can figure out what's going on, my partner or I will be close by."

"What am I supposed to do?" Leigh asked.

"Ignore us," Max replied. "Pretend we're not there. Go on with what you do every day, your normal routine."

"It's pretty normal. And boring," Leigh said.

"Let's keep it that way," Creede told her. "Now, tell us about the money in the trunk."

"It's just a few bills. I left it alone."

Max and Creede began an inspection of the papers and the currency Leigh had found, two $50 bills and one $100 bill. The trunk was less than half-filled with newspapers, and Max began moving them to one side. He stopped abruptly.

"There's something more than newspapers here," he said tersely, and lifted out a bulging plastic bag emblazoned with the words *Trent's Pharmacy.*

§§§

CRESCENT ORCHARD

Chester Leverett sank to the ground, his body weary with aching bones and tired muscles. In the twilight of a late Sunday afternoon, he thought about his predicament. No family—unless he honored Jason Trent with that title and he didn't feel inclined to do so. Although it had been done quietly, Jason had arranged for the right people to know that he was personally channeling money to an account for the benefit of Chester Leverett. Jason had also made the deposit on a room at the Home for the Aging, but Chester flatly refused to go.

Chester stretched out on the damp ground with its mattress of damper leaves. He watched as the first stars twinkled earthward, intrigued with the intricate patterns of stars pasted on the darkening canopy of night sky.

It was this exact area where he had found money a few months earlier. It still puzzled him about that cash, big bills just lying around. Crescent Orchard whispered that Chester had stolen his uncle's money, and even Sgt. Hendley was watching him more closely.

It all seemed so useless. He could refuse Jason's charity, which he had done, and ignore Sgt. Hendley's daily surveillance but that would do nothing for the suspicion breeding in the minds of the fair citizens of Crescent Orchard.

He had a secret, and someday, when the time was right, he would share it.

CHAPTER 18

Phoebe Fain tapped a staccato message on her desk with salon produced fire-engine red nails, stopping briefly to warm her hands over the steam from her coffee. An ailing heating system was unable to warm her office sufficiently, which only added to her ill temperament.

She pulled the preceding week's past-due loan files across her desk, and discovered through a hurried review that the file clerk had not alphabetized them. To Phoebe Fain, that was one of life's unforgivables.

"Well, well. Isn't *this* interesting?"

She opened the file on top, pushed her ebony-rimmed glasses into position, and felt comfortable with the smug expression that settled on her face. Once again, Leigh Parrish's loan had reached the seriously past-due status. Phoebe studied the report. The last payment was made on October 1, which paid the note to August 22. Now, it was almost three months in arrears. She turned to her computer, swiftly converting the thoughts of her favorite mad letter to the screen: *Dear Ms. Parrish: It seems that repeated communications to you have gone unheeded. Your note is approaching three months past due. This letter will serve as the bank's initial notice to you of our intention to foreclose the property unless full payment is made by December 15. Yours very truly, Phoebe Fain, V.P., Loan Operations.*

Phoebe had wanted to make it much more severe, but she would save those descriptive words for the next letter. There was no doubt there would be another, probably more than one. She had nothing personal against Leigh Parrish, and the bank certainly could do without the house on Providence Hill Road, but Phoebe Fain was known in banking circles as *the* loan officer who saw that her customers kept up-to-date with their payments, especially those like Leigh Parrish who paid just enough at just the right time to avoid the foreclosure ax. Her colleagues called her the financial witch, which didn't bother her at all.

She vowed not to be lenient with Leigh Parrish. After all, Phoebe Fain had a reputation to maintain.

§§§

ATLANTA
NOVEMBER 18

Tabitha Parks took a deep breath. She could feel the tears stinging her eyes, and it took every bit of her resolve to keep them from spilling over. For the last hour, her thoughts had followed the same path. It was not a good exercise, of course, but she was powerless to change the route.

With a heavy sigh, Tabitha struggled from her chair. Arthritic knees slowed her steps, but she ignored the pain and began her slow shuffle about the room. There was nothing to do in the way of housekeeping except pinch a few dried petals from the African violet and turn it to catch the afternoon sun.

Why, Lord? Why me? Why now? And poor Leigh. What do I tell her?

She hobbled to the kitchen and filled the tea kettle for her four o'clock cup of mint tea. Before it bubbled out the spout, she had a cup and saucer set out and a Scottish shortbread settled on a royal blue plastic plate.

Soon, the aroma of freshly brewed tea filled the room; it also jogged Tabitha's memory about other times when she had laid the table for her special tea parties. She and Homer had spent their honeymoon in a picturesque village in England and it was there the daily tea ritual had been born. When they returned to America, Tabitha had tried, without much success, to interest her neighbors in joining her for tea. When that failed, she decided to do it alone and found it made a wonderful time for meditation.

She needed that now—time to think about the letter, time to ponder her reaction, time to get over the shock. Time was what she needed. Unfortunately, it was something she did not have.

§§§

CRESCENT ORCHARD

Sue Ellen Burkhalter counted the grocery items on the counter, then checked each one off the list. Eleven items, eleven numbers. She ran a second adding machine tape and compared it to the first.

"It has to be right," she said to her father without looking up. "I got the same total twice—$23.48. So what's the problem with Mrs. Pendergrass? Does she think we're charging her too much?"

"I don't think it's that, exactly," Hannibal said slowly. "She's still in the mindset of 40 years ago. More like the quality of service is faulty."

"How can she have the nerve to complain about *quality*? We fill her phone order, charge her account, make a home delivery. And what do we get? It's too much money or the delivery is slow or we shorted her an item or we took something off sale before she had a chance to get it! What else does she expect—a senior citizen's discount? Good *grief*!" Sue Ellen punctuated her tirade with a Juicy Fruit bubble, then smacked loudly.

"Sue Ellen," Hannibal said sternly, "you gotta stop that gum chewing! That's just not good manners in a respectable place of business. We'll lose customers if you keep that up." He softened. "Mrs. Pendergrass is living in a bygone era. She remembers when common courtesy meant more in business relationships than having the most modern equipment." Hannibal paused to see if he had Sue Ellen's attention. "Come to think of it, she's not too far off base."

"Mrs. Pendergrass is in left field. She needs to face reality. No one else would give her the service we do!"

"Which is exactly why she still shops at Burkhalter's. She just wants the same quality of service she's been accustomed to. And if that means going out of our way to make her happy, so be it." Hannibal was right pleased with the lesson he had just taught. Maybe his Sue Ellen would finally see the light—you get customers and keep customers by doing something a little bit different and a little bit better than the competition. Case closed.

The bell over the door jangled as a customer entered. Sue Ellen ran up the aisle in a flash, her braid swinging in rhythm to her steps. Hannibal swung around and caught a glimpse of Chester Leverett headed to the dairy section where he picked up a gallon of milk and a pound of margarine. Hannibal nonchalantly fell in step behind Chester on his route to the checkout at the front of the store.

"Afternoon, Chester," Hannibal greeted him. "Shopping kinda light today, aren't you?"

Chester mumbled.

"Understand Jason's coming back to sell Marcus' house." Chester's look of surprise caught Hannibal's attention. "Folks say the estate sale cleared everything out of the house, right down to the bare walls. No telling how much history had accumulated in that place." Hannibal bagged

Chester's purchases, but before he could say more, Chester pulled a $50 bill from the bib of his overalls and handed it to Sue Ellen.

"Your groceries came to $4.12. Here's your change of $45.88. Thanks, Mr. Leverett. Please come again."

Chester pocketed the money, then left hastily.

"Strange," Hannibal commented. "What's it been, a few months back, when Chester came in with some hundred dollar bills. Today, he's got a fifty. Where does the money come from?"

"That's a no-brainer. I think it came from Mr. Trent's holdup," Sue Ellen said. She thought about her comment for a moment. "But that really doesn't make a lot of sense," she added slowly.

"What, Ellie?"

"A thief wouldn't be spreading his money around like Chester's doing. Not in his hometown. Where *did* he get that money?"

Hannibal didn't answer, but all the same, he thought it would be a good idea to call Sgt. Hendley and give him an update.

§§§

The door of Burkhalter's closed softly behind Chester Leverett. He stood for a moment on the sidewalk, looking in all directions, then turned and walked slowly away from town, pulling his jacket closer against the November chill. Each step was measured, and all the steps came with a degree of pain, constant evidence of the ankle broken in an auto accident and never properly set.

He trudged along, occasionally shifting his grocery bag, until finally he stood in front of the house where he had spent 30 years of his life. When his parents died, it was

Christine and Marcus Trent who intervened for him and kept him out of an institution. They took him to their home and Aunt Christine began the slow process of teaching him to count. She used rocks and birds and trees—the things he liked most—in her lessons. She would line up small rocks in neat, precise rows for their arithmetic lessons. She taught him to appreciate the song of the birds, and that if he puckered his mouth just right and forced air between his teeth, he could imitate their sounds. Uncle Marcus took him on hikes in the woods, patiently telling him over and over what each tree was, and developing in Chester a powerful love of nature.

Chester stopped in front of the Trent's modest little house just as the postman drove by and waved. The white walls, gray shutters, and roses that climbed profusely on a wrought iron trellis looked the same as they had when he arrived there three decades earlier. He appreciated the simplicity of the house and grounds, but most of all he had appreciated the love and warmth the Trents had given him, and the fact that they had shared their home with him.

Although communication was a real problem for him, he could wonder—and right now he wondered why Jason wanted to sell this special house. Even after he had lost his temper, yelled his unintelligible sounds at Uncle Marcus, and stormed out of the house, Chester knew this would always be home; yet, when Uncle Marcus had come to the shack on Providence Hill and urged him to return, Chester refused the offer.

Few people had ever wanted to be bothered with Chester, and now four of them were gone—his parents, his aunt and uncle. That left only Jason. Surely, something could be done to keep Jason from selling the only symbol of stability Chester knew—the house.

He looked away from the house, past the oak trees that shaded the yard, past the picket fence that enclosed the property to the distant horizon scalloped with the Blue Ridge Mountains.

He continued slowly on his journey to the shack on Providence Hill.

§§§

NORTHEASTERN KENTUCKY

Terrence Elliott slumped against the truck seat, staring straight ahead as he mentally journeyed over the preceding several months of his life.

When he left the BMW at Olnick's in early April and hitched a ride to Tennessee, he had made some momentous decisions, most notably that Olnick would have to search long and hard to find him. If word got back to Olnick that Terrence had taken money from Trent's Pharmacy and not reported it, the results would not be pleasant. Even though Terrence could not find the barn where he had hidden the money, that would be a flimsy excuse to Olnick.

Terrence had closed his bank account, leaving no forwarding address for Olnick's men to trail him. There had been enough funds to buy a 10-year-old pickup truck, with a couple thousand dollars left over, enough to live on until he could develop a plan.

Suddenly, thoughts he believed buried long ago were resurrected: thoughts of a little brother who walked with a limp, thanks to Terrence's irresponsibility with a gun; thoughts of the little three-room house they grew up in, and of the mother who dreamed great dreams for her sons; thoughts of the father who walked out on the family; thoughts of his own vow to escape the life of poverty at whatever the cost.

And the cost had been tremendous. Gambling eventually invaded his life with escalating debts, and out of nowhere came Olnick's offer to settle them in exchange for

Terrence's employment in the organization. Terrence had agreed, and the life his mother constantly warned him against became as natural as breathing.

As Terrence sat in his truck, time stood still. A steady procession marched across his mind: mother, little brother, the three-room house. Suddenly, he wanted to go back, to undo and redo his life. It was impossible, of course.

He pulled into traffic as the breeze showered the road with scarlet and gold maple leaves, not even noticing the road sign that pointed the way to Virginia.

§§§

ATLANTA

"Leigh! Oh, Leigh! Come up here, please. Right away!"

Tabitha Parks waved frantically from the front porch of her house. "Please come! Now!"

Leigh raced along the drive, dashing up the steps as Tabitha disappeared through the front door.

"Tabitha, what is it?"

"Today," Tabitha began, drawing an envelope from her apron pocket. "Today, I received this letter." Her eyes brimmed with tears. "Leigh, I'm being evicted!"

"Evicted! But I don't understand—"

Tabitha caught a tear with the back of her hand before it rolled down her cheek. "I don't own this house, or the caretaker's cottage, Leigh. It belongs to my late husband's brother, bequeathed to Willis in their mother's will. Willis lives in New York, said he would never come back here to live and that Homer and I could make it our home. When Homer died, Willis said I was to continue living here." Tabitha leaned against the wall, cupping her face in gnarled hands. "Apparently, the love of money caused him to lose his common sense. Willis says he's been given an offer he can't afford to turn down and that I must vacate the premises by the end of the year." The tears fell and Tabitha made no effort to conceal her pain. "I'm too old to go house hunting, Leigh. And I sure don't have the money to buy one. If I had known years ago Willis would do this, I would have made different arrangements after Homer died."

"Tabitha, I am so sorry. But the end of the year— that gives us several weeks to find something for you."

Tabitha wiped her eyes. "What about you, Leigh? I know you have your house in Crescent Orchard, but your job is here. What will you do?" Tabitha clasped her hands, then released them and rubbed her face. "I feel so *bad* about all of this—"

Leigh hugged her landlady. "Tabitha, I do appreciate your concern for me. It makes me feel very cared for." She stepped back to look at Tabitha. "Why don't we look for a place to share?"

"Share? Oh, I couldn't complicate your life that way!"

"We don't have to make a decision right now. We've time to look around." Leigh paused. "So your brother-in-law isn't planning to live here?"

"Oh, my goodness, no." Tabitha's eyes flashed. "A business affiliate in Atlanta told Willis a major hotel chain was interested in this property for future development. Willis' letter said all the details were worked out, he accepted their offer, and the deal is closed."

"Not having known this was in progress makes it worse for you, I'm sure," Leigh consoled. "But every situation has a solution."

"Please find it for me. I'm depending on you."

Tabitha's words echoed in Leigh's mind as she walked to her cottage. She fished her key from her purse and pulled the day's mail from the box mounted on the wall by the door. Inside, she dropped to the sofa, sorting the envelopes.

"What's this?" she asked, pulling out one from the Crescent Orchard Bank and lifting the flap.

Glaring back was Phoebe Fain's letter.

§§§

CRESCENT ORCHARD
NOVEMBER 19

The Friday morning staff meeting at the Crescent Orchard Bank concluded at 8:57. For the sixth time in three months, Phoebe Fain's past-due loan list had been the shortest. It also boasted the lowest amount in money owed, but one loan accounted for over 40 percent of the total.

Phoebe shoved her office door closed, dropped her loan files on the desk, and reached for her box of red sticky tabs. She sorted through the alphabetized files, pulling out the one that caused her the most problem.

"There," she said, slapping the tab on the edge of Leigh Parrish's file. She glanced through the copies of correspondence in the file, then flipped to December 15 in her daily planner and circled the date in red, along with the notation *Parrish loan.*

She was collecting all the files to return to the loan department when her phone rang.

"Phoebe Fain," she answered.

"Ms. Fain, this is Leigh Parrish."

"Yes?"

"I'm calling about your letter."

"Is something unclear about it? I try to be concise in my correspondence."

"It's perfectly clear," Leigh replied. "How much do I need to pay by December 15?"

"Miss Parrish, this is no way to handle a financial obligation—paying just enough to get by. When you made this loan, you agreed to make specific payments on a regular basis. I'm sure I don't need to remind you this has not been done."

"There have been other expenses I could not overlook—"

"I'm really not interested in hearing about that. *All* our customers have other expenses, but they make their loan payments."

"Am I your only past-due account?"

"Not the only one, but just about the worst one." Phoebe cradled the receiver on her shoulder and blew on her cold hands to warm them. "Really, Miss Parrish, there's nothing more this bank can do. I cannot emphasize strongly enough the necessity for you to get this note current. When will you do that?"

"I—will try to refinance elsewhere and pay off the Crescent Orchard Bank," Leigh answered slowly.

Phoebe laughed. "Refinance? Really, Miss Parrish. With your payment history, do you think there's a bank *anywhere* that would touch this account?" She paused. "The only hope I see for you to avoid foreclosure is for a fortune to land on your doorstep before January 1."

CHAPTER 19

Some things never change—like weekend traffic on the interstate. Creede had left his house at the crack of dawn for the journey to Nance's Crossing and his appointment with Zachary Bennett, scheduled for mid-afternoon. He maneuvered in and out of traffic, finally reaching the southern limits of Atlanta, and with a moderate burst of speed, claimed the outside lane. Patchy clouds hung in the sky, creating a gloomy gray day. Occasionally, a fine mist of rain peppered the windshield, the wipers creaking agonizingly against the glass.

It was fitting, of course, since it matched his mood. Since Sunday, he and Max and Leigh had explored every conceivable way the Trent's Pharmacy money had found its way to the trunk in Leigh's barn. There were no convincing answers. Sgt. Hendley had come on Monday to take the money back to Crescent Orchard, with a polite invitation to Leigh to come to his office on the following Saturday.

Creede slowed for an eighteen-wheeler just ahead, then pulled into the right lane to pass. The Erin Wintergreen manuscript glared at him, a reminder that he had not yet brought the story to a satisfying conclusion. This would be the last appointment with his editor for this book and if he wasn't mistaken, a synopsis was due on the next book by mid-January. He would pick up a sample contract for his attorney to study.

Creede snapped his fingers. He would also get the contract on the house on the coast he was considering that needed some legal analysis. With the fee his attorney charged, it seemed prudent to get as much advice as possible.

§§§

CRESCENT ORCHARD
NOVEMBER 20

Leigh pulled a chair from the corner of Eve's office, plumped the pillow, and dropped down.

"Bad experience?" Eve asked.

"Not so bad," Leigh answered. "Just—strange. I've never been in the position before of being the accused—"

"Oh, Leigh! You're not being *accused* of anything!"

"Not officially, but Sgt. Hendley didn't try to hide the fact that up to this point, Chester and I are the only candidates for suspects." She paused. "What do you think, Eve? Am I guilty?"

Eve turned the flower container and inserted a chrysanthemum in the middle of the arrangement before responding.

"Leigh, this conversation is not going anywhere because there is no basis for it. You are my dearest friend. I don't even entertain an idea of you being guilty of anything, unless it's being too good! This discussion is now closed." She stuck in another flower. "I'm going to sell Spring Flowers."

The bell jangled as the door opened, and Jason Trent stood framed in the doorway.

"Good afternoon, ladies."

"Well, this is a surprise," Eve said. "Are you campaigning?"

"Not at the moment. I had to complete some of Uncle Marcus' business at the bank—close a couple of accounts and the safe deposit box. Campaigning at the present time is not a priority."

"So the TV rumors have been accurate," Eve guessed. "You are a candidate."

Jason smiled. "Possibly. But for tonight, I'm only me, who would like to take two lovely ladies to dinner. Interested?"

"Interested, yes," Eve answered. "Available, no. Leigh and I already have plans for the evening."

Jason feigned a hurt expression. "Well, obviously, I'm very disappointed. Maybe I'll just check with you when I'm here around Christmas."

"There goes one puzzle of a guy," Eve said as Jason left some 20 minutes later. "You know he wants Chester admitted to the Home for the Aging."

"He what?"

"Actually, *confined* is the better word. Jason says it's for Chester's benefit. Chester refused to go." Eve continued work on her floral arrangement. "I don't know what happened between Chester and Marcus that made Chester leave a comfortable house to live in a shack up in the hills, but I do know Jason is wrong to force his plans on Chester."

"I agree," Leigh said. "And speaking of Marcus' house, I'd like to make a picture of it. Daddy's Mama and Mrs. Trent and I have had some fun times playing on the front porch when I was very young."

"My camera's on the file cabinet," Eve said. "And the van keys are on the desk. If you want to go do that while I finish up here, we'll be ready to head for my house."

"Thanks, Eve. I'll be right back." Leigh started to the door, then looked back. "By the way, Eve. What are our plans for the evening that are more important than dinner with Jason Trent?"

§§§

NOVEMBER 22

Cold air pierced through his jacket and wrapped around his neck like a shawl. Wintry darkness enveloped the yard as he dropped the bike and stumbled over an abandoned flowerbed, then reached wildly for some support to prevent his crashing to the ground. Once upright, he pushed on.

At the rear corner of the house, he paused momentarily to pull a kerosene-soaked rag from a plastic bag. Satisfied that the rag was thoroughly wet, he placed it in a pile of dry leaves at the edge of the house and tossed a lighted match into the center.

When the rag ignited, spreading flames to the trash around it, he stepped back and pulled a handkerchief from his jeans pocket, not even noticing the $50 bill that floated silently to the ground.

It was going to be a good fire.

§§§

Winifred Burkhalter's Pink Lady shift came to a welcome close at seven. Bone-tired and with a splitting headache, she left the hospital and walked to her car, grateful for the security lights at regular intervals that pierced the darkness.

Traffic was light as she made her way through town, experiencing her usual luck at catching both red lights. Minutes later, she pulled into the parking area at the family grocery. It would be another hour before Hannibal would close the store and he and Sue Ellen would be home for supper, which would give her just enough time to cook frozen pizza and make a salad.

Winifred rubbed her temples, hoping to ease the pain. She made her way across the crush-and-run, each step reverberating like a drumbeat in her head, determined that this migraine would not get the best of her.

"Hi, Miz. Burkhalter. Thought that was your car that pulled in."

There wasn't another voice like that on the planet. Winifred didn't turn around. "Hello, Bo. Made your eight-hour day?"

"Shucks, Miz. Burk. My days go from daylight to dark-thirty. And a night shift gets throwed in every now and then."

He held the door for Winifred to enter the store.

"I don't suppose you'd like to come eat pizza, would you, Bo?"

"That sounds mighty fine, thanks a lot." He closed the door. "Want me to bring the Pepsi?"

"Sure, Bo. Tell my husband and Sue Ellen that I picked up a couple of frozen pizzas that'll be ready at eight, so try not to be late. They're both with customers right now and I don't want to interrupt them."

"Will do, Miz. Burk. See you soon."

The night was clear with just enough chill in the air to warn of approaching winter. Winifred slid into her car, turned the ignition, then eased onto Northern Boundary Road, only a black ribbon at night, curving as it followed the contour of the land. The last house before Northern Boundary dead-ended into Providence Hill Road was Marcus Trent's. Winifred glanced in the direction of the house, more from habit than anything else, and winced. Even the slightest motion triggered a new wave of excruciating pain, but something urged her to look again.

"Oh, no!" she breathed and brought the car to a sudden stop. She reached for her cell phone and hit the pre-set for the store.

"Burkhalter's," Hannibal answered.

"Hannibal, *hurry*!" she shouted. "Marcus' house is on fire!"

CHAPTER 20

NOVEMBER 23

By noon on Tuesday, the idle citizenry of Crescent Orchard had acted as judge and jury, and its verdict echoed through town: Leigh Parish was guilty of robbing Marcus Trent's pharmacy and torching the Trent house. The evidence for their verdict was the foreclosure sign that had been firmly planted at Carmela, yet no one seemed to understand the fact that the money from the pharmacy would hardly make a dent in Leigh's financial obligation to the Crescent Orchard Bank. And no one could give a reason for Leigh's presumed arsonist activity.

Lester Miles, Crescent Orchard's self-proclaimed expert on criminal matters, authoritatively delivered his opinion as he conversed with the small gathering at Burkhalter's Grocery.

"Leigh Parrish is guilty all right. The evidence is stacked against her. Money found in a pharmacy bag in her trunk. Now, don't that stand to reason? She was the last person in the drug store before poor ol' Marcus was found. And you know she was seen making a picture of Marcus' house a couple of days before it burned." He drained his Coke can and pitched it toward the wastebasket. "And that last bit Dora heard at the beauty parlor."

Luther Darby whittled an ear on the willow dog head he was carving. "Then your opinion is tainted to begin with. What about the *facts*?"

"Them are the facts," Lester insisted. "Evidence speaks for itself. Cut and dried. She's guilty, I'm here to tell you! I *never* would have thought she'd do something like that. And Chester Leverett was helping her. Firemen found a $50 bill hung in a bush." Lester gave a staccato laugh. "Chester even left his calling card. He shoulda known flashing them big bills around town would one day convict him. Makes you wonder what him and Leigh wanted to hide by burning down Marcus' house." Lester rubbed his chin. "And Jason. Po' boy. Got more troubles piled on him!"

§§§

Winifred Burkhalter used her Tuesday freedom from Pink Lady volunteering to clean her house from top to bottom. Hannibal accused her of being the whirlwind in the bottle. From him, that was a compliment. Winifred knew a spotless house spoke volumes about a woman, and she was determined that her housekeeping reputation would never be the subject of conversation when the town gossips convened their sessions.

She vacuumed and mopped and polished all morning, pausing just long enough to eat a sandwich at lunch. By six o'clock, no dust could be found, and Winifred, showered and dressed, sank into the recliner to rest while supper cooked.

Dora Miles' phone call interrupted Winifred's peaceful R&R.

"I knew you would want to know the latest news, Winnie. My Lester just came back from town and he said—you'll *never* guess what he heard!"

"Tell me," Winifred said wearily.

"He said everybody in town is convinced Leigh Parrish had something to do with Marcus' house burning! And also the drug store robbery! Isn't that something? After all these months, the money turns up and she had it! Lester said she went to the bank to pay on her mortgage—you know she owes a bushel of money on that house and land—and the teller got suspicious when she had that much cash and called the police. And they arrested her on the spot! Her poor old grandmother would be so hurt—she sure tried to raise that girl right. I think it's just *so* awful, don't you, Winnie?"

"Dora—"

"And listen to this. Leigh came to the apple festival with a good-looking man. Somebody she met in Atlanta, I guess. And I heard he's a famous writer. Wonder what *he* thinks of her now?"

"Dora, Leigh has not been charged with any crime. Don't say things about her—"

"Are you defending her? Because if you are—"

"I don't know all the facts, Dora. I can't say anything one way or the other."

"Well, that attitude *shocks* me! But let me tell you this. Lester said Chester Leverett was in on it—him and Leigh are working *together*, Winnie! Chester got some of the money—he spent it at Hannibal's store! Ask your husband if I'm not right!"

"Someone's driving up, Dora. I'll talk to you later."

For one awful moment, Winifred Burkhalter knew she had lied. She said a quick prayer confessing her sin. But then Bo pulled up in his wrecker, and Winifred thanked the Lord for His forgiveness in such a swift, tangible way.

She threw open the door and invited Bo to stay for supper.

§§§

"Are we feeding Bo every night?" Hannibal Burkhalter whispered to Winifred as he helped her carry food to the table. "He was here last night, and here he is back tonight."

"He didn't get much last night," Winifred whispered back, "and it was very late when he got away from the fire at Marcus' house. He got a nasty burn on his arm, too. I'm trying to make amends tonight."

"Steak *and* chicken seems like double amends," Hannibal observed. "Pretty soon, he'll be thinking we're pushing him to propose to Sue Ellen."

"He will not," Winifred shot back. "Bo and Sue Ellen have been friends since kindergarten. They've been dating three years, Hannibal, and if marriage is in their future, it will be their decision, not ours. And after three years of dating, it can hardly be considered a spur-of-the-moment decision."

"I suppose," Hannibal conceded. "Bo does know how to work. And save money, which he does every time he eats here."

Winifred settled all the serving dishes on the table and called Sue Ellen and Bo to come. Hannibal asked the blessing and Winifred sat back to watch the pleased expressions as her culinary specialties circulated the table.

Hannibal cut a piece of steak and dipped it in sauce. "So, how's business, Bo?"

Winifred flinched, wondering if Hannibal knew it was possible to start a conversation any other way.

"Good," Bo replied, retrieving a green bean that fell from the spoon and dropped to the tablecloth.

"Bo's been offered a partnership in the garage," Sue Ellen announced proudly.

"That's a big step," Winifred said. "Congratulations."

"Thanks, Miz. Burk. It all depends on if I can swing the loan at the bank. If I don't get this deal, there'll be another somewhere down the road."

"That's a commendable attitude, Bo," Winifred told him.

"Oh, Mama, did Dora Miles call you? She thought you were working at the hospital and couldn't find you there, so she called the store. I told her you were at home. She sounded like it was earth-shattering news."

"She got me, Sue Ellen."

"What'd she want?"

"To tell me that Leigh Parrish was arrested at the bank."

Bo's fork clattered to his plate. "Sorry, Miz. Burk," he said. "Didn't mean to make a mess. You surprised me about Leigh."

"It's not true, is it, Bo? Dora said she had Marcus' money and that she burned his house—"

"No disrespect to Miz. Miles, but she hasn't got her facts straight." Bo drained his tea glass and waited while Sue Ellen refilled it. "Leigh found the money in a trunk that had been stored in her barn and she called Sgt. Hendley. He went to Atlanta to get it and Leigh went to his office last Saturday to give a statement, or whatever it is they do. She wasn't arrested. As far as I know, she didn't even go to the bank. The fire is still being investigated. Won't know for a few more days what caused it. She was seen there on Saturday makin' a picture, but that's it."

"Why would Dora say such a thing, Mama?" Sue Ellen asked.

"Dora." Hannibal answered before Winifred had a chance. "She hears something and then imagines the rest of it."

"I'd bet my wrecker that Leigh's not involved in any of it." Bo waited as Sue Ellen poured a third glass of tea. "Last summer, I moved a piece of furniture—washstand, I think she called it—from Mr. Trent's house to Leigh's barn. When we left, one of my hubcaps flew off and Leigh helped me look for it. She found a fifty-dollar bill in the grass and got real concerned because somebody had lost it."

"I remember," Sue Ellen said. "It was the Sunday the new piano was dedicated at church. And Leigh was there with that *gorgeous* Jason Trent." She studied Bo. "Why'd you think about that?"

"No idea."

§§§

When the alarm clock buzzed at six on Wednesday morning, Bo had dressed and eaten breakfast. It had been a restless night, thanks to Winifred Burkhalter's steak and onions, topped off with her famous peach perfection four-layer cake. He had been up since three searching for antacid tablets to sooth his indigestion. When it subsided an hour and a half later, sleep was over for the night.

Somewhere in the back of his mind was a thought struggling for words. Bits and pieces of a scene played around, but nothing made sense.

He opened the back door and looked out at the darkness. His wrecker waited proudly under the watchful eye of a security light—and then the thoughts and words came together, merged by the sight of his Blue Bomber.

"That's it! The BMW with all the aerials on the back! The one I towed in 'cause the driver ran out of gas! The one Leigh saw at the pharmacy!"

He dashed out the door, down the steps and raced to the wrecker. He yanked keys from his jacket pocket, unlocked the door, and reached for his record book, flipping pages backward to March. Thirteenth—fourteenth—fifteenth—sixteenth—ah, there it was!

213

"March 16, 8:00 p.m. BMW—Northern Boundary Road—out of gas. Tag number applied for. Paid $55.00 charge with cash. That's it!" He reached inside the wrecker for the receipt book, found the right date, and hurriedly read his scribbling.

"Bingo! No name, but I've got initials. *T.H.E.*!"

§§§

Bo stood on the front walk facing the shell of Marcus Trent's house. The stench of burned materials hovered in the air; blackened timbers reached skyward, silent sentinels to the fiery destruction a few days earlier. The area was still cordoned off with yellow tape, awaiting a final analysis of the charred remains.

Bo walked the perimeter of the tape, kicking the dirt occasionally with the toe of his western boot, but unearthing nothing spectacular. He was headed back to his wrecker when Winifred pulled in behind it and lowered her window.

"Good morning, Bo. You're up and about early."

Bo waved to her. *You just don't know how early.*

"Hey, Miz. Burk. On my way to the garage. Thought I'd stop and see if there were any hot spots, but looks like everythin's hunky-dory."

"Good. How's your arm, Bo?"

He pushed up his shirt sleeve. "It'll be all right."

"Are you putting anything on it?"

"Some burn ointment the fire chief gave me."

"You didn't go to the emergency room?"

"No, ma'am. Chief said this ointment should heal it right up. Shouldn't even leave a scar—"

Bo left his sentence hanging.

"What did you say about a scar?" Winifred asked.

With a shake of his head, Bo came back to reality.

"No scar. Not on me. But that made me remember somethin'."

"About what, Bo?"

He propped on Winifred's car, bending to be on eye level with her.

"Last night at supper, I said somethin' about movin' a piece of furniture for Leigh."

"I remember. Go on."

"Well, somethin' kept gnawin' me—like a thought that I couldn't quite put together. It's been botherin' me all mornin' and I just figured it out. A scar!"

"You've lost me," Winifred confessed.

"The night of Marcus' robbery, I picked up a guy on Northern Boundary who ran out of gas. He had a long scar on the left side of his face. But he was in a black BMW with lots of aerials on the back. And Leigh saw a car like that parked near the pharmacy that same night, but she didn't see anybody." He searched Winifred's face. "What do you think?"

"I think," Winifred said slowly, "that we may have stumbled on a clue, because I also saw a man with a scar on his face."

"Where?" Bo asked.

"A few days after the robbery, he came in the hospital looking for someone whose grandmother had been a patient around the middle of March, but he didn't know the name. I had to answer the phone and when I turned back, he was gone."

"Didn't Miz. Bracken pass away about that time?" Bo questioned.

"The same night as the pharmacy robbery, as I recall."

"Know what I think, Miz. Burk? Leigh may be in trouble."

"Not because of *what she did*, but because of *where she was*."

Bo backed away from the car. "See you later, Miz. Burk. I've got to make a phone call."

"To Sgt. Hendley?"

"No, ma'am. Not yet."

§§§

ATLANTA

Creede Kelly flipped the three pages of the purchase contract for the beach house at Enchanted Harbor, then looked through the pictures of the property. Seven rooms, a screen-enclosed porch across the back, white stucco with red tile roof, a couple of blocks from the ocean. The house was equipped with every known amenity and had a price tag to match.

Zachary Bennett had told him about 1011 Hibiscus Lane during one of their meetings several months earlier. It had been rental property previously. Before Zachary and Louisa had married, Louisa had stayed there for a couple of weeks while researching historical houses in the area. When Creede had expressed a desire to move from Atlanta after Patti married, Zachary urged him to at least look at the property.

It had not stopped with looking, for now he held the sales contract in his hand. Rockingham East would go on the market the middle of December; if it sold quickly, he would be in a position to make further plans. Hibiscus Lane was extraordinary property.

The ringing telephone interrupted his ideas of perfection.

"Hello?"

"Mr. Kelly?"

"Right."

"You probably don't remember me. This is Bo Patton. I met you at the apple festival a couple of weeks ago."

"Sure thing, Bo. You have that blue wrecker with the Georgia Tech emblem on it. What can I do for you?"

Bo exhaled an audible sigh. "I don't quite know how to say this, but since you were with Leigh at the festival—well, I thought you should know."

Creede's throat tightened. "Know what, Bo?"

"About the man with the scar. And the BMW."

"Go on."

"Leigh saw the car parked close to the pharmacy the night of the robbery, and later on I towed it into town after it ran out of gas. The guy rode in the wrecker with me, and he had a long scar on the left side of his face. A few days after that, he was at the hospital askin' about someone whose grandmother had been in the hospital. My girlfriend's mother is a Pink Lady at the hospital and she talked to him."

"Bo, how can I get in touch with the lady at the hospital?"

"She's workin' today—Winifred Burkhalter's her name."

"Thanks, Bo. Leave me your number and I'll be in touch."

Creede broke the connection and dialed directory assistance for the hospital's number. Minutes later, he was talking with Winifred Burkhalter, explaining the reason for his call.

"What can you tell me about the man with the scar?" he asked.

"I only saw him briefly. He asked about the young lady whose grandmother had been a patient, that he was a family friend, but couldn't remember the name."

"Couldn't have been much of a friend if he couldn't remember the name."

"That's what I thought," Winifred agreed. "Anyway, I told him I couldn't do anything without a name. My interoffice phone rang about that time and I turned to answer it. When I turned back, he was gone."

"Wonder why he left so suddenly?" Creede asked. "Do you remember what your call was about?"

"Routine. It was the same night Marcus Trent was brought in and when Jason got there the next day, there was some mix-up about something left in the ICU waiting room."

"Did you mention Leigh's grandmother's name in your conversation?"

"Oh, yes. I said it was sad that Marcus didn't know about Mrs. Bracken's passing since they had been such devoted friends for years."

"That's why Scar Face left. He got the information he needed."

"Oh, Mr. Kelly! I really messed up, didn't I?"

"On the contrary, Mrs. Burkhalter. I think you've provided a valuable clue. So far, the *only* clue."

"I hope I haven't put Leigh in danger."

"Don't worry. We've got something to work with now."

Creede hung up, retrieved the scrap of paper where he'd made a note of Bo's number, and dialed.

"City Garage. Bo speaking."

"Creede Kelly, Bo. I've spoken with Mrs. Burkhalter. One thing came to mind. When you towed the BMW, how were you paid?"

"With cash."

"There goes that theory. I was hoping it was check or credit card that might give us a name and address."

"Don't have that," Bo replied, "but on cash sales, we give a receipt and get the customer to initial our copy. His initials are *T.H.E.*"

"Interesting." Creede hung up as he checked the time. Two more phone calls to go. The first was to Leigh to invite her to lunch, and the second was to his attorney, Regina Compton, who never seemed available to take his calls.

"Hi, Regina, it's Creede Kelly," he said to her voice mail. "I've made a decision about the property at Enchanted Harbor. Let me know when we can discuss it."

CHAPTER 21

"I really think you're making too much out of this."

"Too much?" Creede asked. "Leigh, stolen money is found in a trunk belonging to you. You were the last person in the pharmacy before Marcus' robbery. Marcus' house gets burned and you were seen on the premises making pictures two days before." For the first time, he was almost exasperated with her. "Even Erin Wintergreen would have difficulty proving her innocence with that much stacked against her."

Leigh placed her fork on the plate before replying. "You're the author," she said. "How would you write Erin out of a situation like this?"

"First, she would listen to the people who care about her."

Ignoring the people in the busy restaurant, Creede reached across the table and caught Leigh's hand, held it for a minute, then released it.

"This is not something out of a novel, Leigh, that at some point, when you're tired of reading, you can close the book and put it aside. What's happening now is real. It's happening to *you*, and I care about what happens to you. Very much."

"What do you suggest I do?"

"Remember the handkerchief you found at the barn?"

"Yes, of course. I've laundered it and have it ready to take to the clothing bank at the church. Why do you ask?"

"It was monogrammed. *T.H.E.*"

"I know you're headed somewhere, I'm just not sure where," Leigh said with a smile.

Creede felt strangely rewarded. He smiled back. "The night of the robbery, Bo rescued a stranded motorist out on Northern Boundary. When the guy initialed the receipt for the cash payment, he signed *T.H.E.*"

"So it could have been the same person who took the money from the pharmacy and hid it in the trunk in my barn. But why?"

"My guess is he had to dispose of the money. He saw the barn, hid it in the trunk, and planned to return later to get it."

"But he never did. Why?"

Creede shrugged. "Maybe he worked for someone else, but decided to keep the money for himself. Maybe the someone else found out about it and decided to eliminate his employee." He drained the last of his iced tea. "The important thing is we've stumbled onto the only clue, and that's all we've got to solve this mystery."

"A handkerchief and a wrecker receipt with the same initials. So what can we do with it?"

"Let's backtrack a minute," Creede suggested. "What do you remember about the car you saw at the pharmacy?"

"I don't know what kind it was. I just remember it was black with a row of aerials across the back."

"Maybe a central location, a fleet of cars, and a telephone hookup."

"So what's the next move?"

§§§

By the time Leigh left work at six o'clock, she had more questions than answers as a result of the conversation with Creede during lunch, she was exhausted, and she was

221

facing miles of bumper-to-bumper holiday traffic before she would get to Walnut Ridge.

Once home, she made supper, then settled into her recliner with the newspaper. Just before ten, she checked the answering machine and found the message that would change her Thanksgiving holiday.

"Hi, sweet," Leigh heard. "It's your mom. I'll be dropping in tomorrow. Don't go to any trouble for me. I wanted to do some shopping in the States for the holidays and spend a little time with you. See you soon!"

Just like her. Last-minute call that she's coming.

§§§

Thanksgiving dawned crisp, cold, and cloudless. Leigh and Tabitha shared a pancake breakfast at Tabitha's and by eighty-thirty, Leigh had returned to her cottage where she waited for her mother's arrival.

Waited. And waited.

At five that afternoon, Creede called.

"Thought I'd check on your Thanksgiving Day," he said.

Leigh laughed softly. "It has consisted of breakfast with Tabitha and waiting for my mother to come."

"No Thanksgiving dinner?"

"Not so far."

"Stay where you are. I'll make a quick stop at the take-out foods and see you in 30 minutes."

He was there in 25, laden with turkey and all the trimmings.

"This is so wonderful!" Leigh exclaimed. She put out her ironstone plates and accented them with real linen napkins, department store stainless, and iced tea glasses her grandmother had gotten with trading stamps. A crystal vase held an arrangement of deep bronze chrysanthemums and graced the center of the kitchen counter.

"It isn't the next best thing to home cooking, but it's acceptable on short notice." Creede ladled gravy on the chestnut dressing. "Still no word from your mother?"

"None."

"Where is she?"

"I have no idea. Her message was very brief, and she didn't leave a number where she can be reached."

"But she is in Atlanta?"

"She's here on a shopping expedition." Leigh stopped suddenly. "I thought your sister was spending today with you."

"She did. Arrived at ten this morning from Florida— she's been there since Patti's wedding—and I put her on the plane to Oregon at three this afternoon. We had several hours to visit, which is enough for us."

"Patti seems very fond of her aunt."

"They get along well. After Patti's mother died, Jan moved in to help me raise Patti and stayed until she was 14. The college in Oregon offered her a position, and after thinking about it for 30 seconds, she accepted."

Leigh smiled. "She loves teaching, I gather."

Their leisurely dinner was interrupted at seven by the doorbell. Leigh went to answer.

"Leigh. Let me look at you."

"Hello, Mother. I was getting concerned."

"I should have called. I was just lazy. Spent most of the day in bed catching up on my magazines—" She stepped inside and saw Creede.

"Oh. Am I interrupting?"

"No, not at all, Mother. I'd like you to meet Creede Kelly."

Melanie Parrish moved past her daughter to greet Creede.

"Mrs. Parrish, nice to meet you. Leigh and I had a late Thanksgiving dinner because of some conflicts." Creede picked up his coat from the chair. "I look forward to seeing you again."

Melanie Parrish smiled. "Thank you. So will I."

Leigh walked to the door with Creede. "Thanks for a lovely dinner."

"We'll do better another time. Is your mother spending the night with you?"

"No. She would be very uncomfortable here. She'll go back to the hotel."

"Call me when she leaves?" he asked softly.

"Tomorrow. It will probably be late when she goes."

He caught her hand with a gentle squeeze. "Tonight. I'll be up."

§§§

Melanie carefully scrutinized her daughter and adjusted the recliner before she spoke.

"Is your hair lighter, Leigh? Are you putting something on it?"

"It's sun bleached, that's all. I spent a lot of time out-side during the summer."

"With—what was his name—Creede?"

"No, Mother. Working in my yard."

"You should tell me about this man. He looks promising. But a little older than you, I would guess."

"I've known him about six months. We've had a couple of dates."

"His name is unusual, but it has a familiar ring to it, for some reason." Melanie yawned. "Oh, well, perhaps it will dawn on me one day."

"So how have you been, Mother? And Gordon?"

Melanie sighed. "We're fine." She pulled a pillow from the recliner and dropped it on the floor. "Tell me what's going on in your life."

"I have a job as a wedding coordinator here in Atlanta, and I love it. I spend some time with my landlady, Tabitha Parks. She lives up the hill in the big house. You would love the wonderful antiques in her house, Mother. She has a Tiffany lamp and a lovely table from the federal period that would interest you."

Melanie yawned again. "I've gotten out of antiques and into jewelry. Gordon has a very keen eye for good gems and we've assembled quite an impressive collection." She launched a conversation on the merits of fine jewelry that dragged on for over an hour, coaxing very little comment on the subject from Leigh.

Melanie sank back in the recliner. "You've done very well with your little house, Leigh. My only suggestion would be to use floral drapes here in the living room. It would really make the area come alive. The white ones aren't *bad* by any means, but just keep the idea in mind for later."

"I brought these from Carmela. I couldn't afford new ones."

"Are you still hanging on to that property in Crescent Orchard, Leigh?"

"I want to very much, Mother. It's all I have from my family's history." She slid to the edge of the sofa and looked intently at her mother. "I assume if you and Gordon can buy valuable gems, you must be quite comfortable, financially."

"More that *quite*," Melanie answered without hesitation.

"Then perhaps you and Gordon would consider paying the mortgage on Carmela and let me repay you. If I can't do something soon, I'll lose it."

"Why is there a mortgage?"

"I needed money to pay on medical bills for Daddy's Mama."

A tiny smile brightened Melanie's face as she rose to get her purse and coat. "I'll speak to Gordon about it. He's always intrigued with financial investments." She kissed Leigh on the cheek. "Probably won't see you again before I leave on Saturday, but take care of yourself and have a Merry Christmas!"

§§§

DECEMBER 4

Not one unoccupied space remained on Lenox Square's parking lot. Leigh wove in and out of traffic aisles, then circled back, finally pulling into a spot that was vacated while she waited.

It wasn't that she had an excessively long list: her mother and stepfather, Tabitha, Anna Gibbs, Eve Holliday, a couple more. She had added Creede's name at the bottom of her list with a question mark. He called her daily and they had been out once since Thanksgiving; she knew he was facing a deadline with the book. They had not spoken of Christmas.

She joined the jostling mob in the mall, in and out of stores, looking for just the right gift, and cringing each time her credit card was swiped following a purchase.

By one-thirty, her shopping list was a series of black lines, names that had been marked through. Except Creede Kelly. No bright ideas had grabbed her attention for a gift for him.

Leigh made her way toward the food court, amazed that everyone in the mall had made the same decision. Shoppers laden with bags and boxes suddenly metamorphosed into a tired and weary mob, bent on being first in line. She stepped aside and waited, watching the reactions of those shoppers close by.

To her left and almost on the rim of shoppers waiting to advance to the counter, she saw Creede. Leigh smiled. It must really be a matter of extreme importance to get him to Lenox Square on Saturday, which, according to him, was his day, and the same obstacles that *could not* deter the postman from his appointed rounds *would not* move Creede Kelly from his study the entire day.

Leigh moved in his direction, a warm, happy feeling creeping over her.

It stopped the minute she saw him whisper to the glamorous redhead by his side.

CHAPTER 22

Melanie Parrish cradled the telephone receiver on her shoulder but devoted most of her attention to filing her nails.

"I'm home, Gordon," she said, adjusting the receiver. "Right...I got here an hour ago...Where are you, now?...No, I don't think I need anything from the market." She laid her nail file on the dressing table and shifted the phone to her other shoulder. "I spent a couple hours with Leigh on Thanksgiving night. She proposed an interesting investment idea. You remember the house her Grandmother Bracken had up in the mountains?...Yes, that's the one, with all the apple trees...Well, Leigh has mortgaged the place and can't meet the payments. She wants to know if we'll pay the bank and then she'll repay us...I don't have much business sense about mortgages, but I knew you did...Oh, you think it's a good idea?...Sure, I can get her to send you the amount that is owed...What?...Oh, you're right, we will need wiring instructions to the bank...Anything else I should ask her to provide?...That's fine, Gordon. We can discuss it more when you get home." Melanie laughed. "It took me almost two weeks to get home from my shopping trip. Maybe your shopping at the market won't be as involved."

§§§

Falling leaves sprinkled the lawn with dots of color as gusty, sporadic wind severed fragile stems from their branches. Creede stood at the window in his study holding the final chapter of *Murder in the Mountains*. Erin had solved her case, as she always did, and if he did say so himself, she had brought this one to a stunning conclusion. Smart girl, Erin. He only wished Leigh's problems would be solved as easily.

Creede checked the time. Almost four. He reached for the phone and dialed Leigh's number; her answerer came on after two rings.

"Hi, Leigh. It's Creede. I know this is short notice, but I've just finished the book. Thought if you had no plans, we'd take in a movie to celebrate. I saw you at Lenox earlier today, but before I could get through the crowd, you had disappeared. I wanted you to meet Regina Compton, my attorney, but we'll do that another time. Call me when you get in, please?"

He hung up, turning his attention to a sheet of paper headed *Christmas List* and wrote *Leigh* on the first line.

§§§

At 3:45, Leigh had tossed an overnight bag in her car and headed toward Crescent Orchard. With the shorter days of winter approaching, the sun was dipping low in the western sky and would probably be hidden from sight by the time she reached Eve's house.

Throughout the drive to Crescent Orchard, her thoughts would not move from the food court at Lenox Square and the apparent pleasure Creede Kelly was enjoying with the redhead. *Why did I ever think someone like Creede could be a part of my life? He must know every important person around—and I'm certainly not in that category.*

The miles clicked off steadily, thanks to a cooperative traffic flow. Just before five, she was approaching Marcus Trent's place. On impulse, she slowed and stopped. For several minutes she sat in the car, surveying the blackened remains, then got out and walked around. A moment later, a car stopped behind hers.

"Leigh?"

"Jason?" Her tone gave voice to the surprise she felt.

"It is," he answered, joining her.

"This is unexpected," she told him.

"And for me, too. Pleasant, though unexpected." In the gathering dusk, he noticed a faint smile curve her mouth.

"I have such fond memories of this house," she explained. "When I was very young, Daddy's Mama would bring me here and we'd have the most elegant tea parties with Christine. She would serve real tea and lemon and the most delightful little cakes. And, Jason, she would get out her very best china and dainty little napkins. I felt *so* special." She paused. "A couple of days before the fire, I stopped to make a picture. I'm glad I did, but I was seen by someone, and now I have the distinction of being called an arsonist."

Jason put an arm around her shoulder. "I don't consider you an arsonist. My money goes on Chester Leverett for that honor."

"Chester is not capable of this," Leigh said with a sweep of her hand. "He has a good heart. He would not do this."

"You've heard he was seen around here just prior to the fire, I assume. And he and Uncle Marcus had quite a verbal battle a few days before the robbery. When anyone's as hotheaded as Chester, they may be capable of anything that's destructive." Jason moved toward the corner of the burned house. "I guess some important documents probably got incinerated. I didn't locate them in the safe deposit box."

"Documents?"

"The deed to the store, Uncle Marcus' birth certificate. Odd things like that which I knew about but haven't found."

Leigh began walking slowly to her car, and Jason fell in step. "Are you headed back to Atlanta?" he asked.

"Not tonight. I'm spending the weekend—or what's left of it—with Eve."

Jason smiled. "How about dinner around seven? Just you and me."

§§§

"One thing we don't have to discuss is where we'll eat," Jason said. "Since Crescent Orchard only has two restaurants, not counting the Burger Palace, and one of them closes at noon on Saturday, it's pretty much decided who we'll patronize."

He parked the car under the glowing lights that beamed from the corner of the Valley Restaurant, and moments later, he and Leigh were seated at a small round table near the front of the restaurant. After placing their order, he excused himself to speak to an acquaintance near the back of the dining area.

From where she sat, Leigh had an excellent view of most of the parking lot. As the restaurant door opened and a blast of cold air rushed in, she noticed some slight movement on the parking lot in the vicinity of Jason's car. Instinctively, she rose from the table and walked along the wall of windows that overlooked the parking area, not realizing she was approaching Jason.

"Leigh?"

The sound of his voice startled her.

"Is something wrong? I didn't intend to neglect you."

"Everything's fine, Jason. I—just need to wash my hands. I'll be right back."

"Fine," he smiled. "I'll be at our table."

Leigh nodded, disturbed by a puzzling thought. *That was Chester Leverett going toward Jason's car.*

§§§

"All better?" Jason asked as he rose to help Leigh with her chair. "You looked as though you had seen a ghost," he chided.

"Oh, no. No ghost."

"Good. I apologize for leaving you as I did, but I saw an attorney friend. Tried to get some free advice, but didn't succeed."

"That's too bad."

"Not bad, actually. He passed on some information that may be useful at some point. Seems Chester's been rummaging through the ashes at Uncle Marcus' place." He smiled. "Add to that the fact that you were seen making pictures a couple of days before the fire."

"Doesn't look too good for Chester and me, does it?"

"Oh, come, Leigh. You know if I had to make a choice as to the culprit, it certainly would not be you. I don't think you're capable of arson. Chester, on the other hand, is capable of murder."

"Why would you say that?" she asked.

Jason buttered a roll. "Chester doesn't have the best track record for staying out of trouble. And when something like the fire at Uncle Marcus' house happens, most of the time, he has no alibi."

"Most of the time, Chester stays up in the hills and *needs* no alibi," Leigh pointed out.

Jason's eyes twinkled. "Everybody needs an alibi, Leigh. Including me. When Senator Jorgenstein asks me why I didn't get his speech completed, I'll use you as my alibi—tell him I was trying to coerce you to become a member of his team." Suddenly, Jason was too serious. "That's what tonight is about, Leigh." He pushed his plate aside and pulled his cup forward, refilling it from the decaf carafe. "Come to Washington. I can guarantee you a glamorous life, the likes of which you won't find in Crescent Orchard. Or Atlanta. What do you say?"

"That's not the life I'm looking for, Jason."

"Oh, come, now. You would get accustomed to it. Endless round of parties. Rubbing shoulders with the elite. Exciting job opportunities. It's the life every woman secretly wants."

"I don't think so. I don't fit in the circles where the important-name people circulate."

"Not from what I hear," Jason told her. "Names don't get much more important than Creede Kelly."

Leigh looked up in surprise.

"Word gets around. How did you meet him, anyway?"

"I was the coordinator for his daughter's wedding."

"Apparently, it became a personal matter for him. Again—according to what I hear."

"And who are you hearing this from?"

Jason chuckled. "So there is some truth to it." He added more coffee to his cup, stirring in cream before he continued. "Sgt. Hendley told me he was with you when the pharmacy money was discovered. And before that, he was with you at the apple festival."

"Sgt. Hendley?"

"I've had conversations with him over the last few weeks about the pharmacy deal, and more recently about the fire. I believe it's time to do something about Chester. All the evidence points to him."

"Evidence?"

"The argument he had with Uncle Marcus, the big money he had a couple weeks after the robbery, Uncle Marcus calling his name when the policeman found him. And the very obvious—he was seen near the house a day or so before the fire."

"But all of that is just circumstantial."

Jason laid his napkin on the table and smiled broadly. "Your writer friend has had an effect on your interpretation of evidence. But you are correct—to a point. At the *moment* it's only circumstantial. That could change." He pulled his wallet from his jacket pocket and slipped a ten-dollar bill under the edge of the plate and took a fifty-dollar bill and placed it with the ticket. "Time will tell about a lot of things. Ready to go?"

Leigh nodded, hoping Chester would not be in the parking lot when she and Jason left the restaurant.

The temperature had fallen almost ten degrees while they were eating. The cold was biting and encouraged a brisk walk to Jason's car. He caught Leigh's elbow and guided her around the back of the car to the passenger side.

"Would you look at that!" Jason said, annoyed. "I get a car with a remote that dies in cold weather. I was warned it might not work on a full-moon night, but nothing was said about twenty-degree weather."

Leigh stood back from the car as Jason jiggled the key in the door lock. *This deep scratch on your car makes a faulty remote look minor, Jason. I wonder if Chester is responsible for this?*

CHAPTER 23

DECEMBER 5

"Sure you won't stay 'til after lunch?"

Eve Holliday cleared the last dish from the table and shoved the crumbs of the breakfast casserole into the garbage can.

Leigh set her juice glass on the sink. "I think not, Eve. I want to go by Carmela and check on some things. I've got to decide what furniture to keep, what to dispose of, check the insulation on the water pipes, see if the well has enough insulation—a thousand things I used to do routinely to prepare for winter." She exhaled a long sigh. "Just think, Eve. This time next year, a new owner will be doing that."

"If I could sell the shop, I'd lend you the money to pay the bank."

Leigh hugged her friend. "Thanks, Eve. I had hoped to hear from Mother and Gordon before now."

"Are you *sure* you won't stay on? At least for a while."

"Thanks, Eve, but I need to get back to Atlanta and spend the afternoon with Tabitha. I've neglected her these last few days, and I need to correct that."

"I understand. Drive carefully."

§§§

Long before Carmela came in sight, the familiar feeling of coming home swept over Leigh. It was a sensation so unique, so full of comfort. It seemed paradoxical when she reflected on the fact that soon Carmela would no longer be her home, evidenced by the bold foreclosure sale sign near the road.

For no apparent reason, a comment that Creede had made crept into her thoughts. *The parable of the prodigal son is all about coming home.*

Why did *home* have to be one of those words that made the heart bubble over with joy, but could also squeeze it to the point of tears? Was it really fair for one word to occupy such polar positions? Daddy's Mama had taught her that *home* had two definitions—an earthly house made of wood and stone, and an eternal dwelling made of God's love that began on earth and transitioned to Heaven. She vowed to someday conduct an exhaustive search on the meaning of home.

Brilliant sunshine and a cloudless blue sky turned a late autumn day from frosty cold to almost warm. Leigh slowly made her way to the back porch, noting again the hasty window screen repair. She unlocked the door and entered the kitchen, standing for a moment as she recalled her last visit here with Creede.

Lord, help me move on.

It was a simple prayer, and it was time to pray it. Carmela was going the first of January, and Creede Kelly had already gone.

§§§

By noon, Leigh had completed a tentative inventory: group A she was keeping, group B she would sell. Family pictures, favorite pieces of furniture, and the balance of the linens she would move to Atlanta as soon as she found a place for herself and Tabitha. Group B she would organize for a yard sale to coincide with the house sale.

Everything completed, she pulled on her coat and picked up her purse and car keys. One final, sad walk through the house left her emotionally drained. In every room she saw a reminder of her grandmother, heard echoes of her soft voice, felt her presence vividly.

Leigh sorted through plastic bags in the cabinet drawer, finally locating a mid-size one to hold apples to take for Tabitha. She locked her purse in the car and walked briskly to the orchard, focusing on the bounty that remained on the low-lying limbs. She moved swiftly along the rows, oblivious to anything around her, filling the bag with fruit.

And then, suddenly, something seemed different. An eerie quiet fell over the orchard, stillness invaded the atmosphere. Leigh looked around, her heart thumping, turned, and began retracing her steps through the orchard. Movement just ahead brought her close to panic.

A dark figure stepped from behind a tree and stood directly in her path.

§§§

VIRGINIA
DECEMBER 5

Terrence Houghton Elliott sat on the edge of a lumpy mattress in a run-down motel just outside Washington. From his window he could see the reflection of the red neon sign flashing *VACANCY* on his blue pickup truck that was parked nearby.

He got up and wandered to the dresser, surveying himself in the mirror that bore evidence of hair spray residue left by a previous tenant. His hair was now shoulder length and streaked with some gray. He had opted to grow a beard when he abruptly left his life of crime in the preceding spring and was definitely pleased that the scar on his left cheek was no longer that obvious. The designer label clothes that had been his trademark had been exchanged for faded jeans, a blue-plaid flannel shirt, fringed imitation suede jacket, and western boots. The overall look was nothing short of a miracle, for his own brother would not recognize him.

He had made the sentimental journey to his boyhood home a few days before. His brother had built a mile west of the home place, and he and his wife were raising their family. Terrence had not seen them and had no desire to do so.

He turned back from the mirror and chanced to see the Gideon Bible on the table by the bed. He idly turned pages, stopping midway in the Old Testament where someone had tucked a full-color picture of the man who built his house on the rock. Unfolding that picture evoked memories of a day long ago that he thought had been put to rest. Oddly enough, it had started about shoes.

He trudged doggedly up the driveway from the road, doing what ten-year-old boys do best—kicking at rocks and succeeding only in adding more scuffmarks to the toe of his brown lace-up shoes. Ma had scraped the last of the paste polish from the tin container and covered the shoes the night before, then found a soft white rag and buffed them until they all but glistened.

"Shoes say a lot about a man," she said, explaining her vigorous polishing. "Anybody who looks at your shoes will know that you take pride in who you are and what you do."

"Just because my shoes are polished?" he asked. "They're still second-hand. Somebody wore them before I did."

"Wearing second-hand shoes don't decide your fate. Living a second-rate life does that." Ma carefully folded the polish rag and slid it into an old envelope. "You see, Terrence, your life's a lot like building a house. Remember Reverend's sermon about the two men who built their houses? One was on rock, one was on sand. By and by, the

heavy rains came falling down, and when the good earth couldn't hold no more, floods happened. Now, tell me, Terrence. What do you think happened to them two houses?"

Terrence shook his head and wondered if it was a trick question.

"Use your noggin, boy. That's why God give it to you." Ma watched her older son, willing him to answer her question. When he didn't, she sighed loudly. "What happens when you pour a bucket of water on a little pile of sand?"

That sounded like a reasonable question.

"It washes away."

"It sure does. Now, if you pour a bucket of water on a brick, what happens?"

"Nothing."

"And the lesson here is what?"

A couple of ideas came to mind, but Ma wouldn't like them. He opted for the obvious.

"A rock makes a good foundation to build a house on."

"And what about the sand?" she asked.

"The house'll wash away."

Ma set the shoe polish aside and her brown eyes looked at him so intently he squirmed.

"Don't ever forget you said that, Terrence. And don't ever forget Jesus told this little story for people to understand their lives are those two houses. The rock or the sand—it's your choice to make. And when people see how you live, they'll know if rock or sand was your choice. You may wear second-hand shoes, Terrence, there's no disgrace in that. But if you keep them polished, folks'll know you care about who you are."

She picked up the shoe polish and the envelope with the polishing rag. "Do you understand what I'm telling you, Terrence?"

He didn't, but he would never tell Ma that, so he just nodded his head in a half-hearted affirmation.

A Bible picture and second-hand shoes. What a chain of emotionally charged thoughts that had brought to mind.

He looked again at the picture and found the Scripture reference printed below it. It took a detailed reading of the table of contents and several more minutes of searching before he found Luke 6:46-49 and read the account for himself a total of six times. He closed the Bible, placed it on the table, then stretched out on the bed. He studied the ceiling, creating mental pictures from the dust spots that had successfully escaped the telescoping dust mops from the housekeeping department. Outside, raindrops gently slid down the window, forming a little puddle on the ledge. Traffic whizzed by, ignoring the increasing moisture building on the street.

For half an hour, Terrence looked at the ceiling and listened to the traffic. It had been years since he had thought about that conversation with Ma, and he had no clue why it should come back to haunt him now. Ma wasn't particularly religious as he recalled, but there were times when she had been to church that Reverend's sermons became the yardstick with which she measured the upbringing of her boys. Terrence acknowledged he had not been interested in all that Ma said, but he did know, if only in retrospect, that she had been trying to be a good parent. Pa had walked out on the family, and Terrence had turned to a life of crime. Ma deserved better than that.

Terrence turned on his side, rewarded with a view from the window of the treetops and gray sky. The rain was pelting down, beating a steady rhythm on the windowpane.

He didn't fight the urge to let his thoughts wander down the rock-strewn path to the house where he grew up.

It was considerably off the well-traveled way, an unpainted three-room building that only Ma would have had the nerve to call home. She scrubbed the inside with a homemade brew that disinfected and left the aroma suspended in the air for days. Missing windowpanes were replaced with cardboard carefully cut and shaped to fit. Cloth flour sacks miraculously became curtains strung on cord that twisted around a nail at each top corner of the window. She found discarded chairs and a table outside the Care Haven building in town, loaded them on the rusty truck and took them home where they proudly graced the living room that became the dining room at mealtime. It was Ma who taught him and his brother to cut wood to feed the iron monstrosity that doubled as cook stove and heating system.

Terrence couldn't remember exactly when Pa left the family. One day he was there, the next day he was gone. He never returned. Ma cried one time, and then, as she always did, she rose to the occasion, reminding her sons they would make it.

Just how, Terrence wasn't sure. But he could remember vividly the day he accidentally shot his younger brother in the leg. The wound, while not life threatening, left Roger with a limp. Terrence couldn't stand seeing him hobble around, and so he walked away from Ma and Roger. He was seventeen, a school dropout, and cursed with a rapidly escalating attitude problem.

In the city he had met Mr. Olnick, who hired him to mow the lawn. From there, he began running errands. The night he drove the car from one of Mr. Olnick's "collections" initiated him into his life of crime. It was that night he discovered Mr. Olnick devoted his energies to several illegal enterprises, including an extortion operation with a coded clientele file Terrence only heard about.

Knowing what it was all about didn't help with his conscience, but when he began having hundreds of dollars to send to Ma every month, conscience was easy to ignore. Ma passed away before she made the improvements to the house, and Terrence found the money—all three thousand dollars—sealed tightly in a Mason canning jar and buried under Ma's favorite rose bush. Without any explanation, he gave the money to Roger.

Thoughts could do funny things to a person, especially when they were precipitated by a Bible verse. Ma loved home, no matter what it looked like; and although he had been the wayward son, Terrence knew it was time to repent his past. He couldn't go home, but he could confess to the pharmacy robbery.

He placed the Bible in the drawer, got up from the bed, and flipped on the TV. A couple of minutes of channel surfing offered little in the way of program choice. He settled on the news channel, listening more than watching, until the report of some political activity aired. A TV reporter had cornered a man on the street, albeit, in this case, he stood very near the platform. "Sir," she asked him, "could you give us your opinion on the announcement from Senator Jorgenstein's office regarding his retirement, given the fact that he's just been tapped as the President's choice as ambassador to the U.N.?"

Curious, Terrence watched the picture, then suddenly straightened.

"What's Olnick doing in Washington?"

§§§

CRESCENT ORCHARD

In the shadows of the apple trees, Leigh stopped. Going ahead meant coming face to face with someone, retreating would take her to the edge of the orchard and a brick wall.

The figure began to move toward her, walking slowly, deliberately, his jacket open, his right hand clutching a crude walking stick.

Leigh took a deep breath.

"Chester Leverett, do you know you scared me? Badly?"

Chester smiled broadly and stopped a couple of feet from Leigh, speaking his jibberish.

Leigh smiled. "Have you been walking today, Chester?"

He nodded.

"It's a wonderful day for walking, if you like this cold weather."

Chester pointed to Leigh's car.

"Do you need a ride, Chester?"

He shook his head and began walking toward the house. Leigh fell in step with him.

"Chester, do you need anything? Food? Firewood?"

He shook his head again and began to walk faster. By the time they reached the car, Leigh was gasping. Chester pointed to the car, moved to the back and pointed to the tag. He rubbed his hand across the trunk, walked to the side of the car and touched the top of the rear window. He glanced briefly at Leigh, then stooped, picked up small stones and lined them in a row on the ground. Then, turning back to face her, he jabbered and looked at her with apparent impatience.

"Oh, Chester! You have something to tell me, don't you?"

§§§

The drive back to Atlanta from Crescent Orchard was long and tiring, the interstate buzzing with weekend traffic. When she pulled into Tabitha's drive shortly after four, she had more questions than answers about Chester's visit to Carmela.

Chester knows something that's vital. He can't say it and he can't write it, but he knows he needs to tell someone. What is it that he is so desperate to communicate?

Leigh climbed from her car, gathering her purse and the bag of apples. Her thoughts still focused on Chester, she rang the doorbell and waited for Tabitha to answer.

"Leigh!" Relief faded from Tabitha's face and a stern expression settled in. "You went off and didn't tell me where you were!" she admonished. "I've been worried to death!"

"I did forget to tell you, and I apologize. My trip to Crescent Orchard was a spur-of-the-moment decision," Leigh said as she hugged Tabitha.

"Well, now that I know where you were, it's all right." Tabitha closed the door. "I see you've brought me some of those wonderful apples. Do you mind putting them on the kitchen table?"

"Not at all, Tabitha—" Leigh blinked. Was that Creede Kelly standing by the refrigerator?

"Creede?" she asked hesitantly.

He came to her, smiling broadly and oblivious to Tabitha's presence. "You gave my detective the slip and didn't return my phone call," he offered in explanation. "And your landlady was no help, so I thought I'd wait it out right here. You had to come home eventually."

"What phone call?" Leigh asked.

"Yesterday afternoon. I finished the book and thought we could go celebrate. My attorney okayed my new contract for the next Erin book so that was something else to celebrate. It was going to be a wonderful evening—except I spent it by myself."

"I'm sorry I wasn't home."

"Me, too," Creede said. "But we can still celebrate." He added hopefully, "Can't we?"

CHAPTER 24

They sat around the antique oak table sharing conversation and laughter as darkness crept in silently and the hands on the clock crept steadily toward nine.

Leigh pushed aside the remnants of a corned beef sandwich as she stifled a yawn.

"I really must get to the cottage."

There wasn't much conviction in her statement, but how convincing could one sound when there wasn't much desire to conclude an evening that had been so extraordinary.

"I'll walk with you," Creede said. "I left my truck there."

Tabitha saw her guests out and stood several minutes watching as they descended the path to the cottage.

"Such a nice couple," she murmured as she closed the door.

§§§

"Have a good weekend?" Creede asked as they approached the cottage.

"I suppose it was. I did a little Christmas shopping yesterday morning, then decided to go to Crescent Orchard."

"I saw you at Lenox around one-thirty. I met my attorney there to discuss some contracts. Tried to get your attention but you kept looking the other way."

"Your attorney is a stunning redhead?"

Creede hooked his arm around Leigh's shoulder. "She swears it's her natural color. Where did you see us?"

"At the food court."

He chuckled. "Regina needed to eat before we tackled legal matters. She ran three miles, did gym workouts, and coached a girls' soccer team without eating breakfast. We grabbed a sandwich and discussed my contracts. I got home about four and called, but only got your answerer."

"I left shortly before four." *But I'll never tell you why I left town.* "This morning I went to Carmela and ran into Chester in the orchard." She turned to face Creede. "He tried so very hard to tell me something."

"Any idea what it is?"

"None," she admitted. "He kept pointing to my car and mumbling."

Creede kissed her on the forehead and hugged her. "Think we can have dinner on Christmas Day? Patti and Alex are flying in that morning and after I meet them, we'll come by for you." As an afterthought, he added, "I heard about a neat little place north of Atlanta that's open Christmas Day—if you're not busy?"

"I would love it." She pulled the house key from her purse. "I'm glad you finished the book."

"Me, too. Beat Zach's deadline by three weeks."

"You've not told me much about this story. Are you satisfied with the way everything came out? Did Erin capture the villain?"

"Single-handed. Erin's a pretty smart kid, if I do say so."

"You should know. Do you have plans for the next book?"

He sobered. "Erin's on an extended vacation in the tropics while her creator deals with a matter."

"Nothing serious, I hope."

Creede hugged her again. "Pretty serious. It involves his heart and his future—and the woman he loves."

§§§

Driving home, Creede thought again about his Christmas shopping. Patti and Alex were no problem. He would take them shopping after Christmas and let them make their own selections. Leigh's gift, however, was a problem. When he placed the order, there had been no assurance it would arrive on time. For once, the sales-pitch-ending-with-an-apology was right on the money—delivery of the ring would be delayed indefinitely.

§§§

CHRISTMAS EVE

Leigh closed the drapes and turned the lamp up another notch, then decided it would be more effectively Christmas with only the lights blinking on her tiny ceramic tree. Over the last few hours, the weather had grown cold and windy with rain that had begun slowly, then increased in momentum, lashing the windows with relentless vigor. Inside, it was cozy and comfortable, bordering on warm and fuzzy when she factored in thoughts of home and family.

Daddy's Mama loved Christmas. The baking, the decorating, even the cleaning before and after. She loved the company that came, but most of all she loved the carols. How many times has she told me about Silent Night first being sung to guitar accompaniment? And how many times have we gone caroling on the back of a truck filled with hay? The last thing we did on Christmas Eve was to read Luke's Christmas story and talk about how Mary and Joseph had no

248

home in Bethlehem, how their baby's first bed was a hay-filled manger and not a down-filled bassinette—and how the very first people to know about Jesus' birth were just about the poorest people on earth. Daddy's Mama always said that God had a reason for doing it that way—the shepherds had no money to buy the baby a gift, so they gave what they had—themselves in joyous adoration. And that's really all God wants from any of us—ourselves.

Jeaneen Bracken's words replayed vividly in Leigh's thoughts: *God wants nothing any more than He wants a committed follower, Leigh. He will open the way, provide the guidance, bestow the blessings. Remember the shepherds' story! He did it for them.*

When Leigh crawled drowsily into bed twenty minutes later, her prayer was to better understand the shepherds' story. Perhaps it was divine intervention that kept her prayer focused on the shepherds. For the first time in months, there was no request that somehow she would be allowed to keep Carmela.

§§§

The trees are so huge, the limbs so low. Not much sun can find an opening to warm the chilly atmosphere in the orchard. Better hurry and get the rest of the apples—it's getting late. Well, not really late. It just seems that way because light can't get in easily.

There. The bag is full. One more apple and these handles will break, and I don't want to pick the same apples twice in one day. Okay. Ooops—careful there. You can fall. Watch your step.

Was that something moving just ahead? I'll stop for a minute. Maybe my eyes are playing tricks...no, it isn't my eyes. There's someone behind that tree. I'll leave the apples here and go back down this row. Oh, that won't do any good—there's a brick wall there!

249

They've come from behind the tree. Are they just wait-
ing? Oh, it's not 'they'—only one person. Why, that's
Chester Leverett! What a fright he gave me!

Why are we walking so fast, Chester? Do you need a
ride somewhere? What is it about my car, Chester? You're
pointing to all the dents and scratches, and yes, I know how
most of them got there. But what is it about the rear window?
I've not had that broken out ever. Chester, what is it about
my car…my car…

"My car…my car…"

Leigh flung the covers aside and sat up in bed. "What a
nightmare!" she exclaimed, rubbing her eyes. "And why am
I dreaming about Chester?"

The digital clock display changed to 8:15, and slowly
Leigh climbed out of bed, pulling on a terrycloth robe and
making her way to the kitchen. She measured coffee and
water into the percolator, made cheese toast in the oven, and
opened a can of peach slices.

Today is Christmas. All over the world. Some have no
gifts and some have more gifts than they need. If there's ever
going to be an equity of possessions, it should be at Christ-
mas.

The rain of Christmas Eve had marched into Christmas
Day, and all indications pointed to an extended stay. Clouds
hung low, creating a gray overcast. Leigh smiled as she
wondered what new restaurant Creede had discovered that
would be open today. Over two hours to wait until he
arrived. Maybe doing something would speed time along.

She dressed in dark green slacks with Christmas print
blouse and laid her suit jacket on the arm of the sofa, then
returned to the closet for her long plaid coat. She stopped by
Marcus' washstand.

Now's a good time to decide where to put this wash-
stand. It looks out of place by the door.

Leigh rubbed the top of the chest, intrigued at the natural design in the wood and the intricate carvings on the drawers and door. Antique brass pulls adorned the two drawers and the double doors below. She opened the drawers and discovered that each was neatly lined in sticky-back paper featuring illustrations of garden herbs and seed packets. She smiled.

I'll bet Christine had this liner left over from her kitchen cabinets and didn't want to throw it away. Wonder if she put it in the door section as well.

There was no paper liner behind the doors; instead, a piece of half-inch marble rested on the floor of the washstand.

Maybe this was meant to go on top.

She pulled it out, and although it wasn't heavy, it was awkward to handle.

"There!" she said, positioning the marble on the top. "Well, no, I guess it wasn't meant for the top since it's several inches too narrow. Okay. Back to your hiding place."

After the tilting and squeezing, it finally went back perfectly in place and she closed the doors.

Something wasn't adding up. She knelt in front and pulled the doors open.

This piece of marble is too narrow for the top, but it fits perfectly in this area behind the doors. Why is that? The chest is the same size, top to bottom. Or is it?

She studied the interior, attempting to nudge the marble to the back of the chest. It did not move.

Now, why is that?

Leigh reached inside. Just at the far edge of the marble, her hand struck wood and she discovered four very small hooks.

I need a flashlight!

Gripping the light a moment later, Leigh moved the beam across the interior of the washstand. The tiny hooks were placed very close to the top, latching into eyelets on a strip of wood no more than an inch in width. Carefully, she began working with each one until all were unlatched. The panel tilted toward her.

She focused the flashlight beam on the inside, where folded papers were neatly stacked in two small compartments.

"Now, this is interesting!"

She began removing the papers, placing the first stack on the floor beside her, and unfolding the top sheet.

What is this?

The sheet of paper had been lined vertically and horizontally in pencil, each uniform space containing dates or amounts. At the end of each vertical column was a total.

"Marcus' old pharmacy records, I assume. I'll need to get these to Jason. And I wonder if he knew they were in here."

Leigh opened the next carefully folded paper, studied it a moment, then frowned. There were initials, dates, and amounts of money. The last set of initials was listed a total of seven times, beginning in August of the previous year. The last entry was February 18 of the current year.

"*T.H.E.* That has a familiar ring. But where have I heard those initials before?" She gathered the papers and placed them in the envelope. "I'll take this and ask Creede to look at it before I return everything to Jason."

She picked up the plaid coat to slide the envelope into the pocket. When it stopped midway, she reached into the pocket and felt something.

"What did I leave in here?" Leigh pulled out a small plastic container. "The cassette tape Marcus gave me last winter! I forgot about it!"

Leigh opened the box and removed the tape, examining the label. *"A Serenade of Big Band Music,"* she read. "That's what Marcus told me it was. But why was he so interested in giving it to me?"

A piece of paper was folded neatly to fit the box and placed under the cassette tape, apparently put there to fill the space in the box.

With uncanny timing, the telephone rang.

"Hello?"

There was no response and Leigh repeated her greeting. Within seconds, garbled sounds mixed with muffled noises echoed with frightening familiarity.

"Who is this?"

There was a cry of *"Oh!"*, a low moan, and then a sudden click indicated a broken connection.

Thoroughly alarmed, Leigh dialed Creede's number. The answerer greeted her.

"Creede, I think Chester just tried to call me! I'm going to Providence to check on him!"

§§§

Beyond Atlanta, the rain fell gently and the temperature continued to drop. Pushing the Toyota as fast as she dared on the rain-slicked road, Leigh grasped the steering wheel and fought to keep her concentration on driving.

Shortly after twelve, she reached Providence Hill and pulled into the drive at Carmela. She jumped from the car, not bothering to close the door, and dashed across the road. A well-worn footpath led up the incline that faced Carmela. The opposite side had a crude road to Chester's place, but

Leigh decided weather conditions were not the best for her to attempt the drive. Quickly, she started up the path, only to slip repeatedly. Every step forward was cancelled by two steps backward.

§§§

A pickup truck pulled in the drive at Carmela, parking behind the Toyota. The driver climbed out, weary from hours of steady driving in unfavorable weather conditions.

He looked across the road just in time to see someone struggling along the path and thought it strange anyone would be mountain climbing on Christmas Day.

Not his problem, though. He reached into the truck, pulled on a fringed suede jacket, and mulled over the most effective way to confess a robbery.

CHAPTER 25

ATLANTA

The fog that had hung over Creede's house at six a.m. shrouded Hartsfield-Jackson Airport like a thick veil by eight. It had mushroomed into a monstrous problem, so serious that on his last cell phone call to the airport, he was told that Patti's plane had been delayed leaving Miami and now because of the fog, landing in Atlanta would be late. It was the first breakdown in his plans for the day.

He slumped in the truck seat, turned on the radio to get a weather report, and waited.

"No chance of seeing the sun today," the announcer said. "Visibility is near zero, rain turning to sleet is falling north of Atlanta."

Creede groaned. He picked up his cell phone to call Leigh since it was quite evident he would not be picking her up at eleven. Seven times the phone rang with no answer and no answering machine. Puzzled, he dialed again and got the same response. His next call was to directory assistance for Tabitha's number.

"Merry Christmas," she answered, and Creede could hear the clink of silverware on china. *Leigh went to eat Christmas breakfast with Tabitha, just as she did on Thanksgiving morning.* Relieved, he returned Tabitha's greeting.

"And a Merry Christmas to you, Tabitha. This is Creede Kelly."

"Well, good morning, Creede. This is a pleasant surprise. And I know it will be a good day for you with your daughter coming in."

"Actually, Tabitha, her plane has been delayed. Seems like the weather is rotten across the entire southeast." He paused. "I wonder if Leigh is at your house, and if it would be convenient for me to speak with her."

"I've not seen her, Creede. My brother-in-law and his wife are in town and came by for breakfast. Why don't you hold on for a minute while I go to the front window and look toward the cottage."

"I hate to put you to any trouble—"

Tabitha had left her phone before he could finish his sentence. In less than a minute, she was resuming her conversation.

"Creede, her car is not where she usually parks it. I have no idea where she could be."

"That's okay, Tabitha. Thanks for your help. Sorry to have interrupted your visit with your company."

He broke the connection and dialed to check messages on voice mail at home. With a tremendous sigh of relief, he heard Leigh's voice, but very quickly fear overwhelmed him when she said she was going to Providence Hill to check on Chester.

This moment in his life might just as well have been scripted for a novel: his daughter's plane was hovering in the air over Atlanta, his beloved was traveling north of Atlanta on icy roads, and he sat at the airport, unable to do the first thing for either of them. Who would have thought cliffhangers happened in real life?

Agitated with his situation, he flipped the volume on the radio just in time to hear there was a good chance for an ice storm to blanket the northeastern quarter of the state by nightfall.

"Beautiful!" he muttered. "An icy white Christmas and everybody stranded away from home!"

And, suddenly, one of those light-bulb moments happened. He snatched up his phone and punched a preset number.

"Be there!" he urged.

"Hello?"

"Hey, Max, it's me. I'm at the airport waiting for Patti, and I need your help in a hurry!"

"I'm listening," Max Benedict replied. "But you know the fee doubles on holidays, especially when it's rescuing people who get stuck at the airport."

"It's Leigh. She may be headed for trouble."

Creede relayed Leigh's brief message.

"I have no idea what's up, Max. I do know Chester has no phone, so he may be in Crescent Orchard. I don't know what the problem is, but I don't like what I'm thinking."

"I'm on my way, Creede. I'll keep in touch. And forget the fee. After all, it's Christmas."

§§§

In a matter of fifteen minutes, Max Benedict had strapped on his shoulder holster, checked his gun, got extra ammunition, pulled on his fur-lined parka as he stuffed a ski cap in the pocket, kissed Julia good-bye, and headed his four-wheel drive toward the northeast. Traffic irritated him almost as much as the weather frustrated him.

"Fog's as thick as vegetable soup," he muttered. "Wonder what it's supposed to do for the rest of the day?"

Boom!

It only lasted a second, but as Max concentrated on the steering it seemed like several minutes before he gained control and eased to the emergency lane. He climbed out to confirm his suspicion.

"Blowout!" he yelled.

He dug his cell phone from his pocket and called Tyler Simmons.

"If I'm interrupting anything, Tyler, sorry. I'm stranded with a lame tire and I'm supposed to be protecting Leigh Parrish—"

"I'm on my way, sir."

"Don't *sir* me, Tyler. Just get here—on the double!"

§§§

"Did you call the tow truck to pick up your vehicle, sir?"

Max ignored the title. "Yeah. Said they've got fender benders all over town so it might be a while before they get here."

"You're not concerned about leaving it here?"

"Well, yeah, but I hope for the best. Want me to drive this—what is this, Tyler? From the front it says Chevrolet and from the back it's GMC. What's in the middle?"

"It belongs to my brother-in-law, Louis. He got rear-ended and could only find a GMC tailgate, but it's in good shape—and has mud and snow tires. My car doesn't." Tyler paused momentarily. "With all due respect, sir, I'll drive."

Max nodded as Tyler changed gears and merged into traffic.

"So what's our mission, sir?"

"Creede's lady friend left him a message. Seems like she had a phone call from Chester Leverett that made her think he's in danger. That's all I know and that's why we're headed to Providence."

"That's interesting," Tyler mused.

"What is?"

"Sir, I've been thinking. Didn't you say Miss Parrish inherited some pieces of furniture from Mr. Trent?"

Max nodded. "You have a theory?"

"I remember you telling me when Brian Porter found Mr. Trent, he was saying *chest...chest*, and that Brian thought he might be hurt in his chest, or having a heart attack. And some thought Mr. Trent was accusing Chester of something."

"So?"

"Could it be possible that he was trying to drop a hint that the chest—I think that's another name for a washstand—that Miss Parrish was to get held something important?"

"Tyler, for as long as you've worked for me, you've always had crazy, off-the-wall ideas. And you're at it again. Can you tell me what prompted this most recent observation?"

"Thank you, sir. I accept that as a compliment." Tyler slowed for a van just ahead. "I just sorted through what you had told me and tried to draw some conclusions from that."

"But why would Marcus Trent leave that particular item to Leigh Parrish? What's the connection to her?"

"Perhaps Mr. Trent trusted her. Or maybe it was something hidden inside that he felt she could best handle."

"Like what?"

Tyler sighed. "No idea, sir."

"Aha. So you're not clairvoyant. That's a relief."

"Maybe it's more like—like Mr. Trent had this secret that if it was known, things might not be good for somebody. But he knew somebody needed to know about it, so he puts it in the chest and wills it to Miss Parrish, knowing she'll find it and take the necessary action."

Max cast a glance at Tyler. "Preposterous idea."

"Yes, sir. It is."

Misty rain continued to fall, as did the temperature. Max pulled the parka closer about him.

"Got a heater in here, Tyler?"

"There's a heater, but the thermostat's shot. Lou's got a new one, just hasn't had time to install it." Tyler leaned forward to wipe condensation from the windshield. "Uh-oh. Trouble ahead. Looks like an accident."

He slowed the truck as a state trooper waved him to a halt.

"Eighteen wheeler jack-knifed," the trooper explained as Tyler lowered his window. "Traffic in all lanes will be held up for maybe an hour."

"An *hour*!" Max exploded. He leaned to see the trooper through Tyler's window. "Any way we can get around it? We've got to get to Crescent Orchard—"

"Everybody on this road is trying to get somewhere, sir," the trooper explained. "Right now, there's not a thing I can do. I suggest you call ahead and let them know you'll be late for Christmas dinner."

He stepped back from the truck before Max could reply.

Max pulled his phone from his pocket and dialed Creede's number.

"Creede, we got a problem. There's been an accident and we're gonna be sittin' here for maybe an hour. As soon as we can get through, I'll call you back."

§§§

Creede listened as Max explained the series of events that had plagued his trip to Providence Hill.

"Don't worry about it," Creede told him. "I'll do something."

But what?

He dialed the airport to get another update on Patti's plane.

"That flight should be landing in about twenty minutes."

At last. Something was going to go according to some kind of plan. He almost wanted to whistle. Instead, he held his phone, checked his short list of frequently called numbers, and dialed.

CHAPTER 26

RURAL CRESCENT ORCHARD

Bo Patton took one last peek at the silver ring with its petite diamond perched elegantly on top. The salesman had assured him that solitaires were always a good choice, always in style, but Bo didn't feel convinced. Something with more sparkle would have suited him better, and if Sue Ellen wasn't happy with the solitaire, he would exchange it. She deserved the best.

He closed the ring box and slid it into his pocket. It would be close to a year before they would get married and that would give him time to make repairs on the house he had bought. The economy wasn't booming and foreclosures were happening every day, but still it wasn't exactly a comforting thought to know their first home was possible because another person had lost a home when they couldn't make payments. Life was peculiar that way.

Bo checked to be sure the kitchen light was off. When he got to the truck, he realized Sue Ellen's other present—a CD player—was on the living room coffee table. He retraced his steps to get it, along with the envelope for her mother—also forgotten—with its gift enclosure card advising Winifred Burkhalter that a year's subscription to *Fantastic Southern Cooking* was coming to her, a thoughtful gift from Bo Patton.

With the envelope tucked safely in the inside pocket of his sport coat and the CD player under his arm, he headed out, only to be halted by his ringing phone.

"Hello!"

"Bo?"

"That's me."

"Creede Kelly, Bo. Sorry to interrupt you, but I need a favor—a big one."

"Hi, Mr. Kelly. You're not interruptin' a thing. Need my wrecker?"

Creede laughed. "I wish it was something simple like that, Bo. I don't remember if you live in the vicinity of Leigh's place—"

"Couple miles down the road. Is somethin' wrong there?"

"I had a message from Leigh that she was going to check on Chester Leverett, and I'm at the airport waiting for my daughter's plane. I wouldn't have bothered you, but I don't feel exactly comfortable about this situation."

"Oh, heck, Mr. Kelly. You're not botherin' me. I'll head out there right now."

"Thanks, Bo. Let me give you my cell phone number and you can let me know what's going on. I'll be that way as soon as Patti and Alex arrive."

"Sure thing, Mr. Kelly. I'm on my way."

Bo grabbed Sue Ellen's gift and an extra flashlight from the kitchen counter and dashed for the Blue Bomber, thinking that Mr. Kelly sure must like Leigh a lot.

§§§

PROVIDENCE HILL

The rain had been reduced to a stinging mist as Leigh made her way up the path toward Chester's shack. Walking was impeded by the slippery leaves as the cold air changed

263

the moisture to ice crystals. Several times she slipped, barely missing a bad fall. Where the trees were dense, she grasped low-lying limbs for support, pulling herself from one tree to the next, until finally she was at the edge of the yard and the back of a small building that Chester called home.

Wood smoke hung in the damp air, curling upward from a stovepipe through the side of one wall. Leigh moved stealthily through the trees, finally locating an opening in the undergrowth where she could get to the yard and then to the house. She was about to call Chester's name when she noticed the open door, but did not see him.

Strange. As disagreeable as the weather is, why does Chester have the door open? Unless he's out getting wood for his stove...but he keeps a supply of wood stacked on the front porch, so why is the back door open?

Cautiously, she inched forward, finally stepping up on the small porch. The door moved a few inches, as though gently shoved by an unseen hand, and Leigh heard heavy footsteps from the direction of the front porch. Quickly, she stepped away from the door and off the porch, just as the front door opened, then slammed shut.

"Sit there."

It was all she heard from inside.

Chester has company.

Quietly, she made her way back into the cover of the nearby trees, skirting the area to the side of the shack, until she could see the front entrance, somewhat obscured by the car parked a short distance from the porch. Cautiously, she moved closer.

Rather disturbingly, her courage left as she realized Chester's urgent mumbling about her car a few weeks earlier was meant to tell her about *this* car. The scratches on her car translated to a deep scratch on this black BMW; Chester's animated hand movements to the back window of her car were meant to tell her about the aerials on the back of this vehicle.

Leigh gasped. She had seen this car before, parked close to Trent's Pharmacy the night of the robbery. And Chester must have seen it, as well! He knew who the robber was! And, now, Chester was in great danger.

"Did you see something you find interesting?"

Leigh whirled at the sound of the deep raspy voice, slipped on the icy leaves and fell, twisting her ankle in unbearable pain.

§§§

ATLANTA

Time is of the essence.

Strange how a sentence from a contract picked this precise moment to flutter through his mind, but as Creede hurried to meet Patti and Alex as they came from the airport, he calculated a possible interpretation: one hug for both of them would have to do for now. He guided them toward the truck.

"Hurry, kids!" he encouraged. "We need to get to Leigh!"

"Daddy, what's wrong?" Patti asked, scooting to the middle of the seat.

Creede explained what he knew of the situation.

"But who would harm Chester?" Patti asked. "I don't know him, but I can't imagine anyone doing anything to somebody like him."

"Who is Chester?" Alex asked.

"Marcus Trent's nephew by marriage," Creede explained. "For some reason, he feels befriended by Leigh because she was a friend to his uncle. Chester can't speak so no one has ever taken much time with him."

"Why would he be in danger, Daddy?" Patti asked.

"He may know something."

"About someone?" she persisted.

"Possibly."

"Well, get us where we need to be," Patti urged. "And, oh, by the way, Daddy—Merry Christmas!"

§§§

PROVIDENCE HILL

"Get up!" the raspy voice commanded.

Leigh struggled to stand. Fiery pain shot through her ankle and she fell back.

"I—can't," she said. "My ankle—"

"Then crawl."

Hot tears generated by the pain stung her eyes as she began to make her way across the wet leaves. With effort, she heaved herself up the two steps and across the icy porch. Moisture had penetrated the knees of her slacks and the gloves she wore.

Her abductor knuckled two short raps on the door, then pushed it open.

The interior was dimly lit by a kerosene lamp on a table in the center of the sparsely furnished room. A couple of chairs, an empty bookcase, and a small wood-burning heater claimed their space. Papers were strewn about the room.

As Leigh's eyes became accustomed to the dusky light, she focused on Chester Leverett standing midway across the room. Between him and the opposite door, a figure emerged.

"I didn't expect you to drop in on Christmas Day. I should have said *crawl* in. Such an impressive act of humility."

Leigh prayed silently. *Please, Lord. Help me remain calm. For me and for Chester.*

"Hello, Jason. I turned my ankle outside. It's too painful to walk."

Jason Trent took a step toward her, kicked a chair in place, then extended his hands to help her to the chair.

"You'll be much more comfortable sitting, Leigh. Now, tell me what brings you to Chester's place."

Leigh rubbed her throbbing ankle. "It's Christmas, Jason. I thought Chester might need something."

"Did you drop it outside? You had nothing when you came in."

"I did not bring anything with me. I thought we could go into Crescent Orchard."

Jason came closer. "On Christmas Day, Leigh? You know the entire town closes for the holiday." He turned slightly to glance at the man by the door. "Olnick, take Chester outside. Miss Parrish and I have business to discuss."

§§§

Bo began slowing the wrecker to a crawl at the curve that was just west of Providence Hill. He coasted along, noticing that already patches of ice were forming on the road. He rounded the curve that brought Carmela into view and was surprised to see a truck parked in the yard, directly behind Leigh's Toyota.

Just as Bo pulled into the yard, the driver stepped from the truck. With one glance at the wrecker, the man started to run. When he began slipping, he stopped, then walked back to his truck just as Bo approached.

"Mornin'," Bo greeted him. "Goin' somewhere?"

"Was, but I changed my mind."

"Oh? Why's that?"

"You know me," he said simply.

"I do?" Bo asked.

"Last March. You pulled my car in when I ran out of gas."

"March? March?" Bo rubbed his chin. "What kind of vehicle?"

"BMW. Black. Five aerials across the back."

Bo snapped his finger. "Your initials are *T.H.E.*"

"Right. Terrence Houghton Elliott."

"Mind if I ask what you're doin' here, now?"

"Came back to confess to a robbery at the drug store and a house break-in."

Bo straightened. "What house?"

"This one." Terrence pointed toward Carmela.

"What about the money you took from the drug store?"

Terrence exhaled a long breath. "I hid it in a trunk in a barn somewhere near here. I came back to look for it and couldn't find the barn. I have no idea what happened to it."

"It was found by the lady who owned the trunk and this house. It's come close to wreckin' her life."

"I'm sorry."

"You're the weirdest criminal I ever heard of," Bo muttered. "You had the chance to walk away, but you came back. Why were you waitin' here?"

"Had a problem with my truck running hot. Pulled in to let it cool off. That was when I recognized the house and saw the woman climbing up the mountain."

"A woman?"

Terrence nodded. "Right after I pulled in. She seemed in a hurry."

Bo caught the man's arm. "You've told me the most outrageous story I've ever heard. I'm not sure how much of it I believe, if any. But I'm gonna give you a chance right now to convince me that you're tryin' to be a decent guy. We're goin' up that mountain and find the woman you saw."

§§§

"Well, Leigh." Jason Trent paced back and forth before Leigh, his arms crossed on his chest. "Let's try again. What *really* brings you up here today? As good as you apparently are, it's very unlikely you came in this weather just to bring a Christmas present to Chester Leverett." Jason slapped his hands together. "We've already covered that, haven't we? You were going to take him shopping." He stopped in front of Leigh's chair, crossed his arms again, and looked menacingly at her. "You're not convincing as a liar, Leigh. Care to tell me the real reason?"

"The phone call," she said.

Jason smacked his forehead with the palm of his right hand. "Phone call? How interesting. From Chester? What a novelty!"

"From you. Like all the other anonymous calls I've received the last six months."

"When did you arrive at that ridiculous conclusion?"

"On the way up here. There's not a phone here in the cabin, and Chester is not familiar with using a cell phone.

You have one. And you said you would be back at Christmas."

"It seemed a good time to get back what is mine."

"Which is?"

"Some important documents that are missing. They were not in the safe deposit box, nor at Marcus' house. I've turned this place upside down. That only leaves the chest Uncle Marcus left for you."

"You could have asked me about it. You didn't need to involve Chester."

"Chester *is* involved. *Only* you and Chester. I was confident if you thought Chester was in trouble, you would come. Once again, I was not wrong." He kicked a pile of papers from his path. "There's never been a time in my life that I've failed to get what I wanted. The *how* never bothers me." He grabbed her arm, jerking her roughly to her feet.

"Oh!" She shrieked as pain again shot through her ankle.

"Don't fret over that minor pain," he advised. "Get outside. We're going to take a trip to Atlanta and search that chest."

"There's nothing in it, Jason." *As of this morning, the contents have been moved to a safe place.*

"Leigh," he said harshly, "for your sake, there needs to be something in that chest."

"What are you looking for, Jason?"

He laughed. "Just consider it Trent family history. Ancient history that needs—shall we say—a proper burial."

Leigh hobbled to the door. So many pieces of this strange puzzle were now falling into place, but she still had questions that were unanswered.

"You burned Marcus' house, didn't you Jason? And left evidence to implicate Chester, like the bike tracks and the $50 bill." Leigh knew it was a bold accusation, but now that she had begun, she aggressively pursued the matter. "Why did you burn Marcus' house, Jason? Why did you have to destroy something that meant so much to Marcus and Christine? And to Chester?"

Jason paused at the door. "Surely you don't think I'm concerned with preserving anything for Chester. And as for the house—what difference does it make if anything sits on that piece of land?" His laugh was guttural, his expression sadistic. "My grandfather once told me that fire was a refining tool, a useful instrument in certain conditions. More than once, I've found his advice relevant." He opened the door. "Fire can be illuminating, Leigh. It can bring out the best—or the worst."

Leigh stalled for time. "But if the house is gone, isn't it possible what you're looking for is also gone?"

"It's possible. And I'll know for sure when I search that chest." He pushed Leigh toward the porch. "I believe what I'm looking for is now in your possession—in that chest. And I *will* get it back!"

As he shoved Leigh toward the steps, he yelled to Olnick. "We're going to Atlanta, Ollie. And drive carefully. Our hostages are quite necessary—for the time being."

CHAPTER 27

"Daddy, would you *please* slow down? Just a little? I'm on my very last half nerve!"

Patti wrapped both hands around Alex's forearm and buried her head against his shoulder as Creede struggled to control the direction of the truck. It slid toward the center of the two-lane road, then back to the shoulder, and back to the centerline before it slowed and regained traction on the icing road.

"Sorry, honey. I didn't know I was going that fast," he said, gripping the wheel.

"Well, you were," Patti told him. "Look, Daddy, I know you're concerned about Leigh. We all are. But if you wreck us, we won't be any help to her!"

Alex nodded in agreement, not sure what he should say about his father-in-law's driving. "How much further is it, Mr. Kelly?"

"Two, maybe three miles." Creede glanced in the rear view mirror. "What is that monstrosity behind us?"

Patti turned to look out. "Just a truck, Daddy. What did you think it was?"

He didn't answer, but kept a watchful eye on the vehicle.

Over 30 long, tense minutes elapsed before Carmela came into view and Creede slid into the drive. The other truck followed, and a moment later Creede was greeting Max Benedict and Tyler Simmons.

"What's the plan?" Max asked.

Creede looked around, puzzled. "There's Leigh's car and Bo's wrecker, but I don't recognize that other truck."

"It has Virginia plates," Alex said.

Creede rubbed his forehead and walked to the Virginia truck to convince himself.

"Something suspicious about this," Max mumbled to Tyler. "A car we know with the door standing open, a wrecker we know, a truck we don't know. No humans around. If you had to sum up this scene in one word, Ty, what would it be?"

"Kidnapping."

§§§

When she stepped from the porch to the yard, Leigh winced in pain. In an instant, Chester was at her side supporting her.

"Get in the vehicle," Jason ordered. "You'll ride up front, Leigh. Chester and I will be in the back." He opened the passenger door. "I'm sure there's no need to remind you, Leigh, about the foolishness of attempted escape. With your ankle messed up, you won't get far."

Olnick turned the ignition and the engine whirled to life. He shifted gears and gradually began to descend the incline.

"Jason, what's in the chest that's so important to you?" Leigh asked.

"Inquisitive soul, aren't you?" he replied. "But to answer your question, it's personal property. Family business, if you will. It does not concern you or anyone else. I'm only interested in retrieving what is the property of the Trent family." Jason glanced out the window. "How much further to the main road, Ollie?"

"Almost there."

Leigh leaned forward to rub her ankle that had swollen to twice its normal size. Her thoughts raced ahead, for if they got to Atlanta, Jason would search the chest and find nothing there. His anger would probably explode. She couldn't imagine what would happen to her and Chester. And if Creede didn't check his messages, no one in all the world knew where she had gone.

§§§

Bo blew out a long breath and watched as the vapor hung suspended in the cold air. He paused on the path, waiting for Terrence to catch up.

"There it is," he said lowly. "Just ahead. Somebody must be home. Smoke's comin' from the chimney."

Terrence stopped. "That's where we're headed? To that cabin?"

"*Shack* is the better word," Bo answered. "Let's go around this way."

Frigid leaves slapped their faces as they circled toward the opposite side of the building. Leaves on the ground were crusted with ice particles and crackled as the two men walked along.

Suddenly, Terrence halted, tapping Bo on the shoulder. Bo turned.

"Over there," Terrence whispered. "There's a vehicle. And people are getting in it—looks like a woman and one, two, three men." He paused. "And from here, that BMW looks awfully familiar."

Bo watched intently. "That must be Leigh and Chester. But who are the other two?" He watched as the vehicle began its slippery crawl down the crude road.

"I forgot about that road!" he moaned. "I could've brought the wrecker up that way and blocked their escape!"

"Maybe we can get back down the path before they get to the highway," Terrence suggested.

"Not a chance."

Terrence turned abruptly and started down the path. "We can try," he said with determination.

§§§

"Max, you know this area. What're your suggestions?" Creede paced from his truck to Bo's wrecker.

"There's an excuse for a road on the other side of the mountain," Max answered.

"Then why's Bo's wrecker *here*? Why didn't he drive up? And who does this other truck belong to? And where are they?" Frustrated, Creede increased the momentum of his pacing, regularly punching a gloved hand with the other balled fist.

"Mr. Kelly, why don't *we* drive up?" Alex asked.

"I'll drive, Mr. Kelly," Tyler Simmons offered.

Tyler, Max, and Creede piled into Tyler's truck and after a moment of uncertain coughing and sputtering, the truck jerked forward, spinning momentarily on the highway before entering the road up Providence Hill. Too late, Tyler saw the black BMW approaching from the opposite direction. Both vehicles applied brakes at the same time to avoid a collision, spinning out of control on the narrow, icy road. In a shower of pebbles and wet leaves thrown from the wintry road, the BMW spun again and hit an embankment. The passenger door flew open as the airbag deployed.

Horrified, Creede jumped from Tyler's truck, stumbling and slipping toward the car as he saw Leigh struggling to get out, and the BMW roaring in an effort to extricate itself from the embankment. Just as Tyler and Max began running toward the vehicle, Bo and Terrence came from the path and joined the race.

Unsuccessful in his attempt to dislodge the car, Olnick threw open his door fighting the confinement of the airbag and began to run. He was followed closely by Jason Trent.

"I like these odds!" Bo yelled, racing after Olnick. "Four of us, two of them!"

He tackled Olnick, falling to the ground with him in a slushy pile of undergrowth, pinning Olnick's arms securely across his back.

Terrence stopped in amazement.

"Mr. Olnick!" he exclaimed. "I never expected to see you here."

Olnick turned his face on the cold, wet earth.

"Who are you?" he growled.

"Terrence Elliott. Your driver from long ago."

"You know him?" Bo asked.

"For years. But I didn't know then who the big boss was." Terrence was silent a moment. "It all makes sense now."

"What does?" Bo asked.

"Before I left Virginia and headed here, I saw Mr. Olnick at something political on TV. He was interviewed— some announcement about Senator Jorgenstein retiring and his aide was probably gonna run for the Senate seat."

"You mean Mr. Olnick was an aide to Senator Jorgenstein?" Bo inquired.

"No way. Mr. Olnick's been in the extortion business 30 years. I've been working for him 15 of those years, first as a driver, then as a collector. At the end of every month, I drove him to Washington to take the collections and reports and I saw them in a restaurant a couple of times."

"Mr. Olnick and the senator?" Bo asked.

"The senator's aide. Jason Trent."

§§§

Tyler Simmons knew he was falling the minute he stepped on the spot of ice. No larger than a flattened baseball, his foot hit the exact spot on the run and suddenly everything was upside-down. He hit with a thud, knocking him breathless. He lay still for a moment, willing the ringing in his head to stop. After a few gasps of cold air to fill his lungs, everything began returning to normal.

Two pairs of feet slushed by and he pulled himself to a sitting position, then stumbled to get upright. When he joined in the race, he discovered he was following Max Benedict, who was closing in on a man struggling to shed his overcoat. It slid off with his next effort and Max neatly sidestepped what was meant to be an obstacle.

Tyler charged in a burst of speed to run alongside his boss, who, surprisingly, was not even breathing hard.

And at that moment, it happened. Max dived at his subject, bringing him to the ground, only to lose him, for like a jack-in-the-box he bounced up and sprinted away. Max ran, slipping but not falling, grabbed Jason Trent's arm, spun him around and landed a single right hook to his jaw. Jason sprawled to the ground, unconscious before he hit.

Tyler pulled to a stop.

"Way to go, sir!" he congratulated.

Max dusted his hands together in victory, looked at Jason, then at Tyler.

"I call that my Benedict-tion."

CHAPTER 28

Leigh opened her eyes slightly and was vaguely aware of a hand gently brushing the hair from her forehead, then lingering tenderly on the side of her face.

"Hi."

Dark brown eyes, tender and compassionate, drifted into focus.

"You really frightened me."

"Do I look that bad?" she asked weakly. A blanket was pulled closely under her chin and in a feeble attempt, she freed one hand from the folds.

"No," Creede whispered, catching her hand and rubbing it gently.

"What happened?" she asked.

"There was an accident."

"I'm—so—sleepy," she murmured, turning her head and closing her eyes.

He leaned closer. "Sweetheart, don't go to sleep," he said softly. "Patti's making soup. She'll have it ready in just a few minutes."

She turned toward him but did not open her eyes.

"Patti—is—cooking?"

Creede grinned. She was coherent enough to understand.

"She sure is. At least, she's opening a can. She's become very domesticated since her marriage."

"I'm—glaa—dd—"

She was drifting off again. Creede squeezed her hand.

"Leigh, wake up. Here's your soup." He helped her to a sitting position on the sofa as she opened her eyes slowly.

"What happened?" she asked softly.

"Jason's car hit an embankment."

"Why was I in Jason's car?" She looked at Creede, waiting for his explanation.

"You and Chester were being kidnapped."

The soup spoon paused in midair. "Kidnapped? By Jason?"

Creede nodded. "It appears that way."

She was silent for several minutes as she ate. "I think I remember. I went to check on Chester, and Jason and another man were there. Jason wanted the papers I found in the chest that Marcus gave me." She closed her eyes momentarily, trying to recapture the events that had played out. "Creede, I think Marcus was being blackmailed. I found a list of amounts paid, dates paid, and I guess it was the collectors who came to get the payments—just initials, no names."

Creede sat beside her. "And the last of the collectors helped capture Jason and his buddy." He winked at her. "Bet you can't guess what his name is."

She shook her head.

"Terrence Houghton Elliott."

"Does that name mean something to you?" Leigh asked.

"Not to me, but what are the initials?"

"*T.H.E.*"

"The same as on the monogrammed handkerchief you found at the barn."

"So he took the money from the pharmacy and hid it in the trunk in my barn?"

Creede nodded. "He confessed to his part in the caper. Even to falling down and spilling some of the money, which is probably the money Chester found in the woods."

"But he came back. Why?"

Creede laughed. "Terrence isn't your normal crook. In the first place, he doesn't have a sense of direction. That's why *you* found the money. He hid it in your barn the night of the robbery and came back later to get it, but couldn't find the barn. He also broke in your house looking for the tape Marcus gave you."

"I did find the tape—in my coat pocket," Leigh said. "It was big band music, as Marcus said." Leigh giggled. "This is almost funny." She sipped more soup, then turned to look at Creede. "So what happens now?"

"Terrence is a very cooperative individual. He knew a little about the organization he worked for, which is very helpful to authorities. He just didn't know who the big boss was until today."

"Jason?"

Creede nodded. "A promising political career sacrificed because of greed and vindictiveness. It will be a while before he's a free man, depending on what the investigation turns up."

"So sad," Leigh remarked. "He had it all, yet he wanted more." She set the bowl on a small table. "I keep wondering about Terrence. What changed him from crook to confessor?"

"The way he told it, it had to do with old shoes being polished and a house built on rocks."

§§§

THE BURKHALTER HOME

Bo Patton shoved his chair back from the table, thinking that Winifred Burkhalter must know everything to be known about good cooking. Her Christmas spread would have made any chef envious: roast turkey with chestnut dressing, honey-mustard ham decorated with intricate diamond cuts and studded with whole cloves, vegetable casseroles, layered congealed salad resting on a plush bed of romaine lettuce, and made-from-scratch breadsticks. The only disappointment was dessert. Bo had his heart set on pecan pie with ice cream, but Winifred dished up a fabulous new cheesecake creation dripping with praline topping. Bo decided it really wasn't a bad substitute for pecan pie.

His little escapade at Providence Hill had delayed Christmas dinner until five o'clock, but Sue Ellen had been so impressed with his participation in the round-up that no one seemed to notice the time. When dessert was eaten, they adjourned to the den and gathered at the Christmas tree. Hannibal Burkhalter assumed the role of Santa, distributing gifts and contributing a variety of ho-ho-hos.

Without ceremony, Bo pulled the ring box from his pocket and laid it gently in Sue Ellen's hand. She opened the box, gasped in disbelief, hugged Bo, and cried uncontrollably.

It was an awkward moment for him. When she finally calmed, he figured it was a good time to ask.

"Does that mean you like a solitaire?"

§§§

The gray of midday had softened as the sun timidly peeked out. The rain had stopped before three, temporarily halting the icing on the roads and postponing winter darkness until nearly six.

"Creede," Leigh said softly, "why am I at Carmela?"

"I brought you here after the accident. It was just across the road and your injuries didn't appear too serious—a bump on the head and a sprained ankle."

"But how did we get in?"

"Just think of it as the neat little place north of Atlanta open on Christmas Day."

"Oh. You got my purse from my car and found my keys?"

"Not—exactly."

"I don't think I understand."

"Walk to the window with me?" he asked.

Creede caught her hand and gently pulled her from the sofa, supporting her as she hobbled to the window. They looked out on the winter scene, complete with stately trees shorn of their leaves, and Providence Hill rising majestically across the road. Creede turned her face to look in her eyes.

"I want you to come back home to Carmela—as my wife."

§§§

The door that separated the living room from the hall was cracked just enough for Patti to see the front window. She sighed.

"To be such a gifted writer, Daddy isn't very clever when it comes to wording a marriage proposal."

Alex leaned close to whisper in her ear. "You're eaves-dropping." He kissed her on the forehead. "Behavior unbecoming a princess."

"No argument there," Patti whispered back. She closed the door quietly and caught Alex's hand. "But Daddy could have said, 'I've bought Carmela for you.'"

Alex turned Patti and guided her along the hall to the kitchen. "Wouldn't have worked. Leigh would have seen that as charity. And if he had proposed after that, she would have interpreted it as a tack-on. Like the house was more important than their being married."

"Then why not 'Leigh, will you marry me? I've bought Carmela for you.'"

Alex shook his head.

"Not good?" Patti asked.

"Definitely not good. That sounds like *if* you marry me, you can have your house back."

"Well," Patti said slowly, "I guess my dad did it right. And no matter *how* he did it, I'm glad he did. I was fast running out of matchmaking tactics." She surveyed the results of having made lunch, then turned excitedly to Alex. "Do you realize I have just cooked our first Christmas dinner? And that I'm about to ask you to help me clean the mess I made in the kitchen?"

"Yes, to both," Alex answered.

§§§

EVANGELINE HOLLIDAY'S HOME
DECEMBER 26

"So what did you do with the papers?" Eve asked over breakfast. She propped her elbows on the table, rested her chin on her hands, and stifled a yawn. "Excuse me, Leigh.

283

We must've stayed up too late talking last night. I can't seem to get motivated this morning."

"Sorry to have dropped in unannounced," Leigh smiled.

"Don't worry about it. You couldn't drive back to Atlanta with a sprained ankle. And besides," Eve smiled mischievously, "it seemed to make Creede very happy to have a reason to come back after you today." She reached for her coffee cup. "Now, what about the papers you found in the washstand? What did you do with them?"

"I wasn't very original, I'm afraid. I put them in the washer and piled dirty clothes on top."

"I'd say that was clever. Unless someone came in and did your laundry before you got back."

"Not likely."

"What a Christmas to remember!" Eve exclaimed. "You get kidnapped, survive a wreck, and get engaged in one day. Tell me again how Creede proposed."

Leigh laughed. "Remember when I saw him and the gorgeous redhead at Lenox? That was his attorney, Regina Compton. Creede had been looking at a house at Enchanted Harbor, but decided he would rather visit the coast than live there. He was attracted to Carmela when we came for the Apple Festival, so Regina contacted the bank and made all the arrangements. The mortgage is paid and Carmela is still in my name."

"What *I* want to know is when he was attracted to *you*," Eve prompted.

"Patti said it was when he fired me." Leigh laughed softly. "She said—and this is Patti's opinion—he was determined never to fall in love again and when he saw it was happening, he decided *out of sight, out of mind* would be his motto."

"Well, I'm glad it didn't work," Eve said. "Now, when is the wedding?"

"We haven't made a lot of plans yet. Creede wants to remodel Carmela and build a little cottage for Tabitha. We're thinking the wedding may be sometime around Easter while Patti and Alex are here." Leigh added butter to a blueberry muffin. "I can't believe all that's happened, Eve. Especially that I'm getting married. Wouldn't Daddy's Mama enjoy helping plan a wedding? I wish she could have known Creede."

Eve rose from her chair. "I believe she knows him, Leigh. And I think she's smiling with approval." She stood behind Leigh. "Let me be your crutch. Creede just drove up and in about thirty seconds, he'll be knocking at the door."

§§§

"You would have had a slight catastrophe if your washer had been turned on."

Creede lifted several papers from a plastic box and placed them and the keepsake box on Eve's kitchen counter.

Leigh sorted through the papers. "Did you look at these? What do you think? Was Marcus being blackmailed?"

"Seems that way." Creede pointed to the pages. "And the fact that he had the papers so well hidden."

"But this is somehow incomplete. What was he being blackmailed *for*?"

Creede rubbed his chin. "Just these papers are all you found? Nothing more?"

"Nothing."

Leigh filled two mugs with coffee and handed one to Creede. "Jason told me he had looked in Marcus' safe deposit box for some papers and when he couldn't find them, he assumed they had burned in the house. Do you suppose any other information could be at the pharmacy?"

"Probably not." Creede stirred his coffee. "But if Jason was so interested in locating them, I wonder if it could have been damaging to him if the papers had been found?"

"Where else is there to look?" Eve asked.

"Tell me again about the washstand," Creede urged Leigh.

"I know my grandfather Bracken made it as a gift for Marcus and Christine. Jason said the will specifically mentioned that was the reason Marcus wanted me to have it and the keepsake box." Leigh set her mug on the counter and waited as Eve refilled it. "I never knew my grandfather, but I've been told he was quite talented at dreaming up puzzles."

"Like the washstand with the hidden compartment?" Eve questioned.

"Then what about the keepsake box?" Creede asked as he pulled it closer.

"It was empty and too shallow to have any hidden compartments," Leigh answered.

"So we're back to square one," Eve said. "We feel pretty confident Marcus was being blackmailed, but we don't know *why*. We feel pretty confident Jason is involved, but we don't know *how*." She glanced at Creede. "If you were writing this story, what would happen next?"

"Some kind of diversion to allow everybody to regroup their thoughts."

"Such as?" Eve prompted.

Before Creede could answer, the sound of chimes pierced the kitchen. He winked at Eve.

"A ringing doorbell works very nicely."

CHAPTER 29

"Goodness!" Eve blurted. "Nobody ever comes to my back door. I even forgot there was a bell there."

Before Eve could get to the door, the bell chimed again with three persistent blasts. She returned to the kitchen followed by Bo Patton walking gingerly across the tile floor in his sock feet.

"Bo, for goodness sake," Eve scolded. "Your boots would not hurt this floor."

"Didn't want to track any junk in," he replied.

"Well, your mother raised you right, but it's not like this kitchen has the Good Housekeeping seal of approval," she shot back. "Don't blame me if you catch pneumonia."

"That's a promise," Bo agreed. He turned to Leigh. "Your car has a flat tire. Noticed it when I drove by Carmela just now. If you'll get me your key, I'll go change it for you."

"Wonder how that happened?" Leigh asked, reaching across the counter for her key and making space for a plate of sweet rolls. "Coffee or orange juice, Bo?"

"Always coffee," he answered.

Eve picked up the coffee pot, which tilted and slipped from her grasp, spilling hot liquid along the counter. "Clumsy Cleo!" she hissed. "Don't let it get on those papers, Creede!"

He grabbed for them and slid them along the counter to safety.

"Watch the box!" Eve yelled.

Leigh stretched for the carved keepsake box, barely missing it. With a shattering sound, it hit the floor. The box landed upright, but the top bounced off, separating into two thin layers. The knob on the top popped off and rolled erratically toward the refrigerator.

"Double Clumsy!" Eve fumed. "Is it broken?" She slapped the counter. "Obviously, it is."

Leigh knelt to gather the pieces. "Don't fret, Eve. We'll put it back together. No problem. It's easily fixed—" She paused. "What *is* this?"

"What's what?" Creede inquired.

"This photo. Where did it come from? The box was empty. I *know* it was! So where did this come from?"

Creede retrieved the pieces of the box and placed them on the counter, rearranging the remnants and studying the lineup. "All the breaks are clean. A little glue should fix it up just fine."

When Leigh didn't respond, Creede stepped back from the counter and touched her shoulder. "Leigh? Are you with us?"

"The box was empty," she said slowly, "but the lid apparently was in two pieces and the knob held it all together. With the knob off, the top separated and the picture was hidden between the two layers of wood." She studied the photograph closely. "It's a house. A very large house." Leigh turned the photo over; in the middle of the back was written *Sweetbriar*, and under that *W. Trent*. She turned it back and pointed to a bespectacled youth. "Who is this in the foreground?"

"Looks like a young Chester. But what's he doing in front of that elegant house?" Eve studied the picture. "This is nowhere in this area," she said firmly.

"Where's your cassette player, Eve?" Leigh asked.

"My *cassette player*? How did we so quickly go from Chester and a strange house to cassette players? And why?"

Leigh frowned. "I'm having a little problem putting some things together."

"Like what?" Bo asked.

"To begin with, when I was at Chester's cabin yesterday, Jason said he had turned the place upside-down but hadn't found what he was looking for. Now, I wonder if there's some clue on the tape Marcus gave me. And remember the break-in at Carmela was all about a tape."

"What kind of clue are we looking for?" Bo asked as Eve placed the cassette on the table.

"Any kind," Creede said as he took the tape from Leigh and dropped it in the player. He laid the plastic tape container aside and adjusted the volume as music of a bygone era flooded the kitchen. When the tape clicked off after 30 minutes, he reversed it.

"There's nothing there," Leigh remarked as the tape finished playing. Disappointment laced her words. "Why did I think the tape would be anything other than what Marcus said it was?" She removed the scrap of paper from the bottom of the box before dropping the tape in, rolled it into a ball, and dropped it on the counter.

"What did you find?" Creede asked, looking over her shoulder.

Leigh smiled. "Just stuffing in the box."

Creede reached for the wad of paper and opened it. "Talk about being conservative. Marcus kept a crossword puzzle from a paper four years ago." He smoothed the clipping carefully. "Wonder why he never finished working it. Only two words are not filled in."

Leigh studied the clipping. "Twenty-three down is *light rays through lens*, and fifty-one across is *a group of similar things.*"

"That requires too much thinking for me," Eva said. "How about you, Bo?"

"No talent for puzzles unless it's an engine," he grinned.

"I've got one of them," Leigh said a moment later as she reached for a pen to fill in the spaces. "F-A-M-I-L-Y. Family. That's a group of similar things. But twenty-three down has 10 letters. Let's see. *Light rays through lens.* The third letter from the bottom is *A*." She propped on the counter. "Eve, come take a look and help me guess."

"You know very well I'm not a speller," Eve reminded her.

Leigh snapped her fingers. "That's it!" she exclaimed.

"What's *it*?" Eve questioned.

"Twenty-three down with 10 letters. *Photograph.* Together, twenty-three and fifty-one say *family photograph.*"

"I'm sufficiently impressed with your puzzle-solving ability," Eve said slowly, "but, frankly, I can't see that it's gotten us anywhere we want to be."

Creede had stood silently for the last several minutes. "Leigh, could there be a Trent family photograph?"

"Not any more since Marcus' house burned." It was Eve who replied. "Or there may never have been one."

"Eve, maybe there was," Leigh said. "Remember when Jason took us to Marcus' house and showed us the boudoir chair and the washstand?"

"But he didn't show us a picture," Eve pointed out.

"That's just it. The picture wasn't there. Remember Jason made a comment about a picture. He thought one had hung over the den sofa."

"I do remember that," Eve said. "The picture frame you were supposed to get. But what happened to it?"

"Think Chester knows anything?" Bo asked.

"Probably," Leigh agreed, "since he lived at Marcus' house for many years. We need to get up Providence Hill and see if he can help us."

She hobbled to a chair, sat down, and rubbed her bandaged ankle. Creede knelt in front of the chair.

"Why don't you let Bo and me go to Chester's? If he's got the picture, we'll ask him to bring it to you."

"I like that idea," Eve said.

§§§

Chester pushed past Eve and shoved a large flat package toward Leigh. She pulled the brown paper away and lifted from the folds a picture of Marcus, Christine, and Chester, matted in a rich beige and covered with a glass etched in cracks.

"What a wonderful picture," Leigh said. "And what a handsome family."

Chester beamed as a smile broke across his face.

"This picture is special to you, isn't it, Chester?" Leigh asked. "Did Marcus and Christine give you the picture?"

Chester shook his head.

"Oh, no," Eve said softly. "If they didn't give it to him, how did he get it?" She faced Chester. "Did you *take* this picture, Chester?"

He nodded sheepishly, then steepled his hands and bowed his head.

"The day of Marcus' funeral," Leigh guessed. "No one would have been at the house that day." She looked again at the picture. "Had you ever asked Marcus to *give* you the picture?"

He nodded.

"And he wouldn't do it?"

He shook his head.

"Is that why you were angry with Marcus and moved up to Providence Hill?" Leigh asked, and Chester nodded.

"At this point, I guess it really doesn't matter if Chester stole the picture," Eve commented. "And other than it being his family's picture, I don't see a thing about it that looks like a clue." She rubbed a finger along the frame. "I've never seen a frame with such delicate carving—it's almost invisible. Sure took a steady hand to accomplish that artistry."

"What did you say?" Leigh asked. "About the frame?"

"It's got carving on it. Didn't you notice?"

"No, I didn't." Leigh leaned over the counter to examine the frame. "The carving is very intricate and almost unnoticeable, and yet, the pattern looks familiar." She continued to study the frame. "Now, I know where I've seen this carving. On the washstand and on top of the keepsake box!"

Creede pulled the box closer. "The same, exactly. And your conclusion is?"

"My grandfather Bracken made all three pieces. And since the washstand and the keepsake box held secrets, I'll bet this picture frame has one! Chester, do you object if I open the picture?"

He shook his head and came closer to the counter.

Leigh turned the picture over and gently pulled away the right corner of the back covering where it had been secured with masking tape and glue. She worked slowly, loosening the edges until two envelopes were revealed, taped to the back of the photograph.

Creede whistled softly. "Sesame has opened."

Leigh removed the envelope marked *1*, unsealed it, and removed the single sheet of paper. No one moved, hardly breathed, as she unfolded the page and began to read the enclosed newspaper article, dated 25 years earlier.

"Sweetbriar Mansion was destroyed on Tuesday. The six-alarm blaze was reported by a passing motorist, but the structure was fully engulfed in flames before the fire department could respond.

"Officials estimated the loss of the mansion in excess of two million dollars. Many of the antique furnishings were handcrafted in France more than two centuries ago and were considered priceless.

"Preliminary reports strongly indicate arsonist activity.

"Current owners of the property are Wilton Trent, who was out-of-town at the time and could not be reached for comment, and his brother, Marcus Trent."

"Sweetbriar. That's the name on the back of the small photo!" Eve nudged Leigh. "Isn't there another envelope?" she asked impatiently.

"Right here." Leigh pulled folded pages from the second envelope and began to read.

"The fire at Sweetbriar was not Chester's fault. Jason was responsible for it. He made Chester's picture in front of the mansion just as the smoke started. Jason also knew Chester had been in trouble several times and that he had spent time in a juvenile home for setting fire to a wastebasket in the city park. Jason knew exactly what to do to make sure Chester fit the description of prime suspect by making the

picture. Jason's grandfather—my brother—would have moved mountains to keep Jason from being charged with the fire, even though Wilton knew he was guilty. The investigators were easily bought off from placing the blame on Jason, but one of them knew about the picture of Chester and knew his record, so Wilton paid him extra to discontinue his investigation. That's when Wilton demanded restitution from me. Over the years I have paid him thousands of dollars so that picture would not get published in the newspaper. It would have shortened my Christine's life by many years to know about the picture and about the payments I have made. In a sense, I am as guilty as Wilton for not speaking the truth, but my actions were to protect Christine from a hurt she would never recover from if Chester had been sentenced to prison. And it would have been for something he didn't do. Christine loved Chester like she would have loved her own son.

"This is a tragic account of family hatred generated by jealousy and greed, and by an old man's belief that his grandson could do no wrong. I realize Jason was at that young, mischievous age, but that does not excuse his actions.

"At the back of our family picture is a painting of Sweetbriar, the Trent family home in Canada. The painting was a gift to me from the artist, who was my college roommate. I have no pleasant memories of Sweetbriar, but it would have been very rude to throw away what my friend worked on so hard.

"There is a photograph of Chester in front of Sweetbriar that Jason made the day of the fire. It is in the keepsake box that Samuel Bracken made, at my request, between the layers of wood that is the top of the box. A screw under the lid will loosen the knob and there you will find the picture. He also made the washstand at my request and included the secret compartment. Other documents will be found there. He sure was curious, but he was a gentleman and never asked about my motives.

"This will be found after I am gone. Do what is right with this information. Marcus Trent."

A sepulchral quiet lingered in Eve's kitchen for several minutes.

"This is so incredible!" Leigh whispered. "We were right about Marcus being blackmailed, but we never suspected it was by his own brother."

"And don't forget his great-nephew continued it," Eve said bitterly.

Leigh turned to Chester. "I know you've tried several times to tell me something, Chester. At the Apple Festival when they were trying to get the bonfire going, did it remind you of the fire at Sweetbriar? And the picture of you standing in front of the house?"

He nodded.

"Chester, have you seen the black car with the aerials on the back at the pharmacy?"

Chester nodded again.

"Just once?"

He shook his head.

"Many times?"

He nodded.

"Did you see it the night the pharmacy was robbed?"

He nodded.

"Was it the same car that was at your house yesterday? And that you tried to tell me about when I was leaving the orchard a few weeks ago? And the night you saw Jason and me at the restaurant and you were looking at his car?"

"Wow, Leigh," Eve said. "Are you smart or what?"

Leigh peeled the remaining covering from the back of the frame to expose a painting of an imposing Greek Revival mansion, situated on a gently rolling hill and accented with elaborate flowerbeds and sculptured shrubs. Just above the artist's signature was the word *Sweetbriar.*

"Jason probably burned Marcus' house thinking everything about Sweetbriar would go up in flames. He told me yesterday that fire could be illuminating, bringing out the best and the worst."

"It's not left to the imagination to figure what it brought out in Jason, is it?" Eve asked.

Leigh turned to Creede. "Jason must have thought if he got those records back and destroyed them, no one would ever have known about the payments Marcus has made all these years."

"Which probably explains why Marcus came up with his elaborate scheme for hiding the information in articles he was willing to you," Creede said.

"I can't understand why Marcus let it continue for all these years," Eve said.

"Because of his love for Christine," Creede reminded her. "And, remember, Marcus said in his note he knew it was wrong, but he would do anything to protect her."

"But the picture. I wonder how Marcus decided to use that as a secret hiding place," Eve said. "Tell me, Creede. You're the mystery writer."

"I'm guessing he counted on the picture frame being the outstanding clue—maybe even the first clue. Willing it to Leigh was a natural thing to do since her grandfather had made it. Jason wouldn't have questioned that. And Marcus probably knew Leigh would want to replace the cracked glass and when she took everything apart to do that, she would have found the envelopes." He glanced at Leigh. "Marcus gave you the cassette tape with the crossword clue. If you had looked at that when you first got the tape, it would have led you to the photograph, and the envelopes there

296

would have led to the washstand and keepsake box. Marcus wills specific items to you and gives you the cassette tape, knowing you would listen to the music, discover the paper in the box, complete the unfinished crossword puzzle, and solve the first part of the mystery. After that, everything would fall into its proper place."

"I would not make a very good detective," Leigh laughed. "All the clues that were provided to me and I was so slow to recognize them. And then stumbled on them in the wrong order." She looked up from the picture to Chester. "I suppose we'll never know all the answers, will we, Chester? But if you hadn't kept trying to make us aware of the black car with the aerials, we might not have kept looking for the answers we do have."

"And while Jason is sitting in jail thinking about yesterday's kidnapping charge, we can advise Sgt. Hendley of these latest developments. He'd probably like to know," Creede said.

"Good idea," Eve agreed. "Don't you just love it when justice is done?"

EPILOGUE

Spring had arrived on schedule in the Blue Ridge, bringing the season of new life with an explosive riot of colors as mountain laurel and rhododendron paraded in their finest blossoms.

On Tuesday, April 18, at a ten a.m. service—"How unorthodox is that for a wedding?" Eve had questioned—Creede and Leigh exchanged marriage vows in front of the living room mantle at the remodeled Carmela. The wedding guests—Eve, Tabitha, Max, Patti, and Alex—heard the pastor of Providence Church urge the couple to respect each other, remain close to God, and establish a home built on love. The ceremony had lasted less than 15 minutes; and following a reception of coffee and pound cake, guests had departed to resume Tuesday activities and Creede and Leigh Kelly prepared to depart for a brief honeymoon in North Carolina.

Leigh carefully folded Tabitha's mantilla and placed it gently in a tissue-lined box.

"You know you made Tabitha very happy by wearing her mantilla," Creede said.

"I was delighted she made the suggestion because it was so perfect with Daddy's Mama's linen wedding gown. Just enough lace on the mantilla to complement the simple lines of the dress." She held her hand to admire the marquise-cut amethyst and diamond engagement ring and the gold wedding band. "Engaged and married the same day. Incredible!"

Creede wrapped his arms around her. "Gives an entirely new definition to *whirlwind courtship*, doesn't it?" he asked. "No engagement ring for Christmas, or New Year's or Valentine Day. Barely made it for the wedding."

Leigh's eyes twinkled. "But *so* worth waiting for." She hesitated. "I am curious about your choice of amethyst."

"You don't like it?"

"I *love* it!"

"To match the pin you always wear."

She hugged him. "You are *so* special, Creede Kelly. No one else would have thought of that. I had no idea you even noticed the pin."

"Noticed?" He chuckled. "The first time I went with Patti to discuss her wedding with you—the time I signed that *whopping* check—that pin got engraved on my mind. And worse than that, it totally messed up my writing. I must have shredded 500 sheets of paper because your pin kept popping up in the story. Very distracting."

Leigh smiled. "I will spend a lifetime loving you and thanking God for you—for the way you so wonderfully keep me reminded of the beauty of the past and the promise of the future." She hugged him again.

He returned the hug. "Speaking of the past, would you like to know a secret?"

"A secret of yours?"

He nodded. "It was the past that gave me the future."

"Now, that's poetic. Am I supposed to understand it?"

"A chance encounter on a hospital parking lot. That's my secret. Every tomorrow of our future can be traced to that."

"Isn't it amazing how God has used the little, insignificant things to deepen our relationship? An amethyst pin, apple pie, and especially a little house. I've thought about all these things, and more, Creede. And over the last few weeks, I've thought about the many definitions for home, and how many of them have touched my life during the last year. Daddy's Mama went to her eternal home, Patti went to her home in a new country, Tabitha has a new home because of your generosity. But most special, because of *you*, I'm coming home to Carmela. Life is so good, Creede. So very, very good."

Creede's eyes misted as he looked heavenward for a brief moment. His hands cupped Leigh's face gently and he looked into her eyes, daring to let her see the tears in his own.

"My precious, precious Leigh," he whispered. "Welcome home!"

§§§

At that time I will gather you;

at that time I will bring you home.

Zephaniah 3:20